THE GOSPEL OF THE KNIFE

Tor Books by Will Shetterly

Chimera
Dogland
The Gospel of the Knife

The Gospel of the Knife

WILL SHETTERLY

TOR®
A TOM DOHERTY ASSOCIATES BOOK
NEW YORK

THE GOSPEL OF THE KNIFE

A Tor Book
Published by Tom Doherty Associates, LLC
175 Fifth Avenue
New York, NY 10010

www.tor-forge.com

The Library of Congress has catalogued the hardcover edition as follows:

Shetterly, Will.
The gospel of the knife / Will Shetterly.—1st ed.
p. cm.
"A Tom Doherty Associates Book."
ISBN 978-0-312-86631-0
1. Teenagers—Fiction. 2. Hippies—Fiction. 3. Benefactors—Fiction. 4. Domestic fiction. [I. Florida—History—20th century—Fiction.] I. Title.
PS3569.H458G67 2007
813'.54—dc22

2007009538

ISBN 978-0-312-87539-8 (trade paperback)

First Edition: July 2007
First Trade Paperback Edition: July 2010

Printed in the United States of America

0 9 8 7 6 5 4 3 2 1

Dedications by this book's patrons:

To Bridget K. Houlihan, whose romantic hope that every book she cracks open will be the best that the author has to offer has inspired me to make famous her love of literature, love of reading, and passion for the arts. May you read this with the speed of a thousand thundering turtles!

—TAMMY GREEN

To the men and women of Bravo Company, Tripler Army Medical Center, from whom I have learned much while they were supposed to be learning from me.

—THOMAS A. AMOROSO

To Sarah Kathleen McLaren, who was born while this was being written.

—CHRIS MCLAREN

And by its author:

For Juan, Jelks, Kini, Jed, Ginnie, Kay, Marie, Liz, and especially Barbara. And a special thanks to Stephen Borer and all the readers of my web log.

BOOK ONE

The Wasteland

One

A Coke bottle spins through the air. Thick green glass, curved like an Earth Momma statue, flicking the afternoon sunlight, as beautiful and strange as a space station or a hummingbird.

You're pedaling home. You were thinking of drawing a cartoon about a girl who looks like Cindy Hurly. Would she be impressed? Would she think you're pathetic?

Now a Coke bottle flies through the blue Florida sky.

Toward your head.

You stomp the brake. The rear hub squeals, but you keep moving forward. In the back basket, your books bang like a drunken drummer.

Is a Coke bottle the last thing you'll see?

Beyond the bottle, a gray Chevy pickup is cruising by. In the cab are three boys, old enough for high school, maybe older. One boy's arm sticks out of the cab. He has Brylcreemed hair, pale blue eyes, a pouting lip. Is he pointing at this bizarro thing, a Coke bottle hurtling through the air?

No. He threw it.

Your brake catches. You pitch off the seat and onto the crossbar. Putting your balls on an anvil and hitting them with a hammer would do more damage. It might not hurt more.

The bottle passes an inch from your nose. You barely notice. You drop your desert boots onto the sun-baked ground. You want to fall on your side and lie there gasping.

The bottle shatters in the ditch. That's when you figure it out. The bottle had a target. You.

The pickup roars away. You stand by the side of the road, straddling your bike, curled over the handlebars, gulping air, staring at the truck as it climbs the hill. Its tailgate is thick with bumper stickers: SUPPORT OUR BOYS IN VIETNAM. AMERICA, LOVE IT OR LEAVE IT. The Confederate battle flag over the words AN UNREGENERATE CONFEDERATE.

The Coke-thrower leans out the passenger window and shouts, "You one damn lucky hippie!"

You ram your middle finger at the sky and yell, "Kiss my rebel ass, redneck motherfuckers!" It would sound better if your voice didn't crack, but he's too far away to hear.

Thanks to your finger, he doesn't need to.

His grin drops from his face. He yanks his head back in the cab. You lower your arm and smile. You're a lone dog watching wolves run off. Maybe you only survived, but you feel like you won.

Then the pickup makes a U-turn.

You glance up and down the road. Semis, sedans, and station wagons roll in and out of Gainesville. None of them will worry about a long-haired kid on a bike until the rednecks have done whatever they want.

The pickup cuts across the highway and charges down the shoulder of the road. Gravel and dust stream from it like a cloak. In the cab, the Coke-thrower and two friends with pale crew cuts are laughing. If Hit the Hippie is a game, they want first prize.

You yank your handlebars and take the ditch. Your tires bounce on rocks and ruts and grass. Every jolt sends fire up your spine. A book leaps from the back basket. Your front wheel twists on a hubcap. You slide sideways, nearly dumping your bike, kicking the ground to stay up.

And you're across the ditch. An animal track twists into the woods. You race for it. Weeds slow you. Your back feels as wide as a billboard. Maybe the three kids have shotguns or slingshots. You've heard about rednecks catching freaks to shave their heads with rusty razors, rob them, beat them, rape them, kill them.

The woods close around you. Branches slash and snag at your jeans. A truck door slams. Someone shouts, "Run like a nigger, boy! Ain't nothing gonna save you!"

You're pedaling your fastest. The track's too bumpy and twisty to get up real speed. When you roll up against a fallen tree, you shoot a look back.

Leaves rattle and branches break. Someone falls loudly and yells "Shit!" Someone else screams, "I see the little pissant!" A pale crew cut bobs up over a clump of bushes.

You grab your bike, yank it over the fallen tree, and jump back on. You think, Keep going. Wear 'em out. They're looking for fun. Once they know you're not it, they'll give up. Just keep go—

The track ends at a pond. You brake hard.

The pond is about ten feet across and twenty feet long. You can't guess its depth. It's covered with green scum and stinks of rotting plants. Or worse. There could be bodies in it. Who would know?

You glance both ways: bushes and trees, too thick for anything larger than a possum. If you take the brush, you'll have to leave your bike. You won't make any speed. You'll have to break your own path. Making one for the rednecks, too.

You could hide. Burrow into a palmetto grove and hope no rattlers or coral snakes are nesting there. Scramble up a pine tree and force yourself into its branches. Lie on your back in the water and breathe through a straw if you can find one or make one in time.

You study the pond. You've heard of kids diving into dark water to be caught in barbwire, poisoned by industrial waste dumped by cheap-ass businesses, bitten by cottonmouths, eaten by alligators.

And part of you expects monsters in murky waters, shark-faced mermen and giant octopi who grab your ankle and yank you under. You aren't about to hide in that pond.

Someone shouts, "We got 'im now!"

You look back. The trio comes walking easily, grinning as you whip your head from side to side, looking for any sign of salvation.

You can't guess what they'll do with you. You doubt they know yet. You wish you'd stayed by the highway. They would've gotten in a few punches and kicks, then sped off. Now they can have all the time they want with you.

Someone laughs across the water. You look. So do the boys. You think you have help, but it's only a crow high in a tree.

The boy with Brylcreemed hair laces his fingers and cracks his knuckles. He tells you, "Best say your prayers, boy."

You stomp on the pedals and plunge into the pond. You don't have a plan. All you have is panic, so you're panicking.

Your wheels drop into the pond so fast your fear doubles. Not because of what might be under you. If you can't get far enough from shore, the rednecks will pluck you out like cats at a goldfish bowl.

Your wheels hit something that bounces a little. Maybe that's just the air in your tires. You shoot across the pond, hit the far bank with your front wheel, and fall forward into a tangle of grass and weeds.

You scramble to your feet. You're no worse for the fall, but you're scared worse. The woods are too thick for you to press on, even if you leave your bike.

The Brylcreemed boy reaches the pond first. He stops, looking for the best place to splash through. The others come charging behind him. At the rear, the biggest of the bunch wears a green John

Deere T-shirt stretched tight across his belly. The third boy, with black square glasses like Clark Kent, charges past Brylcreem and leaps. Brylcreem sees him pass and leans forward to follow, with John Deere maybe six steps behind.

You step back. Branches scrape your back, butt, and thighs. You lift your hands in front of your face, maybe to block their blows, maybe to beg them not to hurt you, maybe to keep from seeing what's coming.

The boy in black glasses splashes into the pond.

And keeps dropping.

He has enough time to open his mouth, but not enough time to scream. Dark water and green scum slap over his head, then settles.

Brylcreem brakes at the bank of the pond, throwing his arms back and windmilling, his mouth and eyes wide. John Deere comes up behind him, saying, "What happened?"

If you were drawing this, John Deere would bump Brylcreem, they both would fall in after Black Glasses, and your long-haired hero, the Kid, would laugh and pedal into the sunset while the wet rednecks waved their fists at him. But Brylcreem and John Deere don't fall in, you don't laugh, and Black Glasses stays underwater.

You don't feel a thing as you watch Brylcreem catch his balance and John Deere look from him to the water to you. Something is wrong with the world. You rode across the pond, and Black Glasses disappeared into it. You feel like you're puzzling out a riddle: If you consider the clues long enough, the answer will come.

Or it won't. Instead of an answer, there's a horrible rush in your guts. Someone is drowning in front of you, even if you can't see him. Someone is thrashing in the darkness, knowing he's about to die. Someone is so desperate for air that he'll fill his lungs in a minute or three, and go unconscious, and die.

Brylcreem and John Deere look at you as if you have the answer or are it.

"Get a stick!" you yell. "Get him out!"

John Deere catches on first. He rips a long branch from a willow tree and pokes it in the stinking pond. The water still ripples where Black Glasses disappeared. It feels like you've been standing there all day. Maybe twenty seconds have passed.

John Deere stirs the pond, bumps something, and starts drawing the branch up. It jerks in his grasp. He yells, "Help me!"

Brylcreem grabs on to the branch to pull. You want to do something, but you don't know what. If you try to cross the pond again, will you fall in like Black Glasses? If you make it across and Black Glasses drowns, what will his friends do?

Gripping the branch and streaming black water, two pale hands rise from the pond. A pale crew cut follows. The glasses are gone. The boy's head whips around. He gulps air as his friends pull him near. They tug at his arms and T-shirt to help him, but they probably don't make a difference. He scuttles like a lobster up the branch and onto the bank. Weeds are thick around his sneakers. One leg of his jeans is torn. There might be blood in his white socks, or it might just be mud.

He stands and looks across the pond at you. His eyes are light brown. The right is slightly bloodshot. His face is flecked with pond scum. You half expect him to start cursing you, half expect him to apologize for chasing you.

His eyes widen. He grimaces. Gasping, "Ohgod-ohgod-ohgod," he bolts for the highway.

Brylcreem and John Deere try to grab him. His clothes are too slick with muck for them to get a hold.

"Wait up!" Brylcreem shouts. He and John Deere run after the boy. John Deere never looks back. Brylcreem glances over his shoulder, then runs on. You can't describe his expression. If he had a gun, you wouldn't be reading this.

And you're alone by the pond as if no one else has been here.

You breathe heavily. Your balls drone with pain. Your ribs are cold with sweat. Your throat feels thick. You smell pine from the woods, sweet decay from the pond, the bitter tang from your armpits. You hear cars on the highway, a dog barking at the bottom of the hill, the redneck's truck roaring away. You don't know if you want to puke or cry.

You stand your bicycle up. Overhead, a crow laughs again. "Fuck off!" you yell. It shuts up.

The pond is smooth and still. A dragonfly speeds across it. Shouldn't there be frogs jumping in it, minnows darting beneath its surface, waterbugs dashing over it?

You have to get away, and you have to know what happened. You put your bike on its kickstand and spot a long branch, dry and white like old bone, as thin as a finger. It would break if you snagged it on anything heavy. You like that. You need to know something's in the pond, but you don't want to drag anything out. You take a deep breath and poke the branch in.

It goes deep, touching nothing. You lean over the pond, pushing the branch deeper, then rock back, afraid to get too close. You drag the branch sideways. It hits something and you jerk back, making the sound boys call "squealing like a girl" and girls never call "squealing like a boy." You expect the Creature from the Black Lagoon to appear.

The Creature stays put. You poke the branch back in.

Something solid is there, maybe a foot underwater on the far side of the pond and nine inches under by the bank where you stand. You trace it with the branch. It's about a foot wide. Its top curves. It's long and straight, running the width of the pond—

It's a log or a post or a broken phone pole. You don't need to reach into the pond to learn exactly what it is. It's a pole. Your wheels landed on a pole, and you rode it across. No mystery there. An ordinary pole, hidden by scum and dark water. You're lucky. That's all. Very lucky. Very, very lucky—

You laugh. Not because it's funny. It's impossible, and you have to free the pressure in your chest. What are the odds there'd be a pole where you need one?

You take another breath. You can't look away from the pond. How lucky were you? Enough to use up your luck for the rest of your life. You begin to shake. Sweat bursts out again on your skin. If there wasn't a wall of trees around you, you would run anywhere that's away.

Looking for a place to run calms you. It's a pond, a pole, and a great whopping chunk of luck. You tell yourself you should be glad or grateful. But you hurt, you stink of fear, and someone nearly drowned in front of you.

You slap a mosquito, then another. Shade makes the woods cooler than the highway, but the air is hot and damp. Time to get moving.

You aren't about to try your luck again with the underwater pole. You find the thinnest place in the bushes around the pond and back through, protecting your face while dragging your bike after you.

When you come to a track, you follow it to the path back to the road. At the fallen tree, you stop.

In the theater of your mind, you replay the last minutes: rednecks attack, the Kid runs away. Giving them the finger is dead time in the story. They attack; you run. Giving them the finger is worse than dead time. It's an idiot move, a red flag waved at a bull by a matador without a sword.

You aren't a saint turning the other cheek or a samurai refusing to fight inferiors or a smart kid keeping his clothes and bike safe by running away. You're just a coward running away.

Your nose is wet. So is your lip. You dab the moisture with the sides of your fists, then realize where it's from. You say, "Fuck." You can't say anything else. Something's swelling in your chest and behind your eyes. If you make another sound, it'll break free. Then you'll be a coward who runs away and cries.

A gray squirrel the size of a chipmunk scurries around a tree, sees you, and freezes. You stare at each other. When he doesn't run off, you wipe your fists on your jeans, hold out an open hand, and whisper, "Hey, li'l Reb. You sure make piss-poor moss."

Reb sticks with the statue impersonation. You pat your pockets and find a wadded-up bag of cashews. You thought you'd eaten most of them, but the bag is half full.

You toss a nut near Reb. He darts up to it, touches it with his nose, lifts it in his paws, then pops it in his mouth. You smile, toss him another, and pop one in your mouth.

If Reb minds the salt, he's too polite to say. You throw more cashews until he stuffs his cheeks, wheels around, and runs into the brush.

The woods aren't as hot as the highway, but the air is damp and still. Gnats swarm around you. Your bladder needs emptying. You unzip and check yourself: your left ball is red and sore. Otherwise everything seems normal. Meaning you wish everything was bigger and hairier, but knowing you should keep what you have is good. Your piss is yellow, untainted by blood. That must be a good sign.

You touch your left ball several times, trying to decide each time if it hurts any less. Then you imagine drawing this: The Kid crouches in the woods, his hand in his jeans fly, a cloud of thought balloons over his head: "Does it still hurt?" "Ow!" "Yes." "Does it still hurt?" "Ow!" "Yes." "Does it still hurt?"

Cindy Hurly might ask if the cartoon is a metaphor for the war. If she does, you'll shrug as if she caught you being clever and never admit it's just about being a boy afraid his balls are mashed.

Two

Halloween hit your neighborhood like a storm. Mrs. Moody put a red lightbulb in a plastic skull hanging in a black hood and cape on her porch. The Thornton kids carved pumpkins, five lopsided grins and one scary scowl. The old guy with the noisy black Model A parked it in his yard with a sign: CAPONE'S MORTUARY. YOU STAB 'EM, WE SLAB 'EM.

Homes here are small, single-story, cinder-block boxes. Most have carports. None have garages. Fences are chain-link. Driveways are cement or gravel stained with oil. Yards have grass that's green when it's rained and brown when it hasn't. Gardens are a few flowers under a window or at a corner of the lawn. Lawns tend to have a pine tree or two. Several have a car or a truck on blocks.

Your house: long grass, two pine trees, no fence, no cars on blocks. The front door has a cardboard skeleton, legs and arms bent like it's dancing. Three pumpkins sit on the step: Mom's, Tish's, and George's. Dad thinks holidays are silly. You decided years ago that Halloween is for kids.

The house makes you think of work you hated doing and work you'll hate having to do. You helped paint the walls pink, Mom's second favorite color. You helped turn the carport into the parents' bedroom by walling it with plywood, then painting the outside brown, Dad's favorite color, and the inside red, Mom's favorite.

Parked on the lawn next to the house is a big red Chevy van. You helped convert it from a bread van into a camper by building shelves and beds and chair platforms, then painting the inside and outside red, like a barn on wheels. You don't know what project Dad will find for you next, but there will be one when you least expect or want it.

A pink bike with a chipped white wicker basket and a black bike with a silver banana seat and chopper handlebars lie in the yard—Tish and George are home. The racing bike and the station wagon are missing—Dad's still at school and Mom's still at work.

The grass needs mowing. If you start now, Mom and Dad will think good things about their industrious son. You look at the shed where Dad keeps a push mower. He says it's the "four 'E's": economical, environmental, and excellent exercise. That means he bought it at a yard sale for four dollars. Its wheels jam every eight feet, so you have to stop to yank grass out of the axle. It only cuts one blade out of four, so you have to go back and forth if you don't want the lawn looking like a goat wandered through it.

As you yank open the screen door, Tish calls over the blare of the TV, "Better start mowing, Chris!"

She and George are on the old green sofa with a steel mixing bowl full of popcorn between them. Neither of them look away from the black-and-white screen where Quick Draw McGraw is transforming into his secret identity of El Kabong.

You want to tell Tish she had better start cleaning the living room, but the room looks as good as a place full of secondhand furniture can. This is George's week to wash dishes and clean the kitchen, so you know it's already done. George always does what he's supposed to.

You say, "Better start minding your own business," and head down the hall.

Tish calls, "Chris? Did you do something? In school?"

You stop and look back.

"A man came by."

"We didn't let him in," George adds.

"He wanted to talk to you."

You ask, "Why?"

George shrugs, raising his thin shoulders almost to his ears. Tish says, "He didn't say."

Two days ago, you skipped PE to get high with the Beastman. Would they send someone to your house because you skipped PE? If they knew you'd gotten high, wouldn't they send a cop? "What'd he look like?"

"A man," George says, then laughs at his cleverness and your scowl.

"A man in a suit," Tish says. "He looked like a minister."

You point at your neck. "With a—"

She shakes her head. "He just looked like a minister."

George sings, "Man in black comes, comes to marry, comes to bury, man in black comes, better hide."

Tish says, "He said he would try again after dinner."

You say, "I didn't do anything in school," and keep walking.

Tish calls, "You better get mowing! Dad excused you yesterday!"

"And he can excuse me again today!" You grab your door, and as you slam it, you hear George say quietly, "Oh oh."

You open the door, shout, "I've got homework! Don't bug me!" and slam the door harder.

You toss your books on the bed and see the red-and-white portable record player Mom found at the Salvation Army, undoubtedly because its previous owner realized it was too heavy to be portable and too ugly to keep. The *Easy Rider* sound track is on the turntable. You click it on, twist the dial as high as it goes, set the needle on "Born to Be Wild," throw your arms wide, and whirl around the room. You're a rock-and-roll god, adored by women, envied by men. You're a lone rebel biker, cruising crowded freeways and lonely country roads. You crank the bike's throttle, you slam power chords on an electric guitar, you pound a bank of drums. You jump from the floor to your bed and back again. You could dance everywhere and anywhere without a care for what anyone thinks. You could fight armies of rednecks, cops, and soldiers. You could walk up to Cindy Hurly and ask her if she wanted to see a movie.

The song ends. You turn the player down and look at your schoolbooks. When you jumped on the bed, two bounced off. You bend down to get them. Under the bed, away from the door, as far from Tish and George as possible, is the cardboard box with your comics. You have a new *Nick Fury, agent of S.H.I.E.L.D.* with amazing psychedelic art by Steranko that you've only read five or six times.

So you read it again. Maybe you can't be a super-spy with a foxy girlfriend and a fast car who is always saving the world. You would happily spend your life drawing stories about one.

That reminds you of your notion for a drawing. You get out a sketchbook with a cover filled with doodles of peace signs and marijuana leaves. Most of the pages are full, but you accidentally skipped a few in the middle, so you flip there and start sketching the Kid on a motorcycle, flipping the bird to a dozen rednecks packed into a pickup like the Keystone Cops.

But when you add square-framed glasses to one redneck, you think of Black Glasses looking at you as he crawled from the pond.

You grimace, crumple the drawing up, throw it away, and start another. In this one, in a pool as dark as tar, a scared boy clings to a branch. His eyes and mouth are calm, as if he'll accept anything that happens next. You can't tell if he's rising or sinking.

You stare at the drawing. It isn't a redneck who fell in a pond.

It's a boy trapped by something he can't understand. He doesn't look like Black Glasses. He looks like someone you should recognize.

You hear a knock and Dad's voice. "Christopher?"

You slam your sketchbook shut. "Come in."

The door opens. Dad steps in, leaving a hand on the knob. "Tish says you've got homework."

"Uh-huh. I'm doing it."

He looks around the room, at your schoolbooks on the bed, the comics scattered beside them, the sketchbook on the desk. "It's your turn to mow."

"I'll do it tomorrow. First thing."

He looks at the turntable. The singer pleads soulfully, "Don't bogart that joint, my friend, pass it over to me."

Dad looks at you. "You said that yesterday."

"I got busy."

"You got busy the day before yesterday, too."

You grin. "What can I say? I'm a busy guy."

He doesn't smile. "Your mother works hard so the rest of us can go to school."

"I know."

"When she comes home, she likes the place to look like humans live here."

"I'll come straight home tomorrow and do it."

"Like you were going to today?"

"Uh-huh." Since he doesn't turn away, you add, "Something came up."

"Uh-huh."

If he would ask, you would tell him about the rednecks, but you can't mention them as an excuse. Dad hates excuses. You say, "It's not a big deal."

"What your mother wants isn't a big deal?"

Bad move. You try: "She won't care if it's one more day."

"She shouldn't have to decide if she cares." Dad nods. You think he's going to leave. The record ends. You want to get up and turn it over, but you and Dad have taken positions. Any movement now is weakness or a challenge.

He lets go of the door, looks at the hall, then looks back at you. "What're you working on?"

"Reading, writing, 'rithmetic."

He walks over to you. The rubber soles of his engineer boots make no sound. He reaches for the sketchbook. His hand is big, square, shaded with black hair on brown leather skin, capable of crushing bricks. You think the only thing you got from him is big hands. Your fingers are as long as his, but they're thin, goofy, freckled, and pink with sunburn.

He flips open the sketchbook, riffles forward through blank pages, and stops at the last drawing. "What class is that for?"

He found a lovingly detailed pen-and-ink of a woman carried through the jungle by a gorilla while a man swings on a vine to her rescue. A tattered bit of her skirt and a shredded shirt sleeve are all that remain of her clothes; they don't hide her breasts or butt. Her hair is black and shoulder-length, like Cindy Hurly's. Her muscled rescuer wears a tiny tigerskin loincloth. His hair is as light and as long as yours.

You shake your head. Your face burns. You're blushing, and you hate that.

"Go start mowing," he says quietly.

You should've yanked the sketchbook away when he reached for it. "Now?"

"If it gets too dark, we'll turn the porch light on."

"But supper—"

"You eat when you're done."

"No."

You thought you said it loudly, but he asks, "What?"

You stand. "I'm not your goddamn slave! I've got rights!" Your fists are tight at your side, like you learned in karate class, so tight you feel the pressure on your fingertips.

Dad looks at your hands. You let them open. You're too close to him. He could grab you or hit you easily, but backing away would show weakness.

He nods. "That's so."

You keep staring. There must be a trick. Finally, you say, "Okay."

"Rights come with responsibilities."

"I know."

"You don't act like it."

You walked into that one. You stay quiet.

"Come on." Dad walks out without another glance at you. If you're going to mow the lawn now that the day is cooling down, you ought to put on a work shirt or your jean jacket, but you won't give him a reason to come back for you.

You hurry down the hall. Mom is putting her purse down on the kitchen table as she flips through the day's mail. Tish lies on the living room floor with a notebook open, working through math problems. George is unwrapping a brick of yellow cheese food, which Mom and Dad say is as good as Velveeta and cheaper besides.

Mom says, "What's going on?"

"I gotta mow," you say.

"Now?

Dad, going out the front door, says, "The boy needs to learn some responsibility."

Mom looks at you. "I'll make you a sandwich when you're done."

You nod, following Dad.

George looks at you and shakes his head.

Tish says, "I told you—"

Mom is watching, so you can't even scowl at the kids. You close the door with a little extra force, loud enough that anyone inside will know you're angry, quietly enough that you could say you were just making sure the latch caught.

Dad goes to the garden shed. When he slides its doors wide, you expect him to pull out the push mower. Instead, he hands you a shovel.

You look at him, but he's walking away. He stops just short of the pine tree at the back corner of the lawn. You walk over. He says, "Hand me the shovel." You lift it by the shaft. As he takes it, his hand closing just under yours, you feel his strength. You could never yank it from his grip, no matter how hard you tried.

He puts the blade to the grass, rests a boot on it, and leans forward, as easy as stepping down. He lifts a scoop out of the ground, tosses it aside, takes a pace forward, takes another scoop and tosses it, turns and takes two more paces, scoops a third time and tosses it, then turns and takes another pace for the fourth scoop and toss. He jerks his head at the holes and says, "You don't have to mow inside that."

You know you don't want to hear the answer, but you ask, "Why not?"

"Tomorrow, dig that down six feet. I'll check the depth. Then you can fill it again."

You stare at the holes. Connect them, and they make a long rectangle. You say, "Besides mowing?"

He nods. "You want to be treated like a man, you get a man's punishment. In the army, if you wised off to an officer, you got put to digging pits. That one's yours."

You say, "Because I said 'goddamn'?"

He smiles a little. "Because you're too old to spank and too young to fight."

"You say 'goddamn' all the time."

"One of the few privileges of being Dad. Not having my kids smart off at me is another."

You look back at the rectangle.

Dad hands you the shovel. "Put that away and start mowing."

The shovel is heavy. The rectangle is the size of a grave.

Dad says, "Don't make me tell you again."

You jerk the shovel up, bringing its blade between you and him. He steps back. "Fuck you!" you scream.

His eyes flick between the shovel blade and you. He's waiting for you to attack, ready for it, maybe wanting it. You hurl the shovel aside. It hits the side of the house, loud enough to surprise you both. You scream, "Fuck you! Fuck your bullshit, you motherfucking fuckhead!"

He lunges forward with one hand out to grab you, but you're already turning, already running through the Jacksons' backyard, already crying while Dad yells, "Chris! Get back here! Get back here now!"

The Jacksons keep a German shepherd on a chain, a lean dog they call Buster, but all the kids in the neighborhood call Killer. He rises up barking. You cross the circle of his territory without veering and run on. Killer keeps barking behind you.

You don't know if Dad is chasing you, but you know you're faster on foot. The last time you raced was on a beach near Miami when you were ten, and you beat him.

The red camper fires up as you cross the Jacksons' front lawn. You dart past their truck and down the dirt street. Three routes meet ahead of you: the street, the county road, and the highway. You take the road without thinking, running along the ditch. Snot pours from your nose, tears from your eyes. Between the tears and the twilight, it's a miracle you don't trip and fall, but all you're thinking is, Run. Get away. Dad'll kill you. Even if you escape, you've thrown your life away. Run. Everything's fucked up. It's all fucked up.

You parallel a wire fence, heading for where it ends and the path into the woods begins. You hear an engine coming up fast behind you. It could be a pickup, but you know it isn't.

You cut across the ditch and scramble up the fence. The weather-browned wire forms big rectangles; the fence is meant to keep large animals from crossing it. For you, it's a ladder.

At the top, you hear the camper brakes grind and gravel slide under the tires. Dad yells, "Chris, goddamn it, get down!" and slams the car door behind him. "Now!"

You leap. The fence sways under your feet as you launch out, throwing you forward and sideways. Your right foot twists as you land hard in a cluster of bushes. You fall, scratching and snagging yourself on branches. But Dad is on the fence and climbing. You lurch to your feet and run on.

"This is it!" Dad calls. Something in his voice makes you stop. He's at the top of the fence, looking at you. "You come back now, or you don't come back at all!"

"Eat shit and die!" you shout, and you run on. When you reach the trail, you wonder if Dad knows about it. He could be running down it now like a grizzly after a rabbit. He could drive to the far side and wait for you. He could call the cops and have them hunting you, everywhere you go, like *The Fugitive*. He could drive through the night in the big red camper, hunting without sleeping till he finds you.

Then you remember his last words. He could go home and tell everyone it's good-bye and good riddance. Mom and Tish would cry, but not too hard or too long. They know there would be more peace in the house with you gone. George would laugh. He could move into your room, the second largest in the house, and say you'd sure done a bad job of planning for running off.

Which is too true. You shiver, rub your arms, and walk faster. When the trail forks, you turn on a path you rarely take. As you walk, you rub your nose on the back of your hand. You haven't cried for years. Today you're Captain Snot Rivers.

But you know you'll stop crying soon. Your stomach has started whispering that you haven't eaten since lunch at school, and then you skipped the lima beans and the red Jell-O with marshmallows.

You pull out your wallet. You have a dollar, enough for six comic books or two orders of burgers and fries at McDonald's if you drink water. In your jeans' coin pocket are a quarter, a dime, and two pennies. Make that nine comics or three McDonald's meals. You poke through your wallet, checking every pocket, though you know you didn't tuck twenty dollars away for an emergency. Your emergency money is where you can't get it in an emergency, in a black plastic cube that, when you were nine, you were sure spies would use to hide atomic secrets.

But in the back of your wallet, in a pocket you never use, you find the Penney's card that you were sure you had put in your desk. Mom insisted on getting it for you. You have ten dollars of credit there. You never used it because Penney's is the only store in the universe that is less cool than Sears.

Cool is a luxury now. And who would look for you at Penney's? So you hike to a county road that parallels the highway, then walk along it, sticking out your thumb for every headlight and praying that none of them are Dad's.

Three

As the sky turns red, a dark sedan slows as it approaches. You squint into its lights. It stops precisely beside you. You think about unmarked police cars. Should you take to the woods?

The passenger door opens. A dim overhead light shows the driver. He wears a dark suit, a white shirt, a dark tie, a dark hat. The hat puts his eyes in shadow, but when he smiles, you like him a little. He says, "I can take you to the crossroads."

He seems a bit conservative to be picking up a long-haired kid, but he'll save you two miles of walking. You say, "Thanks," and slide in.

The overhead goes out when you pull the door shut. The car rolls back onto the road. The twilight seems very quiet. The car smells smokey, like pipe or cigar smoke, which makes you think of Dad and wish you had just mowed the damn lawn.

You don't pass any other cars. The man's engine is a well-tuned purr. He drives precisely at the speed limit; you can see his speedometer stay on the forty-five. Dad would approve.

Your hand starts shaking. You want to cry again, but you aren't about to do that in front of anyone, especially not a stranger. You squeeze your fist.

You suddenly feel certain that someone's in the backseat, maybe a lot of people, so you turn. The long backseat holds nothing but shadows.

You wish the radio was on, or the man would talk about something like sports that you could listen to and not care about. You say, "I appreciate the ride."

He keeps his gaze on the road. You think he'll ignore you. Then he says, "I spend a lot of time working. It's nice to do something purely to help someone, no matter how small it is."

"Yeah." You wonder if that includes giving money to runaways, but you won't beg until all you have is gone.

"Where're you going?"

"To the mall." If he volunteers to drive you there, you can accept that without feeling you had asked for favors.

"What'll you do?"

You shrug. You want to pick oranges or hawk newspapers or shovel coal on freighters bound for the Suez Canal. If you discovered a diamond mine in the Andes, the whole family would be sorry they hadn't treated you better. You say, "Hang out."

The man nods. "I wish I could drive you there. I have an appointment nearby."

"You're not from around here?"

He shakes his head. "Business brings me here fairly often."

"What do you do?"

"I'm in collections." He's obviously successful. You don't recognize his sedan, but it's new, clean, unblemished, big enough to carry Catholic families. His suit and hat are made of something soft that soaks up light. You think about asking if it's cotton or wool, but you can't think of a way to ask and sound manly.

You say, "Do you like it?" You can't tell if his eyes flick from the road to you and back again, or whether he has heard at all. You add, "Collections. Is that good work?"

He makes a sound between a cough and a laugh. "People are rarely glad to see me."

"That sucks."

"It's a job."

"You think about quitting?"

"Often."

"Dad says—" You pause, hearing what you're saying, but you've already started the sentence, so you swallow and press on. "You should only do what you want or what needs doing, so long as you don't hurt anyone."

"That's not as easy as it sounds."

"Nope. The old man thinks it just applies to him, anyway."

"Really?"

"Yeah. Like mowing the lawn. It's not fun, and no way it needs doing."

The man's head turns toward you. "Oh?"

"It's grass. What's it hurt to let things grow?"

He looks back at the road. "Weeds sprout up. Old growth strangles the new. The green shoots never see the sun."

"You sound like a gardener."

He smiles, more widely than before.

A traffic light is ahead, glowing yellow, at the first major intersection on the way into town. As the car slows, you say, "Thanks."

"No. Thank you."

"For what?"

"For reminding me it's good to do work that needs doing."

Something swells in your chest. "That's Dad, not me."

"He passed it to you. You passed it to me. All you can do is thank those who give what you need."

"I guess." The car stops. You open the door, thinking you don't want to hear any more about how wise your idiot father is.

"Let me give you something."

You stop, halfway out of the door, and look back. If he offers money you haven't asked for, can you take it and respect yourself?

His hands stay on the wheel. He says, "Enjoy it. Enjoy it all."

You frown. Did he give you something and you didn't notice? Then you understand. He's just giving you advice to make himself feel good. You say, "That's it?"

He nods. "Yes. Because it ends when you least expect it."

"Uh-huh." You look down the road. Headlights are coming, maybe your next ride.

The man waves. "See you later."

"Sure." You close his door, thinking how unlikely that is. You're running away to New Orleans or Los Angeles or New York, Paris or Algiers or Amsterdam, Timbuktu or Fiji or Singapore. His job would have to take him pretty far for him to see you again.

The dark sedan rolls away quietly and turns south at the light. You wait to cross the intersection. An ambulance races by, siren screaming, red lights strobing, heading the same direction as the sedan.

You run across the highway and stick your thumb out, but the next car isn't your ride. Nor the one after that, nor the one after that.

You stand at the intersection for half an hour, long enough for the sun to drop below the horizon, long enough to have walked from where the sedan picked you up, long enough for the ambulance to return, slow and quiet, lit only by its headlights. You wonder if you'll be standing here until the dark sedan passes by again.

You hug yourself, rubbing your arms, thinking you're a fool to run away. You're fourteen and look it, or younger. You could hope to mow lawns, if you had a lawnmower. What else can a homeless kid do? If you're lucky, you could hustle dope on the street. But who would front you the dope? All you have to sell is your small, pimply, graceless, unloved, and unlovable self.

When headlights flash across your face, you try to smile like a teenager who happens to be jacketless on a cool night, who doesn't need a ride but would happily accept one. Cars keep passing. You fight the urge to use the Beastman's technique, lowering your thumb for each car that doesn't stop and raising your middle finger.

You shiver and buff your arms. You wish you had a watch. An expensive one. You could pawn it in Las Vegas, get into a game with high rollers, win a Texas oil field with a lucky hand, and turn over your virginity to a trio of keno girls.

Better yet, find a commune of hippies who'll offer you food, drugs, and sex with all the women. You can give them your art, painting murals, drawing tattoos, designing T-shirts. You'll all live by the sea and swim naked in the sun, then lie on the sand like seals. There'll be music, books, and laughter. When straights see you and the hippies, in your wild clothes and wild hair and wild, wild joy, they'll sneer in disgust to hide from themselves how completely they envy you.

That's the best plan. It only calls for hitching three thousand miles to San Francisco and asking where a commune is.

Headlights come out of the dusk. They belong to a vehicle shaped like a bread box. Like the red camper.

You step back, then see this van's smaller. Its corners are more rounded. It's covered in blotches like an animal's hide. It's a Volkswagen painted in blues, yellows, and reds that swirl around peace symbols and stylized doves.

You thrust out your thumb. The brake lights come on. The van slows and pulls over. You run toward it, grinning because you were thinking about hippies and a freakmobile shows up.

The rear door slides open. Music blares, a tune from *Revolver*. Smoke smells so strong and sweet you know you would see it in daylight. A skinny albino with a huge Afro leans out. "Squeeze in, man!"

Grinning, you obey. The van holds nine people already, two in front, seven on a blue-striped mattress in back. There are three girls, six guys, all older than you, all dressed cool: faded denim, baggy bells, tie-dyed tees, long-sleeved paisley shirts, chambray work shirts, fringed leather vests. They must be a band with roadies and groupies, but where are their instruments?

A skinny redhead in a green and orange dashiki slides over, smiles widely, and pats the mattress between her and the albino. "Going far?" you shout hopefully over the Beatles.

"All the way," says the driver, a young Pancho Villa with a ponytail. Everyone laughs, except for a dark-skinned girl in an army jacket. You laugh, too, and squeeze in beside the redhead. The albino slams the door, turning everyone into shadows.

"I'm gonna make the 'Frisco scene," you offer.

"Far out," says the redhead.

"We're going all the way *to the U,*" says the girl in the army jacket, with a glance at the driver that he misses. You can't tell if she has no patience with you or him or the world.

You shrug. The university is four miles farther from home. "Every little bit helps."

She looks at you, then faces forward as the van bumps back onto the street. Her Afro is smaller than the albino's. Her army jacket makes you think of Black Panthers and Weathermen. Maybe this group blew up a draft center, and you'll all be arrested, and you'll get life in prison like the Birdman of Alcatraz. You'll become a prison lawyer and free yourself, but not till you're ninety years old. Everyone will say it's a tragedy, which will show Dad.

The redhead says, "Do you believe in love?" You can't glance away without being rude. Her eyes are pale green. She has a pimple above her left nostril. Does she mean free sex, a great idea in theory, but which you'd rather not try in the van in front of the others without some private practice? Or does she mean world peace, equally great in theory, but which people like Adolf Hitler and Richard Nixon make you think is impossible? The right answer may get you stoned or laid. You nod hesitantly.

"I knew it!" She clutches your thigh just above the knee. "You have a beautiful soul. I can tell."

Her touch tingles so strongly that you fight the urge to flinch. It's not pain or pleasure. It's just a tingle that's almost too strong to bear. If you jerk away, everyone will know you're a kid who never had a girl put her hand on his leg.

Army jacket girl says to the redhead, "You can tell everybody has a beautiful soul."

The redhead doesn't hear what's under the girl's words. Neither does the albino, who nods and says, "She's special."

"That's sure true," army jacket girl says.

The redhead smiles at the albino, then asks you, "What's your name?"

You open your mouth to say "Chris." You've always been Chris or Christopher or, when Dad or Mom were very mad, Mark Christopher Nix. But Dad never sounded mad when he mentioned Uncle Mark, and Mark Twain is famous, and you could use a link with greatness. "Mark," you say, feeling like a liar.

"Hi, Mark. I'm Tina, and"—the redhead gestures around the van—"that's Juan, Dixon, Bodacious, Lee, Speedo, Sunshine, Nicky, and CC."

You glance at them and nod. The driver's Juan, the albino is Speedo, army jacket girl is CC, the one you might get lucky with is Tina.

You like riding with Tina's thigh against yours. You wish the hippies were going farther than the U. You wonder if they have a place where you could crash. You smile at each of them. They smile back. "This is so cool," you tell Tina, then worry she'll think you're uncool for saying it out loud. She smiles wider and squeezes your thigh. Your jeans are tighter than they were a moment ago.

At the rear of the van are wooden shelves with bungee cord stretched in front of them to keep things from sliding off, like 8-track tapes, collections of *Pogo* cartoons, and a wadded-up motorcycle jacket. The lowest shelf holds a row of dark books and a brass incense burner.

That must be to cover up the smell of burning weed. You hope they'll light up soon. You bounce a bit on the mattress. The Beastman will go bug-eyed when you tell him about a stoned orgy in a hippie van.

The books by the incense burner are identical: shiny black covers, gold lettering. Maybe they're college texts, and the van's full of people taking the same class. The shape of the title looks familiar. Two words. Holy—

You're Wile E. Coyote standing on air, afraid to look down at the canyon's bottom. You're not going to get laid. You're going to get lectured.

Tina's touch on your thigh has less meaning than a nurse's. Her grip tightens as if she's afraid you'll dive out a window. She says, "It is cool. Because the coolest of all is Jesus."

There should've been a warning on the van: Beware of the Jesus Freaks. No sex and drugs. Just tea and hugs. The mall is only a few blocks away. You say, "Hey, I should get out here. I gotta grab some things before I split."

Tina says, "Mark, don't go. When Jesus knocks, you have to answer."

You say, "Or he won't come back?"

Light from a passing car flicks across CC. She's far from pretty: round-faced, gap-toothed, wide-mouthed, small-chinned. But something touches the edge of her lips that's almost a smile, and you like it.

"Oh, he's coming back," says Juan. "For those who don't reject him."

The van slows to turn toward the U. You point at the corner. "This is good."

"Jesus loves you," Tina says. "Don't you want to be loved? You can crash with us, if you want. You can learn with us."

The van pulls to a stop. The 8-track tape chunks to the next song, but Juan yanks the tape out before it can start. He says, "Just ask Jesus into your heart. He loves you."

CC's smile is different from the others. They want you to stay. She thinks this is funny. You say, "Why do I have to go first?"

"Huh?" asks Speedo.

"If Jesus loves me, why won't he say it first?"

CC covers her mouth. Tina says, "He's been saying it all your life. You just haven't heard."

"Maybe he should speak up."

Juan's smile fades. "Maybe you should listen up."

You say, "I'm s'posed to believe without even a miracle?"

"Love is the miracle," says Tina.

You shake her hand from your knee and slide open the door. "Thanks for the ride."

Speedo says, "You're running toward Satan. Turn back now."

"I mocked, just like you," says Juan.

"Mark," Tina says. "Don't you want to be saved?"

You shake your head. "Not by a God who hides, then damns people who can't find him."

You walk toward the intersection. The night is cold after the warmth of the van. Coldness suits you. The world is full of idiots and arrogant bastards, and you will never get laid.

Four

Behind you, Speedo yells, "Hey, where're you going?" The van door slams. You turn fast, expecting Jesus Freaks with baseball bats coming to pound you into the pavement for rejecting God's love.

CC walks toward you, calling back over her shoulder, "Shopping!"

Speedo says sadly, "Thought you were coming to the revival."

She spins to face him, her army coat swirling around her skinny legs, and keeps walking backward toward you. "Next time."

Tina calls, "How'll you get home?"

CC says, "I can catch a bus."

Juan calls, "You're always welcome at the Jesus Pad!"

"Cool!" CC lifts her hand over her shoulder and waggles it, a queen dismissing her subjects.

The van belches smoke as it pulls away. People shout, "So long!" and "See you!" to CC. No one shouts anything to you, not even "Fuck off!" which you would rather like.

CC, walking up to you, looks like a kid in her big brother's coat. In the van, she seemed taller. You catch yourself staring and stalk off. Before you've taken two steps, she calls, "Hey! Wait up!"

She gives the first full smile you've seen from her. You say without thinking, "Cheshire Cat."

She lifts an eyebrow.

You're embarrassed. You can't think of anything but the truth: "In this light, your smile's about all I can see."

The smile disappears.

Does she think you're making fun of her skin? "It's a good smile," you say quickly.

"Good." The smile returns and is gone like a firefly's flicker.

Does she think you think she's hot? You don't. You liked a black girl in sixth grade as a friend, but the only blacks you think are sexy are famous adults: Diana Ross of the Supremes, Peggy on *Mannix,* Uhura on *Star Trek*. You say, "Listen, catch your bus. You're not going to convert me."

"Did I try?" She walks past without a glance. She smells like cigarette smoke and patchouli.

Across the street is the mall, a gray block surrounded by an asphalt parking lot. A glowing orange pumpkin sits over the front door, a beacon for ghosts and witches lost on a foggy night.

Lining this side of the street are low houses made of brown brick or white wood. One yard is strung with cobwebs over wooden tombstones like a cow town's boot hill: Kid Enyew, Daniel Booze, Mild Bill Hickup, the Two-Pun Kid. The house's curtains are open. At a table, a man and a girl laugh as a woman wipes spaghetti sauce from a little boy's chin. They're in their shirt sleeves. Supper must be hot from the stove.

You shiver, stuff your hands into your jeans pockets, and follow CC, asking, "So what do you want?"

That gets you a glance. It's not friendly. "There a law against shopping?"

"You just decided to shop?"

She shrugs. "My cousin's birthday's next week. I don't have a present for him."

"Oh."

"And it gets me away from those fools."

"You're not a Jesus Freak?"

She flashes the big smile. "Gets me out of Auntie's house. She don't want me running around with no boys. But Christians going to hear Christian music, that's different, even if the boys look like no-account hippies."

"Uh-huh." The light at the corner turns red. You both stop, side by side on the curb.

She says, "Why San Francisco?"

"Why not?" She looks at you like that's a stupid answer. You add, "It's cool. Gainesville sure isn't."

"I hear that." The light changes, and she starts across.

You hesitate. If you let her go ahead, the two of you will naturally separate. When she heads for one mall entrance, you can take the other. That'd be the path of least resistance. You walk slowly. The distance between you increases, a few feet, then half the wide street. When DON'T WALK flashes, you run to get out of the intersection.

And find yourself stepping onto the far curb beside CC. She says, "I'd go to San Francisco if I could." She keeps her eyes on the mall as she walks. "I'd go anywhere, if I could."

Is she hinting for an invite? It'll be tough enough for one kid to catch rides. Two would halve your chances. Especially if one was black. You duck that with a question: "Why don't you?"

"Auntie's not so bad. 'Cept when she gets a mad on. Then you got to keep out of her way till she settles." CC tugs up the sleeve of her army coat. The skin of her forearm is blotched like camouflage.

"What happened?"

"Nothing."

"Uh-huh. Looks like nothing."

CC shrugs. "She was boiling pigs feet, and I sassed her. Should've waited till I reached the hall."

You touch one of the blotches. It's scar tissue, harder and cooler than the surrounding skin. "Must've hurt—"

And someone says, "Huh. Is that a white boy and a nigger gal?"

Your hand jerks back from CC's arm. If you were a cat, the hair on your back would point to the sky. You look up, less to see the danger than to find an escape.

About forty feet ahead, two men walk toward you. Their clothes are clean but speckled with paint or oil. One man's potbelly bulges under a jacket with the STANDARD OIL logo. The other is lean and muscular, maybe a one-time high school sports hero. They could be the three rednecks' favorite uncles.

Potbelly carries a gallon of paint. He says, "Or is it the other way 'round?" If he swung the can into your head, he might crush your skull.

Sports Hero says, "Could be two girls. Hard to say."

Ignore them, you think. They just want you to feel like you don't even deserve to be called a— You can't end the thought. What should you be called? What should you do? Running away and getting beat up are equally terrifying.

CC looks at the men, then takes your hand in hers. Her palm is softer and warmer than you expected, softer and warmer than any hand that has ever touched yours. You're too surprised to shake it free.

Sports Hero says, "Think they're lez-beans?"

Potbelly shrugs. "Might could be."

CC tugs to start you walking. Her grip is soft, but strong. You could wrench your hand free and run away, but you don't.

Potbelly says, "Might be they don't know what they are."

Sports Hero laughs and grins at you.

CC stares at the men as you draw near. Her head's high and her chin's raised. The part of your brain that isn't trying to keep you from pissing your pants thinks, That statue. Cleopatra? Nefertiti? You look at the doors to the mall and make yourself breathe slowly. All your attention is on the men at the edge of your sight. You want to ask CC if she knows the risk that she's running. Every story you know of mixed-race couples ends with the boy beaten, the girl raped, one or both dead.

Sports Hero says, "What is this country coming to?"

Your hand is sweating in CC's grip. Your heart must be on a trampoline. CC says loudly, "How 'bout splitting a milk shake at McDonald's, sugar pie?"

The men keep coming without changing speed or direction. CC squeezes your hand and adds, "You fancy chocolate?"

You nod, then cough to clear your throat. "Yeah." Your voice is painfully thin and scratchy in your ears. "I do."

"Christ," says Potbelly. The men turn toward you. Your whole body is a stretched cord. You tell yourself to jerk CC's arm and run.

But the men keep turning, cross four feet in front of you, and get in a station wagon with wood grain paneling.

You and CC walk on. If you draw this, the Kid will tell a beautiful girl with an Afro four times as large as her head, "Chocolate and vanilla, my favorite combination!" And he'll kiss her while twelve giant, milk-white men turn brick red and steam blows out of their ears.

A white woman leaves the mall, dragging a three-foot pirate by the hand. She scowls at you and walks faster. The pirate looks back over his shoulder as the woman hurries away. CC keeps holding your hand. You want her to let go, but you can't be the one to pull free, no more than you could've run from the men.

At the entrance, CC steps ahead to hold the door for an old black man in a business suit who has two heavy Sears bags in his arms. He starts to nod at her, sees you and your hand in hers, shakes his head sadly, and walks out.

CC drags you down the long walk of stores. "Where you wanna go?"

Where no one will stare at me. The thought shames you. You're afraid of your father, you're afraid of bigots, you're afraid of strangers thinking you're strange for holding hands with a dark-skinned girl. You're afraid of admitting you're afraid. You say, "Penney's."

She nods and pulls you down the mall. Maybe she won't let go first. You say, "What'll you do if I have to go to the bathroom?"

She glances at your hands and smiles. "You got to go?"

"No."

"Me, neither."

And that, you think, is a draw. You smile, too. Smiling must be contagious, because two college-aged girls in bell-bottoms grin at you and CC. One raises her fingers in a "V" of peace. You flash the sign back. You would almost think that smiling could bring love to the world, if a security guard's look didn't say, "I know you've been shoplifting and I hate that I can't prove it."

CC pulls you on, past stores selling things no one needs. The music is an orchestra doing an old pop song that no one except you must be able to hear, because if anyone could hear it, no one would play it, right?

CC says, "Where you go to school?"

"George Washington Carver."

"Jefferson Davis."

You nod. Jefferson Davis is the east side junior high. She's younger than you thought.

She says, "What grade?"

"Ninth."

"Eighth."

"Eighth?" She's definitely younger than she looks.

She laughs. "Comes after seventh."

"Thanks. Math's my worst subject."

"Don't pay it no mind."

"I thought you were older."

"How old you want me to be?"

You shrug. You don't care what she wants. She's not just dark and skinny and big-eyed. If she's a year younger than you, she's only a kid.

Without looking at you, she adds, "I can call my auntie and say the concert's gonna run late."

Is she flirting? If she wants to make you uncomfortable, she keeps succeeding. Maybe she hates all whites and wants to see you squirm. You should ditch her when she goes to shop. You shrug. "Where you gonna look for your cousin's present?"

"Penney's."

You glance at her.

She says, "Good a place as any."

"What do you want to get him?"

"Something stupid. Auntie thinks he needs a new tie. He ain't getting no new tie, I can tell you that."

You laugh. "Yeah, you can tell me that."

She lifts her head for a down-the-nose smile. "I can tell you all kinds of things, white boy. You wait."

You stop in the middle of the mall. Shoppers have to walk around you. You don't care. "Why do you call me that?"

"You're not a white boy?"

"You're messing with me."

She nods without a smile.

"Should I call you 'black girl'?"

"Depends."

"On?"

"How you say it."

"Uh-huh."

"Now, don't get all moody. White boys are pretty."

A blond woman with a stroller heads right for you and says pointedly, "Excuse me!" You step aside, pulling CC with you, and glare at her.

"What, you don't like being pretty?" CC says. "Girls like pretty boys. You got it going with that long hair and them soulful eyes." You keep staring. She nods, then adds, "Serious."

"Don't call me 'white boy.'"

"Sure." Her voice has no emotion. Her hand slips out of yours. The air on your moist palm is cool.

You say, "Black girl."

She frowns, grins, and starts to slap you, just fast enough that you have to catch her wrist. You want to tickle her, but the security guard is walking by with a look that says one of you had better buy something soon.

You pull on CC's hand. "C'mon. CC."

"Sure thing," she says. "Mark."

And you head into Penney's, drawing her through the perfumes and women's shoes and kitchen appliances. The store, like the mall, has a typical number of typical families, mostly white, mostly looking like they learned to dress by watching TV shows about white families who looked like like they learned to dress by watching TV, et cetera. The clerks around the makeup counters are ghosts, witches, devils, and catwomen. Deeper in the store you spot a soldier, a baseball player, and a grotesque hippie in a shiny wig, a plastic necklace with a huge peace symbol, a polyester green shirt, and pink flares that look too stupid to be insulting to anyone except the woman wearing them.

Everyone in the store glances at you just a little longer than they would if you were alone. Then they look away. They don't see two kids shopping. They see a long-haired freak and a black militant invading their territory. They fear you because you're the future, and the future is always frightening.

"We're the future," you tell CC.

"You're weird."

"The future is weird." You both grin.

She says, "I'm glad I told 'em to stop for you."

"You did?"

"Juan said the van had enough riders, but I had a feeling about you."

"I thought you didn't like me at first."

"Meaning you think I like you now?"

"Well—"

She smiles. "Yeah, white boy. I like you."

Do you like her? You think so, but you're afraid to say it. You say, "Cool." She grins like that's an answer, and you realize it is.

"May I help you?" says a bride in an ancient gown. Her face is half hidden by a veil. Plastic spiders cling to it. Her accent is as thick as CC's. Under the veil, white wig, and thick white powder, she reminds you of your mother: short, fortyish, maybe twenty pounds over what she thinks is her perfect weight. But you would know what your mother was thinking the second you saw her face. The bride has a smile that wouldn't falter if she shot you.

"Yes'm." CC points at a clear acrylic and string device, five balls hanging next to each other in a frame. "Is that the stupidest thing you got?"

The bride studies CC, then looks fast to either side to see if anyone is near, pulls one ball out and lets it drop. It bangs into the others, and the far one shoots out, comes back, and hits the others, sending the first out again. As the balls clack back and forth, the bride says, "What you think?"

CC reaches over to stop the balls, then lifts two from each side and drops them. As they bounce outward and back, CC says, "It don't get stupider."

CC and the bride smile. CC says, "What're you after, Mark?"

What you need is a jacket and a sleeping bag. You can't get both for ten dollars. You ask the bride, "Do you have ponchos?"

She shakes her head. "Got to go to one of them hippie shops down by the university."

A hippie shop would not take a Penney's card. "How about a blanket?"

"Over here." She leads you away from her counter. CC stays behind, testing bounce patterns with the acrylic balls.

"What were you wanting?"

You think, Something cool. You say, "An Indian print? Or Mexican?"

The bride looks at you. You know she's thinking, Where does this boy think he's shopping? She says, "We just got these."

The blankets look like blankets from Penney's: screamingly synthetic and too ugly to be forgettable. The only one under ten dollars is an acrylic baby blue bedspread. Why didn't you ask for the uncoolest blanket in the universe? Then you would be pleasantly surprised. This is probably only the uncoolest blanket in Florida. "I'll take that."

She pulls it out of the shelf, then looks over at CC. "That girl—"

You brace yourself for a speech about God wanting the races to stay pure. You hear, "She's got more to lose than you. Think on that. You could hurt her bad, just 'cause you want to have your fun."

"I wouldn't do that, ma'am."

She keeps looking at you, then nods and heads back to her counter. "Cash or charge?"

You hand her the card. CC touches the toy of hanging balls, says, "I'll take this," and digs through the pockets of her jacket, finding a tightly folded dollar bill in each. She puts five on the counter and tells you, as the bride hands back your Penney's card, "Didn't know I was out with a rich boy."

"You're not," you say fast, thinking for the first time in days about Grandpa Abner, who died two years ago in northern Minnesota, and Grandma Letitia, who is dying in Sun City, Arizona. If Grandpa Abner was still living, you would hitchhike north and ask to stay with them. Grandpa Abner never wanted you to change a thing about yourself. But Grandma Letitia would make you cut your hair and never wear jeans or T-shirts or anything cool.

As you sign the sales receipt, CC says, "Then I best not ask if you got a couple pennies for the tax."

One dollar, a quarter, a dime, and two pennies, you think. One pair of jeans, a T-shirt, underwear, socks, and desert boots. And Florida's ugliest blanket. You're not rich. You're free. Freedom sure can suck.

You hand both pennies to the bride. She nods as if you've passed a test and rings up CC's cousin's present.

"Y'all come back now," the bride calls as you and CC pick up your purchases in their paper bags.

CC takes your hand, saying, "Sure thing." Having her hand in yours is beginning to feel as normal as everyone-is-staring-at-me-and-some-of-them-want-to-hurt-me-bad can possibly feel.

The smart thing to do would be to drop CC's hand. So you don't.

Walking back through the mall, she says, "Who's the blanket for?"

"Me." She waits, so you add, "I need something to keep warm."

"Thought you were just hot-blooded."

You don't know what to say, so you shrug.

"You're going to sleep in that?"

"That's how much credit I had on the card."

"You going to catch a ride to California tonight?"

You think about hitching at night, unable to see the people who stop until you open the door and the overhead light shows their faces. You're tired. As soon as you leave the mall, you'll be cold. "I'll crash somewhere and take off tomorrow."

"Want to walk me home?"

"Have you got someplace to crash?"

She laughs hard. "Auntie, this white boy followed me home! Can I keep him?"

Her laugh makes you join her. Her lips are a dark rose, her teeth are pearl. Her lips are where her outside ends. Her tongue is her inside flirting. Would kissing her be different than kissing Cindy Hurly?

Her eyes are on yours. Is she thinking about kissing, too? Do you want your first kiss to be with a black girl? You feel bad for thinking about her skin, but the question doesn't go away. You don't know her. You're in the middle of a mall. If Cindy Hurly threw herself into your arms in the middle of a mall and said, "Take me, you fool!" you would be too embarrassed to kiss her while anyone was looking.

You look away. The mall guard is fifty feet back, glaring at you. You're grateful. His presence lets you tell CC, "We're being watched."

She looks away. "Want to give him something to look at?"

For an instant, you're sure that's an invitation to kiss her. And it would be funny to freak out the guard. But it wouldn't be funny if he claimed he saw you stealing something. "We should get going."

"Okay."

Is she disappointed? You're not sure. But kissing her would be a mistake. Leave Florida, go to California, forget you ever had a life here.

Her hand is still in yours. She's definitely playing some game. You should let go. If she thinks that means you're too racist or too straight, so what? In another minute, she'll go home and you'll go looking for a place to sleep.

The mall guard stops following when you go out. Past the parking lot lights, the sky is black. Only the number of cars on the street tells you that the night is early. A breeze rolls leaves under parked cars and across the asphalt. You stop by a trash can and release CC's hand.

You pull the boring blanket out of its bag, stuff the bag in the trash, and shake the blanket out. CC waits. You say, "Do you get the bus here?"

"What do you mean?"

"You told the Jesus Freaks you could get the bus."

"Oh." She hefts her shopping bag. "That was before I found something for Isaac."

"Ah." You throw the blanket around your shoulders. The acrylic settles lightly, not like the wool Navajo blanket at home. You draw it tight around you. If you cut a hole in it for your head, would it unravel? You wish you could add a hood and a drawstring to make it a cloak. A cloak would be cool. You look like a kid who stole a blanket from a Holiday Inn.

"Well," you say. "I'll walk you home."

And her hand is back in yours so quickly you're not sure how it happened.

Five

Porch lights are going dark on University Avenue. The little trick-or-treaters have gone home. No one wants high school kids. You say, "Seems wrong. On Halloween, people should stay up till midnight."

"There's a party at the university. We could go."

You stare at CC. "What about your aunt?"

"She goes to sleep early."

"You could get out?"

CC laughs. "Oiled my window. I be gone like a cool breeze."

"Wouldn't we need costumes?"

"Hippies are too lazy to wear costumes."

"They might kick us out 'cause we're kids."

CC stops and studies you. "A pin would make your blanket into a cape. You can be Batman or the Sheik of Araby."

"What about you?"

"I'll find something." She turns off University Avenue onto a quiet side street. It's the city version of your neighborhood: cluttered yards, peeling paint, old American cars. Music comes too loudly from a nearby house: Motown, not rock. You stop walking.

"What?" CC says.

"Is it all right for me to be here?"

"Why wouldn't it?"

"'Cause, you know, I'm white."

"Thought white folks figured they could go anywhere."

"Stupid ones. I'm all for equal opportunity, but I haven't been beaten up by blacks, and I'd like to keep it that way."

She smiles. "I'll protect you."

"Much appreciated, ma'am."

Fewer houses here are decorated for Halloween, but more of them still have porch lights on. From one comes Dracula and Frankenstein's Bride. He wears a dark purple suit, white turtleneck, gold medallion, white gloves, and a dark cape with red lining. Her hair is as big as her head. The sides are streaked like lightning bolts. Instead of bandages, she wears a sleeveless gold jumpsuit, skintight to the knees where it flares into bell-bottoms. You stare without thinking because every detail is perfect. You wish you and CC were them.

As the couple pass by, Dracula raises his fist slightly in a salute and says in a low, quiet drawl, "Right on, bro."

You stifle the grateful smile you want to give him and say, "What it is."

Frankenstein's Bride laughs, maybe at that, maybe at something else. You don't care. As soon as you're past them, you grin.

CC frowns. "'What it is'?"

"Isn't that right?"

"It's better than 'Howdy-doody.'"

You laugh. "I'll try that on the next brother we meet."

"You wouldn't."

"Sure, I would."

"You'd be scared."

"Nah."

"Yeah."

You spot two teenagers across the street, talking near the street corner. One wears an orange polyester suit with a matching fedora. The other has a brown leather cowboy hat and a brown fringed suede jacket that you wish was yours. Taking a step toward them, you say, "Come on."

CC keeps your right hand in her left and grabs you above the elbow with her right hand, yanking you back. "If you don't want weed or a whore, keep walking."

"Those aren't pimp costumes?"

"Sure they are. With pimps in 'em."

"Oh." You keep walking.

CC keeps your arm in her double grip. "You don't have to prove a thing. Man who'll thumb to California is plenty brave."

"I haven't even started."

"Sure, you have." She stops. "That's my house."

You glance ahead. She means a white brick house surrounded by chain-link. It has a row of bushes along its foundation. The lawn was recently mowed. The windows are dark, except for one, where a dim lamp glows.

CC takes a long-toothed comb from a coat pocket and starts combing down her Afro, parting her hair and giving herself bangs, "Auntie's waiting up, but she'll go to bed once I tell her how we praised Jesus." CC tucks the comb away, opens her coat and takes a pair of glasses with pointed blue plastic frames from an inside pocket. "Don't say nothing," she warns as she puts them on. Under the jacket, she wears a bright yellow T-shirt with bright red printing: JESUS LOVES ME.

She says, "Don't stare. I ain't me now."

She could pass for twelve. A hopelessly square twelve-year-old.

"Who are you?"

She smiles and says in a perfect impersonation of white teenagers on television, "Eula Mae Carter."

"What's 'CC' stand for?"

She shakes her head. "I got to go in now."

"Want me to wait here?"

She looks at the dealers laughing together. "Go through the alley and wait in back." When you hesitate, she adds, "Ain't no dogs or nothing. I'll be out once Auntie's sleeping." She squeezes your hand and starts away.

And you start to doubt. Will she come out again? Did she lure you here so a gang could rob you? Do you really want to go to a university party that you probably won't get into because you look like a kid?

She whirls and says in a soft, hopeful voice that must be Eula Mae, not CC, "You will be there?"

You could tell CC that California is calling, and she would wave good-bye with a grin. Eula Mae would probably wave, too, but the wave would be small and she wouldn't grin.

"Sure," you say, which gets you one of CC's nods, not smiling, just certain, and your doubts are gone.

"You got to climb the fence. It's easy." She smiles suddenly, and before you can ask if this is the best plan, she hurries down the street.

You stop at the corner, a few feet down a side street, just outside the street lamp's cone of light. CC walks to the chain-link gate, opens it, and goes up the sidewalk, never looking back. She seems tiny. The Beastman would think you're crazy. A little black eighth-grader? You should leave. Why did you say you would stick around?

You know the answers. You don't want to be the kind of guy who would do what you want to do. And a girl who will sneak out at night with a boy has got to know where that could go.

But is that somewhere you want to go with her?

What you know is no other girl wants you to wait in her backyard, and you're going to leave Florida and never return. Maybe CC only wants someone to take her to a college Halloween dance. That could be fun. Maybe the wild hippie chick of your dreams will be there, and she'll invite you to crash with her—

The screen door of the white house swings open before CC

reaches the porch. The porch and the entryway stay dark. The house says, "Eula Mae! What time you think it is?"

CC says, "Oh, Aunt Ida, everyone was swept up in the spirit! It was like Jesus took us in his arms! If you'd only heard those angels singing!"

Your heart thumps hard. Someone in a dark house might be able to see you in the dark street.

You head farther down the side street. If anyone notices, you're a shape in a blue blanket. It's Halloween. They won't think you've got the ugliest blanket in Florida. They'll think you've got the ugliest costume.

You stop out of sight of the white house. Its voice carries in the night, loud and low, a saxophone or a tom-tom. "I didn't hear their van."

CC's answers are guitar riffs. "They knew it was late. I told 'em to drop me at the corner and get the other girls home right away."

"They left you at this time of night?"

"Just at the corner. I didn't want the motor to wake you."

"I could never sleep with you out."

"Auntie! You know Jesus looks over me!"

"Just because he's looking doesn't mean bad things can't happen. 'Specially on Satan's night."

CC says firmly, "That's why we prayed extra hard. The devil might have most folks tonight, but he don't have us."

"Doesn't," says the white house. "You're not Negro trash. Don't talk like you are."

"No, ma'am. I'll pray to remember to talk proper. *Lee.*"

"Well. Weakness is all around us. Get in, girl. Going to be morning before we know it."

CC's steps on the porch are drumsticks on a wood block. Then the house adds, "I'm talking to that Juan about when you're supposed to be home."

CC begins, "I told him! He'll just be embarrassed that he got caught up in the spirit. It won't hap—"

Her riff ends with a closing door, not slammed, but pulled firmly, a blow of a beater against a bass drum.

You listen. Nothing escapes the white house.

You walk to the alley. It would be a perfect place for a gang to jump you. But what gang would hide in a dark alley waiting for someone stupid enough to walk down it? As you think that, you see silhouettes ahead: garages, sheds, garbage cans, cars. Thick clouds drift across the sky, but they don't block the moonlight. Most houses have lights on in bedrooms or kitchens. Motown still plays far off. It sounds like "I Heard It through the Grapevine." TV noise comes from nearby, excited voices and anxious music, not loud enough to tell you what show it is. If you knew that, you would know the time. Is it George and Tish's bedtime yet? Is it yours? Your bed would be soft and warm.

You tighten the blanket around you and start down the alley. You can't see your feet. You kick a sheet of newspaper, then step on something soft that you hope is a lost toy. A dog barks as it slams into a chain-link fence beside you, making you scramble to the far side of the alley. The dog is a big lean Doberman. It doesn't stop barking until an old man shouts, "Boris! Hush yourself!"

You expect that finding the white house will be easy, but you walk past it and don't turn back until you're two-thirds down the alley. You're sure the white house is in the middle of the block. So you walk back, looking closer at each lot.

It's where you expected, but not what you expected. You expected to see a light on or going out. It's dark. You expected to see a backyard as bare as the front, short grass surrounded by chain-link. There's a garage and a vegetable garden and a neck-high white wooden fence.

It sits in darkness, halfway between the corner street lamps.

The neighbors have lights on in the sides away from the white house, so light avoids it. You hesitate, then think that's good. No one will see a white boy sneaking into a neighbor's backyard.

You try the gate's latch. It's locked. Are you trespassing if you've been invited to climb into someone's backyard? You remember the Beastman's philosophy: "It's only illegal when you're caught."

You push the wooden fence. It's sturdy. You wrap your blanket around your shoulders like a giant scarf, grip the top of the fence, and leap up. The Kid would soar over the top, somersault, and land on his feet. You lock your arms to hang on the fence and study the darkness. Maybe Aunt Ida bought a German shepherd while CC was out. Maybe there's a cactus right under you, or a rattlesnake pit.

You don't see anything you couldn't see from the alley. You throw a leg over the fence, feel the boards cut into your hands and thigh, throw the other leg over, and drop.

The ground is nearer than you thought. You stumble forward, then turn fast. No snakes, no cactus, no guard dog. No new lights on in the white house or the neighbors. No doors banging open. No one screaming, "Lord almighty, there's a white boy sneaking around the neighborhood!"

The back wall of the white house has two long, louvered windows separated by a small one. In the Kid's cartoon, the windows are the eyes and nose, and the cement walk circling it is a mouth. Its eyes must be bedrooms; its nose, a bath. Which bedroom is Aunt Ida's? Is CC watching to see if you'll really come? Is Aunt Ida staring from darkness into darkness? Is anyone else in the house that CC didn't expect? Aunt Ida could have a big cousin who arrived unexpectedly with big friends who are Black Panthers, Black Muslims, or some other gang that would like having fun with a little white trespasser.

You realize what you're thinking and smile. The Afro-American

League for Beating Up White Kids Who Want to Be Cartoonists is not meeting in Aunt Ida's house tonight. Two people are in there, an old woman who may already be asleep and a girl who wants to come to you.

You look around, thinking of Dad in the car saying, "Always be ready for things to go wrong, 'cause they will. Brakes fail, tires blow, and people swerve into your lane because they're drunk or they had heart attacks or they just want some company when they kill themselves. Keep both hands on the wheel so you're ready to react. Know how to downshift and where your emergency brake is. Always watch what's on every side of you, 'cause you never know when you'll have to head across someone's lawn to save your ass."

Two metal trash cans and a small bush are the only obstacles at the fence. You can scramble over it at any point. If you need to, you can trample the bush. The trash cans have lids. You can hop on one and leap the fence. Better not to plan on that. If a trash can topples with you on it, you'll fall back into the yard.

Escaping on either side is riskier. To the left is the garage. To the right is the vegetable garden. You can't see if there's anything at the front of the garage. The neighbor on that side has a fence that's lower than Aunt Ida's, but even a low fence will slow you. The neighbor on the other side doesn't have a fence, but that yard is cluttered with toys and lumber.

You look past the white house toward the street. The wooden fence joins the house, but the gate by the house is open. You could run through, go over the chain-link in the front yard, and race down the street toward University Avenue.

Staying low, you cross the backyard. There's a gate on that side, too. It's closed. You don't think it's smart to go up to the house to see if the gate's locked. Leave it for a last resort.

The vegetable garden looks wild in the night, a place for land mines and bear traps. Don't cross it unless you have to.

So there, Dad. You go back to the garage, where the shadows are deepest. You brush the ground with your feet, hope there aren't ants or sand spurs, and sit. Dirt can't make the blue blanket look worse.

What if CC chickens out? What if she falls asleep? You wish you had a cigarette. It would look cool to smoke while sitting cross-legged like a polyester Apache. A joint would be cooler. You glance up at the sky and think, The moon was a ghostly galleon—

A cigarette or a joint might reveal you to a watcher. When you were a kid, Dad would light his pipe and say, "Three on a match is bad luck. When the first gets a light, the enemy spots it, and when the second gets a light, the enemy aims, but when the third gets a light—" Then you and Tish and George would shout together, "Bang!" and Dad would tickle you all on the bed while Mom smiled.

You're not a kid now. Wild men raid enemy camps to steal women. You snuck into a backyard to meet one.

CC's not a kid, either. Mom says girls mature faster than boys, but you never saw any proof of that. Maybe CC's the exception that proves the rule. "Proves the rule" means tests the rule. Mom read that in a newspaper. "Can't have your cake and eat it, too," means if you eat your cake, you won't have it anymore. But what good is something you don't use?

You shake yourself to stay awake. You would forgive the blue blanket for being ugly if it were warmer.

Tish and George must be asleep. They'll be glad you're gone. Will Tish get your room because she's older, or will George because he's a boy? Tish will. Dad sometimes gives her advantages because she's a girl, but he never penalizes her. George will get her room. His room will give Mom an office that people aren't always walking through. Everyone will have more space, and no one will have anyone to get mad at, and the whole family will tell people they're sorry you ran off, but they'll know it was best for everyone.

Except Mom. She's probably crying, and Dad's probably telling her not to get excited because you're nearly an adult and pretty sensible for a fourteen-year-old. Mom always wants everyone to be together and happy, even though being together makes them miserable. You could call her and say you're fine, but she wouldn't believe it. She would beg you to come home, and you never can, so there's no point in calling. If Dad picked up the phone, he would tell you to get your ass home now if you know what's good for you. You decide to send Mom a postcard in the morning, so it'll have a Gainesville postmark and not give any clues about how to find you.

Tish might be a little sad. Sometimes she makes peanut butter cookies for you. Peanut butter cookies warm from the oven would be good. You would gladly trade a cigarette or a joint for a warm cookie. You should've asked CC to bring some food, if she can. Was Mom going to make meatloaf tonight? She always leaves the tomato sauce off one end for you, and if anyone complains, she tells them they know how to use a ketchup bottle. Now she can put tomato sauce on the whole meatloaf the way the rest of the family like it.

George might be a little sad at first. He doesn't like things that make trouble. But once he knows you're gone and there'll be no more trouble, he'll be content. At least, you think he'll be content. He doesn't talk as much as the rest of the Nixes. He'll get your stuff, but he doesn't like comic books or rock records. He'll sell them in a yard sale and buy a .22 rifle and never know you spent years putting together a collection that's nearly perfect. He'll just be glad you're gone.

Dad will be mad. He'll know that he looks like a failure because his son ran away. Who cares what Dad thinks? Fuck him, anyway.

You shiver and lie down. The ground is hard and cold, but it's better than sitting up. This is what pioneers and cowboys do. You always liked sleeping outside in a sleeping bag with the family around a campfire. A campfire would be nice. Dad would tell you to make sure it was covered with dirt before you went to sleep, and he wouldn't check on it because he trusted you.

Fuck him anyway.

Does Cindy Hurly know you've run away? Does she wish she'd known how cool you are? Is she sorry you're not her boyfriend?

You've got to send postcards every week to the Beastman. Each one from a different place. Los Angeles and San Francisco and Honolulu and Timbuktu.

CC will come out soon.

It's cold.

Closing your eyes for a little while is a good idea.

It's okay if you fall asleep. You'll sleep like a cat, awake in an instant, alert to danger before it comes near.

A sleeping bag would be nice.

Grass and dirt smell nice.

You'll sleep like a cat.

Six

Something yanks your shoulder. You jerk forward like you're fighting out of quicksand. "Wha—" comes from your mouth, and something claps over your lips. You're in darkness and cold. Your side is stiff. Silhouetted against the sky, a dark figure crouches over you, trapping you—

"Shh!" whispers CC, then: "You sleep like the dead!"

You draw back from her hand. She stays crouched beside you, so you prop up on one elbow on the ground. She wears a frayed and faded terry-cloth bathrobe that might be pink. Beneath its hem is the skirt of an embroidered white nightgown. It looks old. Your grandmothers wore gowns like that when they were girls. CC's ankles are bare. Her feet are in flip-flops. You realize she must be cold an instant before she says, "It's cold!"

She doesn't stand, so you can't. You say, "You want to start walking?"

"No." She sounds like she expects you to figure something out. Bedclothes make a poor costume for a cold night, unless she plans to dance a lot. It must be getting late, even for a party at the U. It'll be colder walking back. You turn your face up to ask what she has in mind. She bobs down, mashing her lips against the corner of your mouth, surprising you. Her lips slide across yours, more gently now that she's found her distance. You think, It's a kiss. She's kissing me. This is what a kiss is like.

You want to pull back. You don't want her to know that you don't know how to kiss on the mouth. Her lips are soft and moist and parted. You've heard about French kissing. Does she think that's gross? Does she expect you to be a good at it?

CC draws her head back. "Never kissed a white boy."

"Never kissed a black girl."

"What you think?"

"Can I have another sample first?"

She smiles the big CC smile, not the little Eula Mae smile. "It's cold."

"Oh. You want to get going?"

She shakes her head.

It would be nice to be a complete idiot. Then you'd never feel stupid for figuring things out late. This time, it's something you like figuring out. You lift the ugly blanket. The air is cool against your T-shirt. "Want in?"

Her smile is a little Eula Mae, a little CC, as she presses in. She's thin and hard and cold. She shivers against you. The knot of her bathrobe belt digs into your stomach. Her weight is on your left arm, pinning it to the ground. Her hair against your cheek smells like soap. It's the softest thing you've ever felt. You thought a black person's hair would be bristly, but it's like lamb's wool or silk or something that is CC's hair and not like anything else at all.

Her lips are on yours, and they've parted. You're not supposed to slobber. What if you do? She must want Frenching. What if she bites your tongue? The idea of sticking your tongue into someone else's mouth is weird. Holding hands and fucking make sense, but the stuff in between is weird. She could give you a cold, if she has a cold.

But as your tongue slips between her lips, you know this would be worth getting a cold for. Her tongue brushes yours. This is what nice girls do with people they love, bad girls do with anyone they want, and what's CC?

Her hands rub your back. You're supposed to do something. You rub her back. The tongue dance is like seals playing. How long are you supposed to French? You're straining against your fly. The Beastman said he Frenched Mary Pitluck at a party and creamed his jeans. You'd thought he was lying, but maybe it was true.

You're supposed to kiss girls' necks and nibble their earlobes. That's as weird as Frenching, but Frenching is nicer than you expected. A little sloppy and very strange, especially when her tongue slips into your mouth, and you don't know if a girl is supposed to stick her tongue in a boy's mouth, but if that's what she wants, fair is fair. You're not going to say anything to stop her.

You slide your right hand along the terry-cloth bathrobe, over her ribs and across her stomach to the knot of her belt. She doesn't stop you. She's kissing you like girls kiss in movies, like the only thing they're thinking about is kissing. Is that what it's like for her? Is that how it's supposed to be for you? Should you talk? They never talk in movies, unless it's to say, "Yes!" or "I love you!" You don't love CC and you don't know what to say yes to. She doesn't seem to have questions.

You finger her belt. You could slide your hand up, feel her breast through the robe, or slide your hand under the robe, then slip it up. Or down. What does she want? You can't ask. Men should know.

The terry cloth is thick. Feeling a breast through terry cloth would hardly be like feeling anything at all. The only thing you know for sure is that when she wants you to stop, she'll say so. You might be telling the Beastman that you got tit on your first date. Is that what this is? A date? Your first make-out session. You might get tit on your first make-out session.

Her belt knot comes undone with a tug. James Bond couldn't do better. Her robe opens, and she presses harder against you. Which way are you supposed to slide your hand? The ground is hard under your hip, but it's another thing not to care about.

There's first base, then second. Up over her stomach and the edge of her rib cage. Slow down to see if she'll stop you. Nibble an earlobe to distract her, then try for second.

You kiss across her jaw. Her breathing is faster. That's good, right? You reach her earlobe. What's the smell of her hair? Prell? Johnson's Baby Shampoo? Something they sell in the section for black women with the hair straighteners? You take her earlobe between your teeth and press down—

"Ow!" She turns her head away.

"Sorry."

"Shh!" And her lips are back on yours, but only for a moment. She's nuzzling your neck. You try again with the earlobe, using lips and not teeth, moving your hand up her body. The top of your hand touches something soft. It's the bottom of her breast. She doesn't stop you. You keep sliding your palm up until you're cupping a breast, a real girl's real breast, a real girl's real nipple pressing into your palm. It's the most perfect feeling you've known. You're so grateful to CC that you don't know how to say it, and you're a little shocked, too, because she's not wearing a bra, and aren't girls supposed to wear bras all the time if they're not hippies?

You stroke her nipple. It gets harder, or CC rubs herself harder against you. Are you doing this right? Making out is easier for women, just hugging and kissing while men have to figure out what to do next.

She hasn't said no. You must be doing all right.

Her hands are on your back, low on your back, pulling your hips into hers. That means something. Is this dry humping, or is it not dry humping unless her legs are wrapped around you? Why do they call it dry humping if the point isn't to stay dry?

Your hand can't go up much higher than her throat unless you're going to pat her head. You start downward. Past the throat to her left breast. Across to the right, stroking them both by spreading your hand. You wish you could pull your left arm free to get a hand on each breast. Maybe that's why she's lying on your arm, so she she only has to worry about one of your hands.

You slide your hand to her belly. Dogs, cats, and girls trust you when they let you rub their bellies. CC will say no at any moment to let you know that this is all you're going to get. You're afraid of hearing her "no," but it'll be good to know the boundaries: first base and second.

She doesn't speak as your hand slips over her navel. She doesn't speak as your hand continues down. She must not think you're thinking what you're thinking. She must expect you to stroke her leg. You slide your hand over her pelvis and down. Her hip and thigh are astonishingly smooth. You should become a sculptor and sculpt that hip and thigh, not for people to see, but for them to stroke. Sight is wonderful, but touch is better.

Your left arm's stiff, and you move it, and realize it can do more than pull CC into you. That hand can slide over terry cloth to her butt. You like her back and hate the terry cloth, and tug at it, hoisting it up, until your left hand has only the thin nightgown between it and her butt. She's not wearing panties.

You stop your hand, but she's not stopping you. You keep stroking. She must be wearing thin panties. Don't girls wear panties at night? You wear underwear under your pajamas. It makes less mess if you have a wet dream. Do girls have wet dreams? She must be wearing very thin panties.

You slide both hands across her buttocks. You should sculpt her hip and thigh and butt. Would people be afraid to touch art like that in public? Or would they touch it and laugh? They shouldn't. This isn't funny. It's wonderful.

What is getting both hands on someone's butt? Not first or second, but not third. Something's wrong with the scoring system, because a butt is nice, as nice as a breast. What if you're supposed to touch her butt on your way between first and second. Are you doing this completely wrong?

If you are, she's forgiven you. Her hands are on your butt, pulling your hips harder against hers. You're tugging up her nightgown. She must be afraid of what could happen, so she'll stop you soon, but touching her bare thigh would be nice. If you were sitting in a public place and she was wearing a miniskirt, you could brush your hand against her bare thigh and no one would think twice about it.

She must agree. Her nightgown is bunching higher and higher. Your hand is on her bare thigh. Her skin must be softer than her hair, but that's impossible. A sculpture might tell how perfect her shape is, but it wouldn't have her warmth or softness.

Shouldn't she be saying no now? Are you supposed to go for third? She must've done this before, because it doesn't scare her. That scares you more. The farther she lets you go, the worse it'll be when you goof up.

But she's not saying no. You can't stop if she doesn't say no. The front of her thigh is as nice as the flank. The inside of her thigh is softer than either. How can anything be that soft? Slide your hand higher. How can it keep getting softer? Are all girls that soft?

She should be twisting away. You're not supposed to go to third until you're going steady. Nice girls don't go to second until they're on a second or a third date, maybe. This isn't a date. This is a make-out session. Men keep going until women say no. Where's CC's "no"? She keeps hugging and pressing and kissing and breathing fast, and that's what you're doing, except for the pressure in your jeans, so intense it hurts, but it's a hurt you don't want to stop.

Your finger touches hair. Your pubic hair is rough and matted. Hers is like fluff. She's not stopping you. Keep exploring. Men are supposed to rub women until they're slick, so you cup your hand between her legs. It's already wet, slippier than you thought women could be, and she doesn't say no. She's slick for you, from your touch, because you didn't screw up too badly except for biting her ear, and she must really like you because she's as slick as you're hard.

If you were older, you would fuck now. If you had a rubber, you would fuck now. But third is good. You slip your finger in, and she's snapping open your jeans and sliding her hand into your pants, and her grip is harder than you like, as if she's afraid your dick will escape if she doesn't grab it hard, but the grip's not so hard that you're about to complain. You slip another finger in, and you remember something about a hymen, so maybe she's not a virgin, and something about a clitoris, but you don't have the slightest idea what that would feel like if you found it.

But she seems to be happy, so you pump your fingers, and she pulls harder on you, and she's moaning, and will she be grossed out if you come in her hand, and is she not saying no because this is what she wants, or are you supposed to pull your fingers out and put your dick in, but how can you know what you're supposed to do? Her moaning doesn't tell you. What if she got pregnant or had a disease and your dick got covered with sores and had to be cut off? But that would be worth it, and you like her because she's letting you do this, only she's not just letting you. She likes it, and maybe you should take your fingers out and see what she says but she doesn't seem to want you to stop so you keep on, knowing something will happen that's never happened before and—

Something is hurtling down toward your head and—

You roll sideways with CC as an iron rake with tines like dull daggers buries itself in the dirt where you were lying. It jerks up high as someone says roughly, almost calmly, "Jezebel. Whore of Babylon. Spawn of serpents."

And the rake falls again.

Seven

The blanket is a trap. CC is wrapped against you. All you can do is keep rolling. The rake grazes your back, the blanket is jerked hard, you think you're trapped, then you and CC spill onto the ground. You know who must hold the rake just before CC yells, "Aunt Ida! Don't!"

The voice of the house says, "You brought the Devil home." The rake rears upward again. You rock to your knees, shove CC away, and fall again. Your jeans are around your ankles. Tripping doesn't endanger CC. The rake is for you.

Your fist drives upward and your arm twists outward and it's not the kind of high block that would make your sensei proud, but it knocks the rake aside. The impact hurts, shivering through the bone. Your block bounces the rake high, into position for another strike.

"White devil. Abomination. Mark of Cain."

You scoot back across the ground, yanking your jeans up, and roll away as the rake falls, just missing your hips, just missing your groin if you hadn't rolled.

"Aunt Ida! Stop it! Stop it! Stop it!" CC throws herself at the shadow. The silhouettes, side by side, are the same height. Aunt Ida's broader. She must be stronger, too. She turns fast, hitting CC with the shaft of the rake, knocking her down.

"Unclean!" the house calls, its voice growing shrill. "Child of filth! Child of the beast!"

The rake is aimed for CC. You throw yourself forward, arms wide, the right high to catch the rake, the left low to grab the darkness wielding it. The shaft of the rake is rough, the wood ancient, hard as stone. You smell lilacs, stronger than any lilacs could be, so sweet that the scent must be meant to hide something vile. Your left arm closes around flannel and a body as hard as the shaft of the rake.

"Stop it," you're saying. "Stop it!" You took the words from CC—

But they're a prayer on your lips, not a plea—

Because this is her aunt, and you can't hurt a woman, and especially an old woman, but you can't let her hurt CC, and you learned things in karate that would stop her, but the price could be breaking her bones or crushing her windpipe, and why won't she stop struggling and let go of the rake and hear CC saying, "Stop it, we weren't hurting no one, it was good!"

A light comes on in a nearby yard. Someone yells, "What's going on? I called the police!"

You should push Aunt Ida away and run, but you can't leave CC, and she's crying as she screams, "I liked it and I like him and you don't know nothing about me or what's good or nothing at all!"

Dogs bark in the distance, and Aunt Ida in your arms is saying softly, "I know you, Devil. I'll go to Jesus fighting you, praise His name!" She's old, at least as old as Grandma Letitia when she broke her hip, and you can't let go of her and you can't keep holding her—

And you say, "Aunt Ida, please listen, you've got to hear, you've got to see, she's fine, I didn't hurt her, I wouldn't hurt her, you don't have to be mad, you've got to know it's all right!"

She collapses in your arms. Did she have a heart attack or a stroke? Your heart beats as if it could fail, too. Then you hear her crying softly.

You look at CC. You can't read what's on her face. You're standing in the cold night with a frail old woman crying in your arms. You don't know what to do. So you stay still while she cries, and she doesn't stop, so you say, "It's all right now," and keep holding her.

CC keeps watching, or maybe it's Eula Mae. She's looking at you as if she wants to run away screaming. Then she steps forward, puts an arm around Aunt Ida, one arm around you, and she's crying. And only then do you realize you're crying, too.

When you hear a car coming, Aunt Ida says, "Police," and steps away. CC's arms drop. The three of you are points of a triangle. You're cold, and you want the ugly blanket. CC smoothes her gown and closes her robe and belts it. You turn away from Aunt Ida, zip and snap your jeans, and turn back, saying, "I got to go." That's what drifters say.

Aunt Ida says, "Who are you?"

"Chris, ma'am. I mean, Mark. Mark Christopher Nix."

Aunt Ida shakes her head. She makes you think of a crow, but you don't know if it's a real one or a cartoon one like Heckle and Jeckle. "No. Who are you?"

"I go to George Washington Carver. Ninth grade."

She shakes her head again. "No. *Who* are you?"

To shut her up, you say, "I don't know," and she nods, satisfied.

You tell CC, "I'll write." You don't know" why you say that, but you can't just go, even if that's what drifters are supposed to do.

"You can't."

"Sure. What's your address?"

"You can't just run off."

"I'll be fine. I—" The car brakes in front of the house. You talked too long. You don't have time to hug CC or kiss her. "I'll write here. Is it Ida Carter in the phone book?"

The car doors swing open, loud and fast. CC is looking at you, like she knows you'll do what's right.

You say, "I'll write care of Ida Carter!" and lope for the rear fence. But as you reach for the ugliest blanket in Florida, CC calls, "Mark! You got a home! Don't run away from it!"

You pick up the blanket.

CC says, "Is something terrible driving you off?"

You pull the blanket around you. You couldn't have bought it if Mom hadn't gotten you a credit card, even if it was just a stupid Penney's card.

CC says, "Is something good calling you?"

You turn around. In her big bathrobe and long nightgown, she's younger than you, and older, and beautiful.

She says, "Don't throw away things if you don't know you don't want them."

You say, "All right."

And the policemen walk into the backyard. They look like Florida policemen, white and short-haired. One's tall, skinny, and young enough to be just out of the army. The other's older, built like a barrel. They look at Aunt Ida and CC and you, then glance around, then squint just at you.

The Barrel turns to Aunt Ida. "Ma'am? We got a report there was trouble."

You hope that's a good sign, a white policeman calling a black woman "ma'am." Aunt Ida smiles and says, "It was just these young ones. You know how it is at that age."

The Barrel says, "Yes'm."

The Beanpole scowls at you. "This hippie was making a disturbance?"

You should've gone over the fence. Can they put you in a cell before letting you call anyone? Can they shave your head and say you had lice? Can they put you in with big men who hate hippies or love boys or both?

Aunt Ida says, "No, sir," to the Beanpole. "He was just calling on my niece."

The Barrel looks at CC. "You know him?"

CC looks down and nods.

The Beanpole says, "What's he got to do with you?" And he smiles like he knows the answer and knows it'll embarrass everyone, CC especially.

You should answer, but you don't go to the same school or live in the same neighborhood or have the same skin color. There's no reason to be here that would satisfy the Beanpole.

The Barrel saves CC from answering by asking you, "How old are you, son?"

You say, "Fourteen."

The Barrel nods. "Out kind of late."

The Beanpole says, "We can take him in. Let juvie decide what to do in the morning."

The Barrel tells the Beanpole, "It's Halloween." Then he tells you, "C'mon. We'll run you home."

"But—" You look at CC.

She nods to say you should go. It's not a pretty face, but you like looking at it, and why didn't you see the beauty of her eyes?

Aunt Ida tells you, "I expect your folks're wondering where you got to."

The Beanpole says, "Sounds like the hippie was trespassing—"

The Barrel says, "You hear anyone make a complaint?"

Aunt Ida looks at you and says, "I got no complaint."

The Barrel nods to her. "You have a good evening, ma'am." He nods to CC. "You don't want to be entertaining boys without telling your aunt, missy." He jerks his head at you to follow and starts walking away.

You could kiss CC good-bye, but Aunt Ida and the Beanpole are watching. The Beanpole says, "Come on, hippie. Can't pass up a free ride provided by the government, can you?"

CC says, "You got to go home."

"I'll call." You look at Aunt Ida. "You're in the phone book?"

Aunt Ida glances from you to CC and back again, then nods without smiling.

"I'll call!" You hurry after the policemen.

The Beanpole holds the back door of their car open. You look at the grate between front and back, then the absence of door handles inside. The Beanpole grins. "What, this your first time getting chauffeured by the city's finest? We got us a hippie virgin here!"

The Barrel says, "Get in, son. It's a long walk to Fifty-fifth Terrace."

You glance at him and realize what your face must look like when he smiles a little. "Your momma reported you. They want you home."

The Beanpole adds, "You sure got a tolerant momma. Mine wouldn't have me back till I got a haircut."

You glance at the dark windows of the white house. Is anyone watching? You wave, just in case, then get in the patrol car. The Beanpole slams the door, takes the front passenger seat, and the Barrel drives away.

The car smells like cigarettes and ammonia. You're in a cage. The people who can let you out are people who took on the job of putting people in cages. You can't decide which would be worse, home or jail. The father of the prodigal son was so happy about his boy's return that he killed the fatted calf for a feast. The only thing Dad will want to kill is you.

The Beanpole says, "So, hippie, how's nigger poontang?"

You feel your face redden in embarrassment at being caught with a girl and anger that you can't stop this man from talking like that about CC.

The Barrel tells the Beanpole, "I'd say you had shit for brains if I thought there was anything up there as useful as fertilizer."

The Beanpole says, "The hippie don't mind a little funning. Do you, now?" When you don't answer, he adds, "What, pussy got your tongue?" and laughs.

The Barrel says, "Let him be."

The Beanpole says, "Didn't think you had any use for hippies."

"You never run off to see a girl?"

The Beanpole glares at him. "Not a nigger girl!"

"Then you might not want to be flaunting your ignorance."

The policemen stop talking. They take you back the way you came, up University Avenue, past the mall. When you pass the point where you ran out of the woods, your heart beats faster. If there was a crank, you would roll down the window, for air or to flee.

Surely the police won't want to wake anyone up. They'll drop you off, and you can wave good-bye, then sneak into the woods, and sleep in your blanket. You can still go to California. Or you can live in the woods. The papers will write about the Gainesville Wild Man, and mothers will warn their children to watch out for you. You begin to smile.

Then you see your home. The houses in your neighborhood are dark, except for yours.

The Beanpole says, "I ran off once. Daddy tanned my hide good."

The Barrel says, "There's all kinds of folks. Thank God."

The patrol car stops in front of the drive. If George is watching, he's probably disappointed that there aren't flashing lights and sirens.

The front door of the house opens a second after the car stops. Dad steps out, looking grim. Mom follows, looking as upset as the time Dad took a shortcut on a logging road that got narrower and steeper till the only possibilities seemed to be getting stuck on the mountain or falling off it.

As the Beanpole gets out, the Barrel says, "They don't look like monsters."

You say, "They aren't, sir."

The Barrel nods, and the Beanpole opens your door. Staying in the car is tempting, but you're not going to let anyone see you want to hide, least of all Dad. You step out fast.

Mom starts forward. Dad catches her wrist, but she yanks free. She's hugging you and kissing you and crying and smiling and saying, "We were so worried, Chris! Anything could've happened to you!"

"I'm fine, Mom," you mumble, hating that she's treating you like a child and hating that people are watching so you have to push her away. You say, "Hi, Dad."

"Christopher." His tone only says he acknowledges you. That's good. If he wasn't going to let you come back, he would tell you. It also says he hasn't forgiven you, but you knew he wouldn't. He believes in taking responsibility for what you do, and accepting a fair punishment for doing something wrong is part of being responsible. What's a fair punishment for this?

You think you know the hardest part of your punishment already. You have to stand there knowing he knows you had to come home. He would've respected you if you'd made a new life. Coming back is defeat.

The Barrel says, "You want to keep him?"

Dad says, "I'm thinking about it."

Mom says, "Luke!"

Dad looks at you. "You prepared to live by the house rules?"

"Yes, sir." Saying that is accepting more punishment than anything he can give.

He tells the Barrel, "Damned if I know why, but we'll keep him."

The Barrel says, "Since no one's pressing charges and this is the first time, you're welcome to."

The Beanpole says, "All that hair might be keeping the oxygen from his brain."

You hadn't thought that cutting your hair might be part of your punishment. But Dad studies the Beanpole, long enough to say that he thinks what his kid does with his hair is no one else's affair. When the Beanpole looks as if he's figured out he went too far, Dad says, "Thanks for bringing him."

The Barrel says, "Slow night. You folks be all right now?"

Mom says, "Yes. We're so grateful to you!"

The Barrel smiles. "Then you have a nice evening." He jerks his head at the Beanpole. "Come on, Deputy Dawg." The Beanpole scowls and follows.

You stand with Mom and Dad, watching the police car drive away. Then Dad says, "It's late," and heads in.

Mom catches the screen door as she follows and says, "You must be hungry."

You glance at the woods and the stars, at the lawn and the clutter of bicycles. You say, "A little," and hold the screen door for her.

Eight

The living room is smaller. You search for signs that something changed, but nothing has. Dad reaches for his pipe and says, "Missing supper was his choice."

Mom keeps looking at you. "Do you want a cheese sandwich? Or a hamburger? I'll fix you something."

Dad tamps tobacco into the pipe. "You don't have to reward him for running off."

Mom says, "He's home, Luke! Don't you understand? He's home!"

Dad snaps open the top of his lighter. "There's still a price to pay."

Mom watches him flick the lighter and put the flame to his pipe bowl. She shakes her head once and opens the fridge.

You say, "I can do that. If it's okay."

Mom says, "I will."

Dad says, "Best not argue when she's like that."

You nod.

Dad puffs his pipe, then says, "Why'd you come home?"

You say what you've heard him say, "Home's where they have to take you in."

You hoped he would smile. He nods, sits in the big easy chair, and puffs on the pipe a few times. You don't know if you should sit, so you stay standing.

He says, "If you don't abuse the rules."

"I won't."

He studies you and nods. "Your mother and I talked it over. You come straight home from school for the next two weeks and don't leave the yard without her permission or mine."

You nod.

"You dig that hole three times."

You glance at him.

"Once 'cause I told you to. Once 'cause you didn't when I told you to. Once 'cause you swore at me. It's that, or we fight to see who's captain of this ship."

"I'll get my own ship in three years."

He smiles. "I expect you will."

Mom brings a glass of milk and a sandwich, American cheese on white bread, cut in quarters, with pickle slices on the side. She says, "Sit down, Chris! Eat!"

You sit at the table. You're not hungry as you think about what the next three years will be like. But Mom's watching, so you start eating, and you think maybe the years won't be too hard, if you can just get through digging the three holes. Being grounded means you won't be able to see CC. You're not going to ask for permission to visit a girl. You're not going to tell them you want to visit a girl. You say, "I met a girl. At the mall. Can I call her?"

Mom says, "Now?"

You shake your head. "If I got to follow rules, I got to know 'em."

Dad says, "You can call anyone you want after homework's done and the first hole's dug. Any visiting will have to be at school."

You say, "Okay."

Mom says, "What's she like?"

You say, "A girl."

She sighs. "You're worse than your father."

Dad says, "Let him be, Susan." Then he adds, "Where'd you get the blanket?"

"Penney's. With the charge card Mom gave me."

Dad says, "You can pay it back."

Mom says, "It was a gift. He doesn't have to."

You cram the last pickle slices into your mouth, then the last quarter of the cheese sandwich, and wash it down with the last half of the glass of milk. "Thanks, Mom."

She says, "I'm glad you're home."

You nod and stand.

Dad says, "Anything else you want to tell us?"

"No, sir. Good night."

You expect the folks to just say good night, but Mom hugs you again, and Dad says, "Sleep well, Christopher." And for some reason you can't figure out, you think that maybe he respects you after all.

The hallway is shorter than you remember. The bathroom is smaller. Tish's door has the Wonder Woman sticker that you gave her two Christmases ago, and George's has the Superman, and your own has the Batman that you kept for yourself. You reach up to peel the Batman off, then decide to leave it up.

Your room is a little smaller than you remember. You pile your clothes on your chair and crawl into bed. The last thing you notice is CC's smell on your fingers.

The next morning at six thirty, Dad knocks on the door and calls, "Work's waiting." You want to yell that it's Saturday, then remember why you're exhausted.

You don't want to face anyone. The morning is almost too typically Saturday. Dad is reading the paper. George and Tish are watching *Popeye.* Mom is making French toast. Tish says she's glad you're home, George says he's sorry you're home, and they both go back to watching Brutus running off with Olive Oyl.

As you flip through the phone book for Ida Carter's number, Dad says, "After the first hole's dug and filled."

He only said "dug," last night. If you argue, someone will say "You should be a lawyer!" and laugh. You don't want to hear anything you ever heard when you were younger. If you have to fill the hole before you call CC, you'll fill the hole.

The ground is harder than you expect. You have to chop through heavy clay, stones, and roots. Your hands blister as you shovel, but the most annoying part is when little neighbor kids come to ask what you're digging. In the Kid's cartoon, you could steal from Mark Twain and say you're digging for treasure and get them to dig while you sit in the shade. That's not the kind of initiative Dad would reward. He might laugh, but he would make you start over.

You tell the kids, "A hole." When they ask why, you say, "To bury little kids in." Jimmy Beasley runs away crying, and you have to tell Mrs. Beasley you're sorry you scared him, and listen to Dad say the real reason you're digging the hole is you're too big to spank and the damn government won't let a man sell his own child into slavery anymore.

Dad sees you rub your hands and says to put Band-Aids and gloves on. That helps, but the blisters still hurt. Your shirt is soaked with sweat. You peel it off, though now you look like a scrawny white kid with a soft stomach. Mom makes you put on suntan lotion. You keep working, wondering what you can get a tan from besides the sun.

The dirt doesn't get softer. The distance you have to throw it grows. When there's dirt heaped on every side of the hole, you have to get out and shovel it back to make room for more. The hole isn't done by lunchtime. You eat fast while Tish and George watch *The Archies*. Two hours after lunch, you measure the corners. They're all six feet below the grass line. You climb out on the kitchen stepladder and get Dad. He measures the middle and says you've got three more inches to go.

You think you should never have come home, but you keep digging.

It takes another half an hour. Dad nods, and you start filling. That's easier, but not as easy as you hoped. Each shovelful is still heavy. Your arms and back and legs ache worse than after any karate practice or mountain hike.

You move the last dirt onto the hole, think it looks like a fresh grave, and get Dad. He sees the mound and says to pack it down. You're too tired to wonder if that's fair. It's stupid, but it fits the terms of the punishment. That's as close to fair as you can expect.

You tromp over the mound, mashing it under your boots. You hit it with the shovel. You get a piece of cardboard and sit on it, bouncing on the dirt. When it looks like an old grave, you tell Dad that's the best you can do. He stands on the mound. It doesn't sink. He says, "Okay."

You're exhausted, but you run for the phone. You've been repeating the number all day, silently when anyone was around, softly when no one was near. You run into the kitchen, call to Mom, "Can I use the phone in your bedroom?" As soon as she says, "Yes," you add, "Don't let Tish pick it up out here!" Tish yells, "I wouldn't do that!" as you run into the bedroom, grab the phone by your parents' bed, and dial.

It rings five times. You're ready to say hi to CC when Aunt Ida says, "Yes?"

You say, "Uh, Ms. Carter? Is C, uh, Eula Mae in?"

You hear nothing. You were an idiot not to expect the person who rents the phone to answer it. Then Aunt Ida says as if she knows the answer and doesn't like it, "Who is this?"

"Mark Christopher Nix. May I speak with Eula Mae, ma'am?"

"No. And don't you call back." The *click* of disconnecting isn't loud. It's just final.

Will calling back make her think less of you? Can she think less of you? How can you talk to CC if you can't call her? You dial again.

"Ms. Carter, please, I'm back home and you can talk to my parents if you want. I make good grades and I try to be polite and all I want is to talk to Eula Mae for one minute, please."

She says, "No. Don't you call back. Find yourself a nice white girl and forget about Eula Mae. Good-bye."

You dial as soon as you hear the disconnect. The phone rings and rings and rings. You hang up, dial again, even though you know you dialed the right number. After seven rings, you hang up. You dial the number and listen to seven rings for more times than you count.

When you hear Dad saying, "I don't care who he's calling, I'm not staying out of my own bedroom all day," you give up and go out.

Mom's smiling when she looks up, but her smile fades and you go straight to your room. You've got to give Aunt Ida time to realize this is all right. You write letter after letter to her, explaining that you respect CC and you know it's tough for a white boy and a black girl in the United States, but the world is changing. When Mom knocks and says dinner is ready, you go out. Everyone looks at you and no one asks questions. Dad says, "Dealing with women and going to war are rites of passage. I'm not sure which is tougher." Afterward, you write more letters. None of them convinces you, so they won't convince Aunt Ida. At bedtime, you can't smell CC anymore.

In the morning, Dad says you can go to church and start digging afterward. You like the Unitarians, except when they have tomato juice instead of orange juice, but you say you want to get the holes dug. Mom says, "Luke—" and Dad says, "It's his decision."

You dig while the family dresses for church. You did a good job packing the dirt, and you ache worse than yesterday. As soon as everyone leaves, you run inside and dial Aunt Ida's number. The phone rings and rings.

They must've gone to church. You dig harder and faster. What church do they go to? Are all poor blacks Baptists? Two black families are Unitarians, but one's headed by a doctor, one by a professor. Maybe you could go to Aunt Ida's church and be the only white boy there, and finally Aunt Ida would let CC talk to you.

You run inside every fifteen minutes, call Aunt Ida, then run out and dig. The hole is six feet deep, all around and in the middle, before the family returns. When Dad says it's okay, you tell them you don't want lunch. Mom says you'll get sick if you don't eat, so you eat fast and get to filling in the hole. By the middle of the afternoon, it's tamped down tight, you're back on the phone, and Aunt Ida's number rings and rings and rings.

You go in the living room and say, "If I can go for a bike ride this afternoon, I'll dig an extra hole."

Dad says, "Punished men don't make deals."

"Two extra holes?"

"Is it about that girl?"

You nod.

He says, "If this one doesn't work out, there'll be another along in a bit."

Mom says, "Luke!"

He looks at her, then at you. "All right. No extra holes if you're back by six. One extra hole for each hour after that."

You say, "Thanks!" and run for your bicycle. Pedaling to CC's house is mostly uphill. It takes an hour. Your heart keeps pumping hard and your breath comes even harder, but you don't stop to rest.

Aunt Ida's blinds are closed and her house is dark, but that just makes it seem like it was last night. You go through the front gate, put your bike on its kickstand so they'll see you're being respectful, smooth your hair, tug on your shirt to make a dirty, sweat-stained T-shirt look as good as it possibly can, walk up to the front door, and knock.

After half a minute, you knock again.

After another fifteen seconds, you knock a third time.

There's no one in the house. You know there's no one here. You knew it before you knocked, but you didn't want to know you knew it.

You knock again. And again. And again.

A man comes out of the house next door and calls, "Who you looking for?"

"Ms. Carter."

"They're gone."

The words are clear, and you're expecting them, but you still say, "What do you mean?" When the man frowns, you add, "Sir?"

"I mean they ain't in that house and they ain't coming back to that house."

"Where did they go?"

He frowns again. You say, "Eula Mae and I are supposed to do a science project." You're surprised at how easy it is to lie when you really want something.

The man says, "Better find someone else for your project. They left last night."

"Did they say where they were going?"

He frowns again.

You say, "She lent me five dollars. I could mail it to her."

He smiles. "You can give it to me in case they write. If not, I expect I can find something to do with it." You ought to smile with him, but you can't.

"Does anyone know where she went?"

His frown comes back, deeper this time. "You're an awfully honest young fellow."

"I just—" you start, then finish, "She's nice. I don't want her to think I don't care. About her money."

"Yeah," the man says slowly. "But there ain't no point in worrying about that now."

You thank him, then go from house to house on the block, asking everyone who's home about Eula Mae and saying you need to pay her back her five dollars.

You concentrate as hard as you can on seeming like a nice boy, so they'll want to help you, even if your hair is long and your clothes are dirty.

Everyone is helpful. You learn Aunt Ida came from Georgia, or maybe Alabama, in the countryside near Jackson or Louisville, in a small town named Conroy or Delroy or Winslow, and she could've gone to see relatives in Louisiana, or maybe Texas, or was it someplace north like Chicago? The most useful thing you learn is that the house was rented from a family on the corner. They give you your only certain information: Ida Carter left a note saying they wouldn't be back. The note didn't include a forwarding address.

You get home forty-five minutes after six. Dad looks at your face and says you don't have to dig an extra hole.

Nine

Monday drags. You don't want to talk to anyone at school, not even the Beastman. You pass Cindy Hurly several times. Why didn't you ever notice she's so pale? When the Beastman says you seem bummed, you tell him you ran away from home and now you're digging holes and grounded. You don't mention CC. You don't know what you think of her. But if she were around, you would spend all of your time with her to find out.

You pedal home and start digging. Work goes faster when you pretend it's Dad's grave. You're the Man with No Name. Soon you'll bury your worst enemy. Heavy clay flies from your shovel.

A car slows near the house. Wondering if Mom's home early, you look up. The car is boxy, foreign, and conservative with a star on the hood, something a TV diplomat would drive on his way to betray his country or be killed. It should be in a big city, not Gainesville.

The driver gets out. He's young, as stocky and strong-looking as a Clydesdale. His dark suit makes him look like a lawyer. He sees you in the hole. "Christopher Nix?"

"Yes, sir."

Something bad is about to happen. You decide that can't be right. How can things get worse?

"Sorry I missed you Friday. I'm Ralph Fitzgerald." He reaches into his jacket. You expect to see his FBI ID and hear you'll do twenty years' hard time because you and the Beastman scored a nickel bag. He hands you a pamphlet. "Have you heard of the Academy?"

The cover shows smiling, short-haired boys in sports coats and ties on a campus like a movie set for an Ivy League university: wide lawns, big trees, large old brick buildings. "No, sir."

"Well, the Academy's heard of you. Are your folks around?"

Is he from a reform school? Is there more to your punishment than Dad said? The catalog confuses you. You thought boys' schools were junior versions of prisons or army bases. "Mom's working. I'll get Dad."

You cross the yard, flipping pages. Academy boys play rich people's games, tennis and golf and something with long sticks that the caption calls "lacrosse," which you thought was a town in Wisconsin. They put on plays in a theater with professional equipment. They swim in an indoor Olympic-size pool. There's a science center, an observatory, and an art building. The teachers are from Oxford, Cambridge, Yale, and Harvard. You would love to go there, if boys didn't have to wear ties and there were girls. But uniforms and no girls turns anyplace into a prison or an army base.

The house is quiet since George and Tish are out. Dad, in his favorite chair, puts a book aside. "All done?"

"No, sir. There's a man from this school to see you." You hand him the catalog.

He sets the book aside, leafs through the catalog, frowns at it, then at you. "Is there something you want to tell me?"

You shake your head.

He glances back at the catalog, then nods. "Let's see what he wants."

As soon as you and Dad step into the sunlight, Mr. Fitzgerald comes forward. "Mr. Nix? Ralph Fitzgerald." His hand is out. His smile's pleasant.

Dad shakes the hand, saying, “What can we do for you?”

“You can enroll Chris at the Academy.”

Dad smiles. “Didn’t know you folks went door to door.”

Fitzgerald laughs. “You’ve heard of us.”

“I read a little.”

“Then you know we’re not desperate, Mr. Nix. Your son is special.”

Dad nods. “That’s one word for it.”

“We value diversity at the Academy.”

“Huh. I didn’t see any black or brown faces in your brochure.”

Fitzgerald blushes. He’s not much older than the college kids you envy. “We started a scholarship program for minorities. We have six colored students this year.”

“Out of?”

“The student body’s just over five hundred. It’s true, we’re not representative, but then, that’s not our purpose. We seek the best. Our boys go on to greatness, in private life and public.”

Dad glances at you. You can’t tell if he’s sad or amused. “What kind of minority is Chris?”

“He’s a promising student. With the right motivation—”

Dad frowns. “Who’ve you talked to?”

Fitzgerald blinks. “A few of his teachers. We wanted to know if he would benefit—”

“They said we could afford to send Chris to a private school?”

“The cost is no concern, Mr. Nix. Your family has a benefactor. He’ll cover all expenses.”

Dad looks at you. You shrug. Dad asks Fitzgerald, “Who?”

“Jay Dumont.”

“Never heard of him.”

“He’s indebted to your family. To your wife’s family, that is. Her father saved his life during World War I.”

“Grandpa Abner?” you say.

Fitzgerald smiles as if he's relieved to escape Dad's doubt. "Your grandfather was a medic. Mr. Dumont would've bled to death, if not for your grandfather."

Dad says, "Abner Uvdal's dead."

"That doesn't lessen Mr. Dumont's wish to repay his debt."

"What's in it for you?"

"Excuse me?"

"You said you're with the Academy, not this Dumont."

"He's been very generous to the school. His son was a student. The new art center is named for him. His daughter's one of our students."

You say, "There are girls?"

Dad laughs. "The school produces presidents, and you want to know if there are girls. That's my boy."

You shrug. "There aren't girls in the catalog."

Fitzgerald says, "We just went coed. The Academy embraces change."

"Do boys still have to wear ties?"

"Only to chapel and dinner."

"Chapel?"

"It's nondenominational." Fitzgerald grins. "Haven't lost a boy during chapel yet, though the headmaster can go on for a bit. Don't quote me."

You smile, imagining the Academy being controlled by a giant head in a vat, connected by cables to thousands of heads, and look at Dad. He says, "If the offer's legit, it's a hell of an opportunity, Chris."

You look at the unfinished hole in the back of the yard. CC's gone. Dad's impressed that you're being offered this.

And something's calling. You don't know what, but you know you have to know.

BOOK TWO

The Academy

One

JFK Airport looks like a spaceport: everything's pristine plastic. Travelers rush by. Most are businessmen who sell things and tourists who buy them, but you see a few hippies, a few soldiers, and a one-armed man in a VIETNAM VETERANS AGAINST THE WAR T-shirt. Everyone's louder and faster than anyplace you've been. Their clothes are flashier. You scan the crowd, expecting to see movie stars or rock gods.

A porter says, "Sir?" You're about to say you don't need help when he asks, "Did you drop this?"

He's holding a sheet of paper. It says, "Tell nobody. Nobody can help you."

You frown and shake your head. He says, "Sorry to disturb you, sir," and walks away.

Someone calls, "Mr. Nix?" A man almost as dark as CC comes toward you. He is wearing a black suit, white shirt, and tie. "I'm Gabriel. Mr. Dumont sent me."

You get your suitcase and walk into the early September heat. In a no-parking section sits a sleek black sedan. Gabriel opens the back door. Having someone do things you could do yourself feels wrong. But you're entering a new world. You need to learn its ways.

The seats are covered with the softest leather you've ever felt. There's a cassette player and a radio, New York newspapers, a stack of magazines, and a small refrigerator with beer and wine. Gabriel says no one will mind if you have a drink. None of the labels are anything you've seen on TV, so you pick a beer at random. It tastes as bad as the Budweiser that Dad sometimes drinks, but it's part of riding in luxury into New York, so you like it.

You like it all. This city is where the Shadow fought and King Kong died, where the Beatles came when they were rich and Bob Dylan came when he was poor. You're torn between looking at the buildings and the people. Pretty young women from every part of the world are here. They wear miniskirts, hot pants, or cutoff jeans. They make you think of CC. After the Academy, you'll go to Harvard, become a lawyer, make a fortune, and use your wealth to find her.

Gabriel stops at a department store that looks more expensive than Sears. Old movies told you about Macy's and Gimbel's. This isn't either. "Why're we stopping?"

"Mr. Dumont said you need clothes."

"I've got clothes."

"You have clothing. You don't have clothes."

"I don't get it."

"You will."

You glance at yourself. Brown corduroy bells, a green-and-yellow tie-dyed T-shirt, desert boots. "What's wrong with this?"

Gabriel rolls his eyes. "At school, you may wear whatever you like. Within the dress code. For now, accept what you're due."

In the store, everyone looks rich, even the help. In the men's section, an unsmiling man in a dark blue suit says without warmth, "Mr. Nix. Welcome."

Another man takes your measurements. If you draw this, they'll be mad scientists preparing to build your robot double. When they're done, the unsmiling man says, "Everything will be delivered in an hour."

You say, "What will?"

Gabriel says, "What you need."

The unsmiling man says, "And should you require something more, we have your measurements." He nods. "It is an honor, Mr. Nix."

"Uh, thanks," you say as Gabriel leads you out.

The next stop makes you think Gabriel is visiting a girlfriend. It looks like a beauty salon, but not one Mom would go to. Colors are subdued, seats are leather, and music is classical, not pop. A pretty woman meets you with a very wide smile.

She says in a French accent, "Mr. Nix, please be seated. You have such beautiful hair." You take a second look at the salon. You thought women went to beauty salons and men went to barbershops, but either New York is different, or rich people are.

The woman adds, "A handsome young man like yourself must hear that from many girls."

You tell Gabriel, "The dress code says collar-length is fine. Mom cut it just the other day."

The woman says, "Ah, but mothers do not cut to show how sexy young men truly are. You will like it."

You will hate it. The woman must be twenty-five or thirty. She's too old to know what's cool, and Gabriel is too straight.

The woman calls over more pretty women, an Asian who smiles shyly and a Scandinavian who laughs often. The Scandinavian washes your hair, which feels nice, but embarrassing. If you'd known a woman was going to touch your hair, you would've washed it this morning. The Asian cleans and trims your fingernails, which you had thought were clean and trim. Who notices a guy's fingernails? Then the French woman lifts a strand of your hair and a gleaming scissors.

You say, "Uh, not too much."

"But of course not. It would be a crime to deny young women the pleasure of running their fingers through such beautiful hair."

The other women laugh. You blush and decide to be quiet. The French woman cuts quickly, taking such small snips that you don't expect to see a difference. But when she turns you to the mirror and says, "There. Who would not flirt with this man?" you can only stare.

The kid in the chair is hip, but not a hippie. He knows what to say and when to say nothing. Anyone who sees him will like him.

CC wouldn't recognize him.

The women are waiting. You nod and mumble, "Thanks. It's good." The women laugh and whisk your neck and shoulders, sweeping your hair into an immaculate dustpan, then pouring that into an immaculate bin that's quickly closed and put away.

Gabriel looks at you and nods. "Ready to meet the Dumonts."

It's not a question. You grin and say, "Why not?"

The amazing thing about New York City is that it looks exactly like New York City. You don't think that thought would impress Gabriel, so you don't mention it. You just keep staring at people and buildings. New York is hot, humid, and smelly, but it looks so much like New York that no one cares. Besides, in the car with the air-conditioning on, only sight matters.

Gabriel drives you to a blandly impressive apartment building among many other blandly impressive apartment buildings. A doorman opens the car door and says, "Good afternoon, sir." Are you supposed to acknowledge servants? You thank him, and his smile grows a little wider.

A second doorman drives the car away. The first lets you into a small lobby. Gabriel leads you to an elevator that seems small for such a big building. Eight people would fill it. It stops at a small windowless room with dark wainscoting. A bench and a small table make it look like a sitting room. You're confused. Where's the hall for people to get to their apartments? There's only one door. It must open on the hall.

The far door opens. A silver-haired man in a suit and white gloves says, "Welcome." Beyond him is a large room like a hotel lobby. Do a few big apartments on this floor share a lobby?

You say, "Mr. Dumont?"

He shakes his head. "He's expecting you, Master Nix. This way."

Gabriel says, "Thanks, Jonathan."

This is a butler. You've seen butlers on TV. Also, Martians. It wouldn't feel stranger to be met by a man with antennae.

As you cross the room, you ignore the chairs and sofas and marble floor and enormous Persian rug. You stare at statues and paintings. A red-bearded man drives a chariot pulled by goats through a storm, a black-bearded man topples a pillar to kill himself with everyone in a temple, an Arab with a glowing face rides a flying horse, a samurai fights a demon, a woman with four arms dances with weapons in each hand, a man in white robes stands in front of cave.

You want to linger, but Jonathan walks briskly toward a hall. Then you see this room isn't a lobby. The Dumonts have the whole floor.

In the hall, the art continues: Chinese vases, Roman busts, a beach with fishing boats like a Van Gogh, bright squiggles and blobs like a Miró, a cowboy feeding a horse like a Remington, a cartoon space monster saying "Squa Tront!" like a Lichtenstein. You whisper to Gabriel. "It all looks so real!"

He replies, "Don't say that to Mr. Dumont."

Jonathan opens a door at the end of the hall. The air inside is warm and humid, the light is soft, and you know the smell of a swimming pool before you see it. Three people are on the far side of a pool that's bigger than some you've seen at motels.

A tanned girl in a red bikini reads a book in a lounge chair. Her hair is long and dark brown. She probably thinks she should lose ten pounds, but she would be beautiful if her frown didn't say she hates being interrupted, especially by you.

Near her, a pale woman in a white terry-cloth robe sits sipping a wineglass. She's as thin as a model. You can't tell if she's Scandinavian blond or white-haired. Her smile barely touches her lips.

Nearest to you is a stocky man in tight black trunks. He stands, arms akimbo, backlit by windows with all of New York behind him. His short hair is iron gray. His jaw and nose make you think of warriors, Apaches or Arabs. He's shorter than you. He reminds you of Dad. He grins like a man whose team just won.

As you head toward the trio, Jonathan says, "Master Nix? Do you swim?"

"Sure."

Before you can add that you didn't pack a suit, Jonathan says, "Forgive me," and shoves you into the pool.

Two

The water's cool. Chlorine stings your eyes. The pool lights are dim. You float in pale green space, infinite beside and below you, capped by a translucent ceiling where the water meets the air. You're surprised, not afraid. Falling into water hasn't scared you since you were five.

You swim easily upward. You must've misunderstood. Jonathan must have bumped you, then said, "Forgive me." You'll apologize for being clumsy, and he'll insist it was his fault, and everyone will laugh. Will he get in trouble for bumping you? You hope not. Accidents happen.

As you rise at the side of the pool, you see a silhouette above you. The shadow of a hand reaches out. You smile. Everyone will be surprised when you ignore the help and burst from the pool like a seal.

But as you reach the surface, the hand catches the top of your head, holding you under.

This must be a joke. The hand will let go in a second, so you don't struggle. Why embarrass everyone by panicking?

Your lungs throb for air. Your heart pounds, filling your ears with the sound of drums. You've been held too long for a joke. You kick to drive yourself upward. You only churn water. You sweep both arms to sink below the reach of the hand. The fingers hold your skull too tightly.

You've read that people see a far light as they die. Perhaps they see what they expect to see. Perhaps sight goes like the flash of a dying lightbulb. Is that what you're seeing?

The light's above you. It comes down as you rise. When you meet, it fills or empties you, then is gone or is always present.

You hear a voice. "He pleases me."

You open your eyes. You're standing, breathing comfortably. The man in dark trunks is smiling at you.

You frown. What pleases him? Having Jonathan push you in the pool? Who held you down? How did you get out?

The woman in the white robe is squinting at you. The girl in the red bikini, with a grimace of disgust, turns her eyes back to her book. You look at Jonathan and Gabriel. Jonathan is bowing. Gabriel is staring at your feet.

You glance down. You're standing on the water.

You gasp. What felt like firm ground is like carpet, like a mattress, like mud, like glue. You're sinking. Bogs suck people under to suffocate and never be seen again.

The man in trunks is laughing, rolling laughter that fills the room. The girl laughs, too, a deep, delighted laugh that makes you feel as if you failed a test she knew you would fail. You want to scream, but who will come if you do?

The water is syrup midway up your chest. Will you drown before it's water again?

The man walks toward you, strolling on water like crossing a lawn. You've sunk to your neck and tipped your head back for a last gasp when he bends down and grabs your hand.

He tugs lightly. You rise as if the water is rejecting you. As soon as you're standing on it again, the girl says, "Daddy, that wasn't funny."

He laughs. "It could've been a furnace."

You smile. You see yourself terrified as fire fails to burn you. You laugh. You see yourself a moment ago, thinking you would die in the water. You laugh even harder.

The man is grinning. You would do anything he asked. Dying for him would be a privilege, because he might remember that you had given everything for him. You say, "Thank you. I'm so—" What are you? "Everything. Thanks for everything."

He nods and walks away, leaving you standing there. The water quivers under you. You look down. Has the man abandoned you? What does he expect? Are you more likely to plunge back in if you stay still or walk away?

Jonathan is at the side of the pool with a large white towel. His sleeve is wet. He held you down. He looks apologetic. He would probably look apologetic while strangling a baby.

You glance at Gabriel. He shrugs to say he just does what he's told. You understand. You would do what you were told by the gray-haired man. Why doesn't he tell you what to do now? Should you ask? Would asking be wrong?

The water softens under your boots. You take a step. Water ripples. You take another, and that ripple is greater than the first. You run, splashing with each step, until you reach the side of the pool.

You begin to shake. Having tile underfoot is not more comforting than water. If water can hold you, can earth swallow you? You look across the pool at the man, the woman, and the girl. They look like people, but the water in the pool looks like water. You say, "What are you?"

The man smiles. "First ask, what are you?"

You're wet, shivering, furious, and terrified. Deal with the easy ones first. You reach for the towel in Jonathan's hand, then say, "Will that turn into a snake or something?"

Jonathan smiles. "No, Master Nix."

You take the towel and scrub your head and hands. You like the rough terry cloth against your skin. It defines the world: If the cloth is real, then you are.

You hand the towel to Jonathan and walk toward the others. Your clothes cling to you. Your boots squish with each step. The girl is back to reading. The woman is sipping her drink. The man watches you.

You say, "Are you Mr. Dumont?"

He nods. "I am who I am."

"How did you do that?"

"I told Jonathan to push you."

"No. How did you make—" All of the words to finish that sentence are impossible to speak. "Was I hypnotized?"

The girl's sigh might be a comment on something in her book.

Dumont's smile widens. "There are many ways to make things happen. The best only call for a push. Now, go with Jonathan. Dinner will be ready soon."

When you hesitate, he adds, "Your questions will be answered. Don't worry. So long as you're with us, everything's fine."

Jonathan takes you through several hallways to a bedroom with a view of the city and Central Park. There's a button to call him if you need anything, but what could you need? There's a four-poster bed, a color TV, and a rolltop desk. There's a private bathroom with a clawfoot tub and a toilet that's flushed by pulling the chain. The closet is as big as the room you shared with George before you and Dad enclosed the carport. Someone's clothes hang there. You say, "Where's my stuff?"

"That is your stuff, sir."

There are three suitcases worth of a rich boy's wardrobe, from a wool winter coat to a small nylon swimsuit.

"All of it?"

"Indeed, sir."

"It won't fit in my suitcase."

He indicates a leather trunk and a matching suitcase. "Those are yours as well, sir."

"Where's my suitcase?"

"I'll fetch it, if you wish. Or those things can be given to charity."

You start to say you can't accept this. But as you glance at what you're about to give up, you see a pad of fine paper, pencils, pens and nibs, and bottles of Japanese ink. You've seen them in art stores, in the cases that you passed when you went to get the cheap supplies.

It would be rude to refuse Mr. Dumont's kindness. You're starting a new life. Why not start fresh? You say, "Charity's a good idea."

Jonathan suggests you wear a dark blue suit, low leather boots and a belt as dark as oxblood, a light blue shirt, and a silk tie the blue of midnight. He knots the tie, helps you with a silver tack and cuff links that show two knights riding on one horse, and brushes your hair. You want to say you can do this yourself, but you know you can't do it as well.

When you look in the mirror, you think the people who called you handsome might mean it.

As you use the toilet, you wonder, Why is this happening? Did Mom and Dad secretly adopt you? Did Mom have an affair with Mr. Dumont? Were you born on another planet? Are you invulnerable? Can you leap tall buildings? Run faster than a locomotive? See through women's clothes?

You stare at the wall. You can't see through it. You stand still, thinking, "Up, up, and away!" Nothing changes. Does your levitation only work on things that are thicker than air? If you filled the tub with bubbles, could you walk on them? On smoke? Is standing on water the only thing you can do?

It's a stupid power. It would be better to be Batman and have a cave and a car and a utility belt than be Waterbug Boy.

Jonathan calls, "Master Nix?"

"Coming." You dry your hands and go out.

As you walk through the halls, you feel like a passenger in a car skidding on ice. There's nothing to do but accept what comes.

Jonathan opens a door and stands aside. You step into a room in shades of brown and gold. You see a painting of men in robes riding over the desert, a sculpture of a hawk, another of a horse, and shelves of old books with dark bindings. You smell tobacco and alcohol. You hear a jazz record playing on a big stereo cabinet.

Dumont rises from a leather chair. The pale woman stands by the window. The dark-haired girl sits cross-legged on a sofa reading a book. Dumont and the woman wear black evening clothes, but the girl's in a white dress.

You hesitate by the door, looking for clues to what they are. Vampires have fangs. Elves and Vulcans have pointed ears. Werewolves have hairy palms. What are the signs of people who walk on water?

Dumont says, "Christopher!" He indicates the woman. "My wife, Charlotte."

She offers her hand. "It's a joy to have you in our home, Christopher." She sounds like an actress who's tired of her role. Her skin is taut like leather on a frame. Her accent sounds slightly Germanic.

Dumont says, "And my Heller. Heller, greet the boy."

Without looking up, the girl says, "Hello, boy. You don't mind if I read?" Her voice is husky, more American than her mother's, more exotic than her father's.

Mrs. Dumont says, "Heller!"

You say, "It's all right. I hate being interrupted when I'm reading." You add, "What're you reading?"

Heller glances at you. "That's an interruption."

Dumont laughs. "That's my girl." He claps your shoulder, and you think of strength like mountains.

Heller closes her book. It's Shakespeare's *The Tempest*. She says, "What'll you be? A third-former?"

Third form equals ninth grade. You shake your head. "Fourth."

"Oh, good. You can be the little brother I never had." She slaps her book down on the couch, stands, tells her parents, "But he's not Josh."

Mrs. Dumont says, "Heller!"

"He's not!" she says louder. You want to excuse yourself, but where would you go?

Dumont says, "He's not replacing anyone. He's the grandson of the man who saved my life. That's enough to make him welcome here." He glances at the door as Jonathan enters and says, "Have all our guests arrived?"

Jonathan's nod suggests a bow. "Yes, sir."

"Then we should go."

You say, "I've got some questions."

Dumont glances at the bookshelf, then says, "How did you learn to swim?"

"Dad threw me off the end of a dock. Why?"

Dumont laughs. "He and I have much in common. Come. It'll all be clear in time."

Going down the hall, you ask Dumont, "Did you invite a lot of people?"

"I wouldn't call it a large gathering."

"Good. I'm terrible with names."

He smiles as Jonathan opens a pair of doors carved with olives and leaves.

At least sixty people stand at a long dining table. Most of them look like diplomats from the U.N. You see dark suits, evening dresses, robes, caftans, saris, and Nehru jackets. Two Chinese men wear Mao suits. Most of the guests could be your grandparents' age. Some are young and long-haired, but they aren't hippies.

Their clothes are expensively fashionable. Their hair is Hollywood perfect.

Everyone bows toward the door. You think they're bowing to the Dumonts.

Four empty chairs are at the head of the table. The Dumonts go stand there, leaving one seat between Dumont and Heller. At the far end of the table is Gabriel. You would happily sit by him, or anyplace inconspicuous, but every other seat is taken.

Dumont says, "Christopher, be seated."

An old man asks in a thick Italian accent, "Christopher?" then laughs.

Dumont tells him, "A coincidence."

A woman in a turban smiles. "How could it be otherwise?"

A gray-bearded man in a heavy suit says, "If he was called David, would you let us claim him?"

As the three laugh, you look at the Dumonts. Heller watches you with narrowed eyes and tight lips. Mrs. Dumont watches with a cool smile. Everyone else is waiting for something.

"Sit," Dumont says. "You're the guest of honor."

Thinking the best way to get this over with is to get through it, you sit.

Dumont steps behind you. As he says, "See my heir," something drips on your head.

Startled, you look up. Dumont shows you a small bottle, then puts it in his pocket. "Olive oil. People have done this for over three thousand years."

You touch the top of your head. There are only a few drops. "Heir?"

"My son died. I owe your grandfather a great debt. Let me repay it."

"But my family—"

"You'll inherit all I have. You may treat your family well, if you wish."

"All?" You glance at Heller and Mrs. Dumont. They don't look amused. "Is this a joke?"

The guests laugh. Heller says, "*I* think so. But Daddy's serious."

You're rich. You don't know how rich, but any rich will do. You can buy a motorcycle. Or a car. All the art supplies and comic books you could want. Could you buy a castle? An island? A comic book company? A movie studio? You grin and smooth the oil into your hair.

A young Englishman raises his glass. "To Christopher Nix!"

You start to reach for the glass before you. Mrs. Dumont catches your eye and shakes her head slightly. Toasting yourself would look vain. So, as everyone toasts you, you smile like an idiot.

You're relieved when Dumont turns to Jonathan and says, "A demonstration is in order."

Jonathan looks at Gabriel, nods, and begins to smile. His smile falters slightly as Gabriel draws a pistol from a shoulder holster.

You think the gun looks surprisingly real.

And Gabriel fires two shots into Jonathan's heart.

Three

Jonathan slumps to the floor. He looks more surprised than hurt. Blood spreads on his shirt where his tie is tucked into his jacket.

The people near him draw their chairs back. They're very calm, like everyone else in the room.

Gabriel watches Jonathan, then holsters his pistol.

No one's upset. Why isn't anyone upset?

Dumont says, "Breathe." You think he's talking to Jonathan. Then you gasp and take quick, deep gulps of air. Dumont says, "Slowly," and you grow calmer.

Everyone's watching you. Why? You didn't murder anyone. Oh. You're the only one who didn't expect this. You're the witness. Will you be killed next? Gabriel holsters his pistol. Will someone else kill you? Will you be killed differently? Will you be hurt first?

You say, "My parents know I'm here." As soon as you say it, you think that's a mistake. If they're not afraid to kill Jonathan, they're not afraid to kill anyone.

Dumont says, "There's nothing to fear."

You want to ask if this is a trick. Blood pools around the back of Jonathan's jacket. It's not a trick.

Dumont says, "Bring him back."

Sounds take ages to become words. Words take eternities to become sentences. Heller Dumont has a look that might be pity.

Mrs. Dumont's look is contempt. Everyone else seems simply to be waiting. But Dumont is smiling, and something fills you, a light or its absence.

You walk to Jonathan and stop beside him. He's wrong. You can fix him. You just don't know how.

Dumont says, "The longer you wait, the harder it'll be."

You touch Jonathan's shoulder. He's still warm under the jacket.

Dumont says, "Spit on your hands, then touch his skin."

You spit, rub your palms together, and put them on Jonathan's cheeks. You're in darkness and cold, like being lost at night in an arctic storm. You would turn back, but something flickers just ahead of you.

You stumble on. The dark and the cold grow more intense with each step. The flickering flees faster than you can run. You leap for it and catch something tiny, delicate, and beautiful.

Cold darkness is comforting. You could rest here, but you've left things undone. You turn back.

And Jonathan jerks up from the floor, screaming. You're in the Dumont's dining room. You scramble out of Jonathan's reach. He doesn't seem to see you, or anything.

Dumont says, "Tell him he's healed."

You say quickly. "Jonathan! You're healed."

He gasps, then sees you and whispers, "Master Nix?"

"Yes. It's me."

"You brought me back."

You look at your hands. Something revived him. You want to be glad he's alive, but you remember the moment he died. Horror filled you, but so did something else. It felt like strength.

That can't be right. You must've felt adrenaline telling you to flee or fight. That panic seemed like strength in your memory.

Jonathan touches his chest. He stares at the blood on his fingers, then looks at Gabriel.

Gabriel shrugs. "You knew you'd be fine." His voice is flat. You think he would've shot Jonathan no matter what he expected to happen next.

Dumont says, "I thank you both."

Jonathan nods and goes out. Gabriel, with a sponge and bucket, begins cleaning the floor. Did the bullets pass through Jonathan, or are they still in him, or did bringing him back dissolve the bullets or send them away? Did reality change, so the bullets were never in Jonathan, even though his blood is on the floor?

You look at the others. The oldest guests are satisfied. The youngest are awed. Dumont smiles. "You're truly my heir."

He turns to the guests. "So you all may know this is so, I give him the one thing I truly love, the finest fruit of my loins, my child, Heller."

She stares at him. Her jaw shifts. You're sure she'll protest. Then she glances at you, and you see the plea in her eyes. You say, "I'm only fifteen."

Dumont nods. "An adult in most cultures."

"But I don't know Heller."

"Then your marriage begins as an adventure." His smile disappears. "Don't you find her attractive?"

Agreeing would trap you. You say, "I love someone else." Is that true? You've wondered about that for ten months now. If saying you love CC will get Dumont to forget about you and Heller, you'll tell the world you love CC. You know you want the chance to find out if you love CC. Maybe that's all that love is.

Dumont shrugs. "Love as you wish. In countries that allow it, take many wives. But your heir will be of my blood."

Mrs. Dumont says, "He thinks you mean for them to marry tonight."

Dumont laughs. "Ah! No, Christopher. When you marry, everyone who matters must be there to know the line continues. Marry for the world in, say, ten years. Now is your time to learn what you may be. Using what you learn will come soon enough." He hands you a goblet. "Let's have wine."

You look in the goblet. "This is water."

"At the moment," he agrees. He picks up a steak knife. "Hold out your wrist."

You would ask why, but you see the answer. You can bring back the dead. Why fear a knife? He asked for your wrist, not your heart. Maybe he means to show that knives can't cut you. You extend your arm as the guests lean forward. This interests them more than killing Jonathan.

Dumont pushes your sleeve back. You stifle a gasp: knives still cut you, and you still feel pain. He holds the goblet under your wrist. A drop falls. You hear a soft inhalation from the guests. Another drop falls, then more.

When the water is as red as burgundy, Dumont touches your wrist. The blood stops flowing. The cut closes. He says, "Healing others is easier than healing ourselves."

Dumont gives the goblet to the Italian man, who sips, smiles, and says, "Ah, the best wine that's served last."

He passes it to the woman in the turban. She says, "Sometimes I think this is the wine we were told not to drink." She drinks, then smiles.

The gray-bearded man laughs when the goblet reaches him. "Sometimes I think this is the blood we were told not to drink." After his taste, he laughs louder and passes the goblet on.

When it completes the circle, you expect the Dumonts to drink. But Jonathan, in a clean shirt and jacket, comes to take the goblet away.

As soon as it's gone, conversation springs up again. Servants enter to refill people's drinks. In the bustle, Dumont tells you, "Now that they've drunk to you, you have protectors."

You say, “Do I need protectors?”

Dumont shrugs. “Probably not.”

Heller says, “They drank to Josh.”

Mrs. Dumont says, “Let’s discuss this later.”

Heller says, “Why? Everyone here knows he was killed!”

The room falls quiet.

“He drowned,” Dumont says. “Nothing suggests it wasn’t an accident.”

Heller says, “We don’t have accidents.”

Dumont smiles. “You know the Icarus tale. Overconfidence kills.”

Heller says, “And I know the Balder tale. Trust kills, too.”

Mrs. Dumont shakes her head. “Don’t trouble yourself with this now.”

Heller says, “Of course not. Why should we trouble ourselves with feelings?”

Dumont says softly, “We love, daughter. As strongly as we hate. If Josh was killed, our justice will be terrible.”

You repress a shudder and the thought that whoever killed Josh might come for you. Then Dumont smiles, and you know you’re being silly. You’re not Josh. No one’s sure he was killed. Enjoy this evening. It’s for you.

The first courses include caviar, steak tartare, lobster salad, and chicken leek soup. Each has a different wine. You want to look grateful, so you drain every glass. Several pretty women smile at you in ways that no one has smiled at you since CC.

Dumont talks with the nearest guests about international trade, the climate, and whether it would be better for Russia or China to rule the world next. Mrs. Dumont only speaks to suggest better ways for Heller to sit (“Always erect!”) and hold a fork (“Left hand, darling! Do you want to be thought an American?”). Heller ignores her mother and finishes everything on every plate that’s brought to her.

Dumont turns to you. "Do you like the meal?"

You think if caviar were cheap, no one would eat it, but you like everything else. "It's great."

He nods. "The world's for our use. We kill, we eat, we—" He looks at Heller, then says, "Once a man gives his child, she's given."

Heller says, "I don't want him."

You're slightly insulted and greatly relieved. Before you can say that's cool, Dumont smiles at Heller. "How do you know?" He reaches across you to squeeze her hand fondly. "Find out if you want him."

She glares at him. "Daddy!"

"It's purpose, daughter. You'll have parties and praise when the world should know. But why waste a moment until then?"

You say quickly, "I'm not—" When they both look at you, you know your mouth was, as usual, faster than your mind. You say, "I don't want anyone who doesn't want me."

Dumont's smile grows. "See? You should both find out what you want."

Heller snaps, "Fine."

You say, "Fine?"

Dumont nods. "She said, 'fine.' Jonathan! Bring the best wine in the house! We have a union to celebrate!"

The nice thing about wine is that when life is confusing, all you have to do is drink. You like the taste and the effect. You like people who bring wine to you. You like the way guests talk happily in many languages. You like the way Heller ignores you. That's funny. Everything's funny.

You look down. A plate is before you: a pink slab of venison in a pool of its juice. You take your knife and fork and, like Zorro, cut boldly. The slab slips. Hot venison juice shoots from your plate, missing Dumont, who is turned away to speak with a guest, and splashing Mrs. Dumont's face, shoulder, and breasts.

She stands, saying something quick in German that you don't want to have translated. Dumont looks from her to you. So does everyone else.

You say, "I'm sorry, my knife slipped—"

Dumont says, "It's nothing."

Mrs. Dumont pats herself with napkins that Jonathan brings. "I'm nothing? My dress is nothing?"

Dumont says, "Charlotte—" as you say, "I'll save up to buy you another—" and Mrs. Dumont says, "You are not worthy of my daughter!" and Heller shouts, "Mother, stop it! It was an accident!"

Mrs. Dumont whirls toward Heller. "Don't raise your voice to me!"

Heller shouts, "You should apologize to him!"

Dumont says, "Heller, be quiet."

Heller says, "She started this!"

Mrs. Dumont says, "Your ignorant foundling started—"

Dumont says, "Be still."

And everyone is. You think of Dad and how people know to be quiet when he has had enough.

Heller shakes herself. "Daddy, can't you see—"

Dumont tells her, "Apologize to our guests."

Heller squints at him, then says, "What did I—"

And you say, "I'm the one who should apologize. It was my fault."

"No! It's wrong, Daddy!" Heller runs for the door. A servant standing near looks at Jonathan, who looks at Dumont, and Heller yanks open the door herself.

Dumont says, "Stop."

Heller hesitates.

You say, "It really was my fault."

Dumont glances at you, and Heller's through the door. She slams it behind her, and her footsteps race down the hall.

Mrs. Dumont rises, saying, "I shall change." The servant at the door doesn't hesitate to open it for her.

Dumont sighs and tells the guests, "Our family drama is over. Forget this little disturbance and enjoy the evening!" He nods to Jonathan, who looks toward the kitchen. Servants flow into the room with small crystal glasses of golden wine and silver bowls of ice cream that smells of cinnamon.

Everyone acts as if nothing happened. People laugh, and the two pretty women smile at you, and servants have already cleared Heller's and Mrs. Dumont's places. You feel terrible about Mrs. Dumont and worse about Heller. Her troubles came from taking your side.

You tell Dumont, "Excuse me," and stand. As you rise, the party falls silent.

Dumont frowns. "Are you ill?"

"I'm fine. Tell Mrs. Dumont I'm sorry. It was a great dinner, and I'll see you in the morning."

Dumont says, "Stay."

You stop with your hand on your chair. His voice, like Dad's, demands obedience, but there's nothing in it that you love. If he never forgives you, what do you lose?

You walk toward the door. The servant there seems confused, but you nod to him. He opens it without a glance at Jonathan.

In the hall, you wonder what you've done. Dumont will take away all that he offered, and you'll go home knowing you bungled everything. You'll live the rest of your life knowing you could have been great.

You feel sober. Correction, you feel afraid. Being afraid is remarkably like being sober.

You're walking down a hall you haven't seen before. You're hunting for a way to make things right. When did you decide to do this? When you left the party? You're not sober. You're just afraid.

You hear sobbing behind a door. You stop, feeling entirely helpless, but you knock lightly. When no one answers, you call, "Heller? I'm sorry—"

"Go away!" You hear her run across the room. You step back, expecting her to burst through and start hitting you. The door swings wide. She says, "Go home and forget about this!"

She wears a red bathrobe. Her feet are bare. Is she wearing anything under the robe? You would like to draw her standing in the doorway. You would rather draw CC, but you'd like to draw Heller. You think, "You're beautiful when you're angry" isn't entirely a cliché. You say softly, "Would your father let me?"

Her face calms. She wipes her eyes with her sleeve, then says, "You poor kid," and stands back. When you hesitate, she says, "Come in. It'll make Daddy happy and Mommy furious. It's perfect."

You shrug. "I guess that's the least I can do." You step in.

Her walls are almost hidden by bookcases filled with books, a jumble of hardbound volumes and paperbacks. She says, "Some of those were Josh's. We liked reading the same things." The tops of the shelves are covered with teddy bears. She adds, "When Daddy went away and felt guilty, he would bring me a bear."

He must have gone away a lot, but you don't say that.

She says, "Close the door."

You turn and push it until it clicks. You think this is probably a mistake, but since everything you can think of looks like a mistake, this may be the best.

When you turn back, Heller has dropped her robe. She's not CC, and she's heavier than a *Playboy* model, but she's beautiful.

You're staring. You turn around and say, "Sorry."

"Come on," she says. "Let's get it over with."

"We don't have to."

"Of course we do." You hear her throwing the sheets back, then sitting on the bed. "Are you queer?"

You whirl without thinking. "No!"

"It's cool if you are. You can have boyfriends or girlfriends or dogfriends, I don't care. As long as we do it now and then, everyone will be satisfied. That's what matters."

You shake your head. A beautiful girl is naked before you, and for the first time since you learned how babies were made, you have zero interest in sex.

She says, "Have you done it before?"

You think of CC. "Almost. Not really."

"They say the first time is worst. So we'll be doing each other a favor."

You shake your head. "I'm drunk."

"Too drunk to do it?"

You know that's not true, but you nod.

She says, "We can turn the lights off. It says in *Everything You Wanted to Know About Sex* that it's normal to be shy."

"It's not— I like seeing you. But I don't think this is what you want."

"Who always gets what they want?"

"I should go." You turn back to the door.

"Can't you feel it?"

You want to say you don't know what she means, but you do feel something. You want to stay with her, but it's not that you like her. You want to have sex with her, but it's not that you desire her.

You look back. She nods. "It's the blood. It knows its own. Daddy would've died in France. He was in the bushes where no one knew to look. But your grandfather was of a lost line, so he came looking without knowing why. It's the blood."

You watch her and don't know what to say. You want to draw her breasts and stomach and thighs. You want to touch those curves and close your eyes so you could draw them in the darkness. But there's something in her face that you don't understand, an intensity that makes you sure that whatever this is to her, it's not sex or love or anything you want. You say, "What lost line?"

"I don't want to talk about it."

"So I should go away and forget it?"

"No." She looks out the window, then at the robe on the floor. It's closer to you. You hand it to her. She slips it on, and the part of you that wants to draw her is sad, and maybe another part is sad, too. She says, "You must think I'm weird."

You shrug. "Who isn't a little weird?"

She hugs one of her teddy bears. You think she isn't going to speak again. You're about to leave when she sets the bear aside and pats the bed lightly. It's a suggestion, not a demand.

You feel the pull, what she named the "call of the blood," as a whisper. It's not the desire you felt with CC. It's easy to ignore. You sit.

She says, "We're elohim. That's why they worship us."

"Elo—heem?" She nods. You say, "Your family?"

"And you, now you're anointed."

You test the name. "I'm an elohim."

She smiles. "An elah. Or an eloah. 'Elohim' is plural. It means the mighty ones. The four of us."

"I'm a mighty one?"

She nods, and you grin, thinking, I'm the Mighty Elah-Man! Your grin makes her laugh, which makes you think she's nicer than she seemed. You ask, "We can do things because of our blood?"

"That's what Daddy would say. Mommy would say it's a mystery. I say it's genetics."

"Are there other elohim?"

She smiles again, and you definitely like her smile. "That's like asking if there's another royal family. People with the blood are nefilim."

"Like my family?"

"It depends. Being from an old line doesn't mean there are other nefs in your family. If there's a nef gene, it's really recessive."

"Can something be really recessive?"

"Sure, if it's like being a color-blind left-handed albino dwarf."

"How many nefs are there?"

"Of the known lines? A few hundred. The blood's weak in most of them."

"Is that who was at the party?"

She shakes her head. "Daddy only invited worshippers." She sees your frown and adds, "Useful humans. Daddy wants them to see the elohim is complete again. They expect that."

"Complete how?"

"The four of us. King, queen, prince, and princess."

"Prince and princess?"

She nods.

"Do we get our own country?"

She sets her hand on your thigh. It doesn't seem sexual. It's intimate in a way that's more than sexual. "We get the world."

You study her to see if she's lying. She nods and leans closer. You think you should leave, but why? You're an elah, the elohim prince, the prince of the world, worshipped by people who are rich and powerful. The world's princess wants you. The blood is calling, stronger than you thought it could.

As your lips meet, you think of CC. Will you see her again? Was CC a virgin when you were with her? If you see her again, wouldn't it be best if you weren't a virgin, either? You would be equals, then. For CC's sake, you should have sex with Heller.

The logic is flawed, but what logic is perfect? Heller has your pants open. You're not too drunk. Your hands are in her robe. Her breasts feel good in your palms, fuller than CC's, though you shouldn't compare them, but how can you not compare them?

Heller squeezes, and you say, "Not so hard."

Her touch changes. "Better?"

You want to laugh, because you're both so awkward, but you say, "Yeah," and you mean it, because awkward is still nice, and you'll finally get rid of your virginity—

"Wait!" You leap up.

"Chris, no!" She grabs you, pulling you back. "I want you."

You twist free and find your pants tangled in the sheets. "I've got—" You find your wallet and pull out the rubber that you carried for ten months, hoping to use it with CC. "So you don't have to worry."

"No."

You rip open the package. Should you have practiced putting it on? It's supposed to unroll, but what does that mean? Then you hear what Heller said. "No?"

"We don't need that."

"It's being safe."

"We're nefs. If we caught something, we could heal it."

"What about catching a baby?"

"Nefs don't get pregnant easily."

"But you can get pregnant?"

"Sure, but—"

"Okay, then." The rubber doesn't want to unroll. Oh. You're holding it backward.

"Don't," Heller says. "Not for the first time."

"But this is for you!"

"I thought guys don't like rubbers."

"That's why it's for you."

"So don't."

"It's no big deal." You don't want to admit you want to wear a rubber. You hate the idea of being a teen dad, and rubbers are supposed to be slightly desensitizing. Making the first time safer and slower seems like a good idea. You want her to want to do this again. You don't care if it won't be as great for you. It'll be sex. That's great enough. If you're her first, you hope she'll tell her friends someday, "He was wonderful." Or even, "He wasn't as bad as some guys I've heard about." That would be good, too.

The rubber is on. It feels silly, like a dive suit for your penis, but it's on, and suiting up for action makes a strange, sexy sense. You reach for Heller.

Only now she's the one who twists away. "I want the first time to be natural."

You stare at her. You want to say, "What's more natural than sex?"

"Take it off. I'll do anything you want. Just take it off."

You keep staring. You know you're an idiot. You've been honorable. Maybe she's on the pill. Maybe she's got an IUD. Her body, her choice, right? She made her choice; now you can have her body. Do her!

You say, "Are you on the pill or something?"

"Don't worry about it. Come on."

You start putting on your underwear. You'll figure out what to do with the rubber later.

"Chris? You're leaving?"

You nod.

"Just like that?"

You nod again.

"Did we talk too much?"

"Maybe not enough."

"Okay. We can talk some more."

You look around the room to see if you're forgetting anything. She's still beautiful, and you're still an idiot, but you're the kind of idiot who does stupid things like this. You say, "Sorry," and leave.

You go to your very lonely room, where you dress in silk pajamas and climb into soft cotton sheets and think about CC and Heller and elohim and babies.

Eventually, you fall asleep or pass out.

Four

No one is building battleships beside your bed. Someone is tapping lightly on the door. You say, "Yeah?" or maybe you just growl.

Jonathan steps in. "Breakfast will be ready in thirty minutes, sir."

Then you remember leaving the party and refusing to have sex with Heller. You were tested, and you failed. They'll send you home.

Or kill you to keep their secret.

But why bother? If you told what you know, who would believe you?

You could walk on water to show that much is true, but your power is weak. Dumont woke it. He must be able to take it away. Maybe that would be best.

You want your old clothes, but Jonathan says they've gone to charity. The new wardrobe does not include jeans. You try to pick the cheapest things, but you can't guess the prices. You end up in Top-Siders, khaki trousers, and a green polo shirt.

Jonathan says Dumont is in his study, and he takes you to the room where you met the family. Dumont sits in a red leather chair, eating a bagel with cream cheese and lox.

As Jonathan goes, you tell Dumont, "I'm sorry about last night. When I get home, I'll pay you back for your wife's dress and the plane tickets and everything. I'll have to save up—"

He laughs. "What're you talking about? You're going to the Academy!"

"But—"

"I've had to learn a great deal about patience, Christopher. You'll make mistakes. Then you'll work harder to overcome them." He gestures at a platter of food. "Go ahead. Sometimes it's good to be served, sometimes it's better to take."

You choose fresh orange juice, a bagel with cream cheese and lox, strawberries, and a slice each of cantaloupe and honeydew. If you were home, the selection would be based on what's cheapest: Tang, Wonder bread, Velveeta. You're glad Dumont has not changed his mind about you.

Then he says, "Someone may try to kill you."

Your appetite is gone. You set your plate aside.

He says, "We have enemies. Some want to rule in our place. Some prefer chaos to order. The motives only matter if they help us win."

"So Josh was killed?"

"I believe so. I won't tell the women. Nothing useful comes from having them worry. I won't tell our people. Never remind serfs that the king can die." He sips his coffee.

"Who would kill—" You're not sure whether to finish with "Josh" or "me."

"Why limit the possibilities? There's only one person to trust at the Academy."

"That teacher you sent to Florida? Mr. Fitzgerald?"

"Yourself. Fitzgerald doesn't know what we are. The headmaster does, and he's served us loyally for ages, but anyone might grow ambitious. Heller said she told you about us."

"A little."

"Several families of the blood have students at the Academy. Any of them would wish you dead, if they knew who you are."

"Because I'm the prince?"

He laughs. "That's how she explained it?"

"I'm not the prince?"

"I would've said consort, but, yes, you're the prince. If you die, another youth of the blood will be Heller's mate, and someday, El Elyon."

"El Elyon?"

"The highest of the elohim."

"Oh. You said if they knew. Only Heller will know who I am at school?"

"And the headmaster."

"What about the people last night? The worshippers?"

He smiles. "Call them stewards when they might hear. They won't tell anyone what they know. If we fall, the next elohim will choose new puppets. Our stewards know that."

"Puppets?"

"When things go badly, they're blamed, we install new puppets, and life goes on. You only need to worry about other nefilim."

"So I'm bait?" Your voice cracks. You're not sure if you're more afraid or angry.

"If that was all, I'd never tell you this."

How much of what he says can you believe? Something calms you, making you trust him. You feel it happening, and you think you shouldn't, but you do trust him. Why be suspicious when he eases your suspicions? Your suspicions are wrong. It's good of him to ease them.

You ask, "Who are the nef students?"

"You'll know them, by the blood. You'll recognize them as easily as you recognize Heller."

"Won't they know me the same way?"

He shakes his head. "Your line's older. They don't know its signs. You're safe so long as you don't reveal yourself."

"Can I tell my family?"

"It's a dangerous secret, Christopher. I wouldn't share it with anyone I loved."

"Oh."

He laughs. "Cheer up! In a few years, you may share it with the world, if you like."

You try to imagine keeping a secret so long. "A few years?"

"That's not even a moment to us. Nefilim can live for a thousand years."

He's not joking. He's not crazy or lying. What happened in 970? What will happen in 2970? You ask, "Are you that old?"

His face darkens. You think he's angry, then know it, then know his anger can kill you as easily as you can flick a gnat. Will he spare you if you beg him?

Before you can speak, his face lightens. He's handsome and good. You would do anything to please him. He is pure light, so bright and hot you can't be near him because you're mist before the sun. You're about to drop to the floor and hide your face—

And he's a man sipping coffee. He says, "I'm older."

"Oh."

"Heller didn't tell you everything."

You shake your head. He wants you to treat him like a man, and you want him to be pleased with you, so you will. You ask, "Could she be in danger?"

You see his surprise. Then he says, "What did she say about the elohim?"

"Just that it's the four of us."

"Sky Father, Earth Mother, Spring Bride, Summer Groom. With the consort dead, the only hope for continuity is through Heller." He studies you, then adds, "The enemy might show himself by courting her."

You swallow. Are you supposed to be ready to fight someone

over a girl you don't like? You ask, "If they, uh, attack me, and no one else can stop them—"

"Remember bringing Jonathan back?"

You nod.

"Sending people away is easier."

One is going into the dark storm to save a firefly. The other is throwing a firefly outside and slamming the door. Why is the easy one so much harder to imagine doing?

Dumont says, "That troubles you?"

"You say it so casually."

"Is the lion casual? It is what it is. We give life, and we take it. That's the heart of our power. It's why they fear and love us."

The door opens. Jonathan says, "Gabriel is ready."

You glance at Dumont. Who is Gabriel going to kill? You? But Dumont wouldn't have spent time with you if he wanted you dead, and Gabriel does other things for Dumont than kill.

Dumont says, "I like you, Christopher. You have much to learn, but the Academy will teach you what you need to know. When your time comes, you'll rule well."

His nod says you may go. You have many questions, but remembering his anger, you decide you don't need to ask any of them now.

You follow Jonathan out.

Gabriel waits by the elevator. Your new suitcase is beside him. In a butter-yellow shirt and purple bell-bottoms, he looks like an actor or musician.

Jonathan tells you, "Your trunk will be delivered to the Academy. I look forward to serving you again, sir." He bows and goes, as quietly as ever.

Should you have given him your blessing? You hope he wasn't disappointed. It's not easy being the prince of the world.

Gabriel hands you a piece of paper and a coin with a hole in it.

"Train ticket, subway token. You'll attract less attention at the Academy if you arrive like you're no one special. But that makes it tougher to get you there safe. So we take the elevator down together. You have any last questions, ask them then. I go out. Count to thirty and follow. When next you see me, you don't know me. Walk to the subway station. I'll follow. Go to Grand Central. That's when I disappear and you're on your own. Don't stand close to the tracks or do anything that'd make it easy for someone to arrange an accident. If you talk with any Academy students, keep it simple: Dumont owed your granddaddy, so he bought you some clothes, put you up for the night, and sent you on to school."

Gabriel's coolness falters. He adds, "You and Miss Heller—"

You nod to let him know it's okay.

"You met here, but she's a sixth-form girl and you're a fourth-form boy. In public, say hi and move on. Follow her lead, and you'll do fine." He says softly, "She's seventeen, but she's got a head on her shoulders."

You like Gabriel for a second, then remember how calmly he shot Jonathan. He says, "All set, sir?"

"You can call me Chris."

"Not when I'm on duty, sir."

"When aren't you on duty?"

He grins. "Good question, sir."

You pick up the suitcase and enter the elevator. "Guess I'm set." As you descend, you ask, "How long have you been on duty?"

"I was called to be Gabriel on July 18, 1863."

You glance at him to see if he's joking, but why should he? In the Dumont home, he's probably a kid. You remember him drinking last night. "Are most stewards that old?"

"No, sir," he says proudly. "Most of 'em just get a few extra healthy years. The exceptions are agents like Jonathan and me."

"You were a soldier?"

"Mr. Dumont likes soldiers."

"There was a Gabriel before you?"

"I expect there were many."

"What happened to them?"

"I don't think much on that. Either they died serving well, or they died 'cause they didn't. I'm not planning on either, but I'll settle for the first." The door opens, and he walks out.

On the way to Grand Central, you hardly notice New York. At first you're afraid you might be killed. Then you're afraid you might have to kill someone. If Dumont had said this is the price of being the world-prince, would you agree to pay it?

What would a killer look like? New York is full of very rich people and very poor ones. You study everyone you see. Would you prefer to kill someone who is clean and well-dressed or filthy and ragged? A man or a woman? An old person or a child?

Either no one tries to kill you, or Gabriel does his job extremely well. As you board the train, you think about the people who never appear in TV shows or movies, the poor and the homeless, and you smile. Their suffering will end soon. You'll be the best prince the world has ever known.

Five

On the train, you look for an empty bench. The car's half-full of business types and college kids and preppies who might be going to the Academy. You'll have to sit with someone.

You see CC. Your heart swells, and you grin, and you think the elah magic is working overtime.

But the woman who glances up is old enough to be CC's mother. Only her silhouette is similar to CC's. CC's gone to New Zealand or Never Never Land for all you know.

A man says loudly, "Don't look sad, lad. Got a seat right here." He's in shades of brown, from his pale shirt to his dark suit. His hair and his clothes are rumpled. His face is too red. His smile is too bright. His breath says he's been drinking.

His bench is turned to face another. Across from him is a kid who wears round wire-frame glasses and smiles like he's high. His black hair hangs from a center part to the middle of his T-shirt, where what looks like the Ford logo actually reads FUCK.

The drunk seems like a happy drunk, the longhair seems cool, and you need a seat. Then you look across the aisle.

Heller, in a window seat, is reading *Siddhartha*. Should you keep walking? All the other seats are with straights or preppies.

You jam your suitcase into the rack over the longhair and sit.

The drunk looks like he's passed out. The longhair says, "Hey, man. Going far?"

"Near Boston." He could be going to a university. Maybe he'll think you are, too.

The drunk, without opening his eyes, says, "Boston. Excellent party town."

The longhair says, "Is that home?"

You hadn't thought about what your home is now. Does two families mean two homes? You shake your head and say, "Gainesville, Florida."

The drunk says, "Gainesville. Excellent party town."

"What's up north?" The longhair grins wider. "A girl?"

"I wish. You live in New York?"

"No way, José. Visiting a sweet, crazy chica."

The drunk says, "New York. Excellent party town."

The longhair says, "Man, you think every place is a party town."

The drunk opens his eyes. "Sometimes you have to bring the party."

The longhair laughs. "Right on!"

A jock in an Academy sweater walks by. Either he's concentrating on his balance or he sneers at you, the drunk, and the longhair. The longhair says, "No one's bringing a party where he's going."

The drunk nods. "Parties aren't for the weak of will."

The longhair says, "Fucking preppies. They wipe their butts with money and think it makes their shit smell sweet." He glances at you. "Nothing personal."

You curse your new hair and clothes and shrug. "They can't all be like that."

"Some crooks rob you; some con you. It's all the same in the morning."

The drunk says with delight, "You're a communist!"

The longhair nods warily. "It's a free country."

"Ah, yes. You have Democrats and Republicans so you may vote for the prowar, antidrug capitalist you like."

The longhair says, "Man, you're the one who talks like a red."

The drunk laughs. "I talk like a drunk. You say what you think, and people hate you. I say what I think, and people laugh."

"What good does it do if they laugh?"

"They remember what I said when they think I was funny. Speak bluntly, and they only remember you're a boor." The drunk pulls a flask from his jacket. "Want a shot?"

The longhair looks down the aisle. "Conductor."

The drunk slips the flask back in his pocket, glances at you, and smiles. "If it's hidden, does it exist?"

Across the aisle, Heller looks up from her book and says, "Oh. It's you, Chris."

"Uh, hey, Heller." It's nice that she's talking to you. Then she smiles at the longhair and you see why. What's he got that you haven't? You're the prince of the world. He's just a guy who happens to be older, taller, handsomer, and cooler than you.

The longhair says, "Heller. Nice name."

She says, "For a preppie?"

He grins. "Especially for a preppie."

The drunk says, "Introductions are in order! And I would gladly make them, if I knew your names."

While you wonder if giving your name to a strange drunk is wise, the others say, "Elverado Sanchez" and "Heller Dumont."

Elverado blinks at her. "As in Jay Dumont?"

She frowns. "You know Daddy?"

"By name."

"How?"

Elverado looks sheepish. "I go to the Academy." He glances at you. "Mama teaches science. That's how."

You say, “I’m, like, on a scholarship.”

“You a brain or a jock?”

“Just lucky.”

The drunk says, “Did I offer you good people a drink?”

Elverado laughs. “Yeah.”

You say, “What about the conductor?”

The drunk says, “I fancy a stroll. Anyone care to join me?”

“I could do that,” says Elverado.

“Sure thing,” you say.

“Since you ask,” says Heller. You and Elverado glance at her. She sets down her book. “You did ask.”

“Indeed!” The drunk looks at you. “There was another introduction to be made.”

“Oh. Christo— Chris Nix.”

“Christochris Nix,” says the drunk. “A pleasure.”

“Um, it’s just—”

“Onward!” The drunk rolls to his feet. “Mother Earth’s nectar awaits us!”

Heller and Elverado nearly bump as they spring into the aisle. You’ve been forgotten. You don’t like Heller, Elverado thinks he’s cool just because he’s cooler than anyone else here, and the drunk’s annoying because he’s a drunk. You can read or watch the scenery in peace now. Arriving drunk at school would be a terrible beginning to your new life. You should stay here and make a list of ways to make the world better.

But you’re an elah. Maybe you can control how drunk you get. You really should know as much as possible about what you can do.

The drunk has one small flask. He probably means to give you each a sip. A sip is only being social.

You scramble after the others.

The platform between the cars has the upper half of its outside door open. It’s loud, cold, and windy. The train rocks like it’s galloping. A sign says passengers may not stand between cars when the train is in motion. Being here is perfect.

Heller has the flask to her lips. The wind whips her hair. You like her profile and want to draw her, the countryside, the frame of the doorway. She lowers the flask and smiles. "Single malt. Highland Park?"

Elverado takes the flask and swigs deeply. "If that's Canadian Club, it's mighty smooth."

You're next. Flasks are cool. Warren Beatty drinks from flasks, shoots cops, and screws Faye Dunaway. You sip. You're afraid you'll cough, and you don't want to know Elverado's definition of rough. Then you understand. It's like drinking from a stream of melting ice. "That's whiskey?"

"Scotch," says Heller. "The twenty-five-year-old?"

The drunk raises the flask in a salute or a prayer and sips.

Elverado says, "It'll get you off."

Heller says, "Canadian Club? Is that a blended? Daddy says people who drink blended should pee in the bottle because the effect is the same and the taste is better."

Elverado says, "Your daddy can afford to sneer at people who can't spend a month of groceries on a bottle of booze."

"He's only pointing out a fact. You must admit it's silly to drink a Scotch from Canada."

You say, "Does that make it a Canuck?"

Elverado and Heller laugh. You were serious, but you laugh with them. Green woods roll by. It's good to roll through nature in a cage of civilization.

The drunk says, "Wish we had something besides whiskey."

Heller says, "Sobranie?" She pulls a cigarette pack out of her jacket.

The drunk waves it away. Elverado plucks a cigarette. "Thanks."

You take one. It makes you think of Camels, which are cool

because of the art deco drawing of Egypt. “They don’t have these in Florida.”

“I got them in Monaco.” She snaps on a lighter that looks more like jewelry than a lighter, then sees your glance. “Stole it from Mommy. She has dozens.”

The Sobranie doesn’t taste better than a Camel. “Don’t they kick you out of the Academy for smoking?”

She nods. “That’s why everyone smokes.”

Elverado says, “They make stupid rules to teach us to break them.”

Heller shakes her head. “They make stupid rules to teach us not to get caught.”

Elverado smiles. “You’re not so straight.”

She meets his smile. Why does that annoy you so much? Because you can’t have CC, and maybe you can’t have Heller, either. You say, “Cigarettes should cover the smell of a jay.”

Elverado asks, “You have weed?”

You had a jay under the flap in your wallet. When the Beastman threw you a good-bye party, a shitload of dope was smoked. Did you smoke it then?

“Maybe.” You open your wallet, hoping it’s still there. The world-prince should have all the weed he wants.

You pull a flattened joint from under the flap. “Eureka!”

Heller says, “Is that marijuana?”

You nod, pleased to have her attention. New problem: Can you light the jay in the wind? Do elah powers include starting fires?

Elverado solves that, snapping open a Zippo and cupping his hands as if he’s done this often.

The smoke is as smooth as the liquor in the drunk’s flask. As it fills your lungs, Elverado says, “Know why they banned hemp? To sell more nylon and oil products. Fact. Hundreds of people OD every year on hard liquor, but no one’s ever OD’d on weed. Fact.”

The drunk says, "Your rulers ban hemp because rulers love to ban."

You offer the jay to Heller. She says, "Bad things should be banned," and takes a hit.

Elverado says, "That's why you're Miss Straight Arrow?"

She coughs, and her eyes stream. She says, "Rules aren't for those who make them. Everyone knows that."

The drunk takes the jay from Elverado. "So many gifts of the earth." He inhales so deeply you're afraid he'll finish the joint.

He hands it to you, and a car door opens. A girl in glasses steps out in a blazer and skirt like Heller's. As she glances at the four of you, you cup your hand around the jay to hide it. The girl says, "Heller?"

Heller says, "Blaise!"

Blaise sniffs, then glances at you. You want to ask if she wants to get high. Does her brown hair make you think of seals? But Heller doesn't make introductions.

She tells Blaise, "You smelled tobacco. We'll talk at school."

Blaise nods and walks into the next car.

Elverado frowns. "That was fucking freaky."

Heller says, "No, it wasn't."

Elverado's frown disappears. Heller looks at the drunk, who laughs and says, "What's not fucking freaky?"

You hand Elverado the jay. As he inhales, you ask Heller, "Who was that?"

Heller bites her lower lip, studying the drunk, then you. "Blaise Selby. I don't know her well."

Elverado says, "It's cool. She didn't notice the joint."

The drunk takes his hit and says patiently, "Best to dispose of the evidence." The jay goes around again, and so does the flask. When the jay's only a roach, Elverado offers a tiny brass pipe, and you smoke the roach, cupping it from view whenever people pass.

Heller says, "I don't think it's working. I think I'm just a little drunk."

You know it's working. The train platform is better than a carnival ride, and you've found the best companions of all. You watch telephone poles flick past and think about Blaise Selby. Why?

Because her hair is the color of CC's skin. You need a girlfriend to forget CC.

When you announce you're the world-prince, getting girls will be easy. But now girls think you're a zit-faced kid with a weird sense of humor and a pathetic love of comic books. You would give anything to know if CC liked you because you fooled her into thinking you were cool or if you never fooled her and she liked you anyway.

You say to no one in particular, "Yeah, this is some good shit."

The drunk says, "All part of the cycle."

Heller grins like a six-year-old. "It's not shit. It's good!"

Thinking is funny, you think, then think that's funny. You see an approaching telephone pole and think this could be the moment of your creation. The pole flicks past. How could you know if you were created approaching the pole, or passing it, or only when it had been passed? Can something be passed if there's no past? All you know is you're here now.

Elverado is telling Heller, "You're the coolest straight chick I ever met," and she's saying, "Long hair's best on boys," and you're wondering what madness made you agree to cut yours, and Elverado and Heller are kissing on the train platform, and the drunk, heading back toward the train car, is saying, "My work here is done."

Giving Heller and Elverado some privacy is right. If you stay, you'll get jealous.

Does Elverado have the blood? Is that why Heller is responding to him?

No. You would know if he was a nef. She's answering a different call.

Let them be happy. You would rather stay on the platform in the wind than in the car with the cigarette smoke and the straights. But you go in and see all the straights, most sitting quietly, a few talking, all lonely and human and trying desperately to do what they think is right. The world is so fucked up that you can't just yell, "I love you all!" without everyone thinking you're drunk or stoned or both just because you are both.

That makes you giggle. As people look at you, you cough as if you had something in your throat. Then you're back in your seat.

"They're so straight," you tell the drunk.

"No one's straight all the time."

"They're scared that people will know how fucked up they are. That's fucked up."

"True."

You grin. "They wouldn't be so fucked up if they got fucked up sometimes."

"Sometimes."

"Maybe all the time."

He shakes his head. "Sometimes you're driven, sometimes you drive. If you're doing the same thing all the time, you're dead."

"That's far fucking out."

He smiles. "Ride the wind, Christochris. You can't fight it."

"Cool."

When Elverado and Heller return, you look up. The drunk is gone. You say, "Where's that guy?"

Elverado says, "What guy?"

You say, "That drunk."

Heller says, "What drunk?"

You laugh. They're goofing on you. The drunk must've gotten off at the last stop. That's funny. You all got off, then the drunk got off. You want to explain the joke, but people would overhear and not understand.

Six

The town rolling toward you is old New England, with two-story houses of wood, brick, or stucco. The station is a classic train set, a shoe box with a wraparound porch.

The train jerks to a stop. Preppies pour onto the platform. You hadn't realized how many the train held. They look alike: mid-teens, clouds of hair, suntanned skin, gleaming suitcases and back-packs. They're healthier and handsomer than regular kids. Only a few are fat or zitty or dark-skinned. Is life harder or easier for prep-pies who don't look like Hitler Youth?

You step off the train from shade into sunlight. The air is cool and moist. The sky is gray. It'll rain, but not soon. Heller says, "We can share a taxi, but then you're on your own, okay?"

"Nope. A gentleman gets the taxi."

"Don't be stupid."

"Oh, man, don't make this harder than it already is."

Elverado laughs, and Heller shakes her head. You follow her around the station and down the steps to a mob of kids in blue blaz-ers surrounding three taxis.

You can feel the blood, though it's weak. In the crowd, you can't tell nefilim from human.

A boy tells everyone, "Why don't they ever send enough taxis? Someone in this town should be able to figure out how many taxis to send on opening day."

Another boy says, "Cooper, how can you expect anyone to figure out anything when you can't figure out you're a prat?"

A girl calls, "Heller! Room for one more!" If you drew her, she would be a basset hound in the company of a cat, a fox, and a squirrel. The four scramble into a taxi while the driver does geometry exercises with their luggage.

Heller is looking at you and Elverado. You say, "How far is school?"

Elverado says, "About two miles."

"It'll be nice to walk. See you there!" You stride away, trying to look like a bold adventurer. The truth is you want to save the taxi fare, and you'd like to be alone to think.

"Wait up!" Elverado runs toward you with his pack on his back. You're jealous; your suitcase handle is already digging into your palm.

If elah powers include walking on water, can you cheat gravity? You think, My suitcase weighs nothing.

The breeze catches the suitcase, flipping it upward. You think, My suitcase weighs what it weighs! And you keep raising your arm as if you're waving to Elverado.

You think, My suitcase weighs a pound.

It's a good compromise. You could carry it all day.

Elverado, grinning, says, "Nice to get away from the plastic people."

You hear a horn honk as a green VW bug slows beside you. It takes you a moment to recognize the driver: Ralph Fitzgerald's hair is a little longer than when he came to Florida. He calls, "Chris! Pete! Want a ride?"

Elverado says, "No, thanks, Mr. Fitzgee! Got to stay fit for track!"

Fitzgerald looks at you. You say, "I like walking. Thanks just the same!"

"See you at school then!" He drives away, and you and Elverado walk on.

You say, "Pete?"

He looks embarrassed. "I'll legally change it when I'm eighteen. Mom doesn't understand wanting to be proud of your people."

"What do they call you at school?"

"Mostly, Elverado, but shitheads sneer when they say it. Masters call me Pete."

"Elverado's cool." As he smiles, you add, "Does everyone call the teachers 'masters'?"

"Yeah. Freaked me out till I saw the logic. Public schools have teachers. Private schools have masters."

"'Cause they're like upper-class English schools?"

"Sure. But why are upper-class English schools like that?"

"Tradition?"

"And again, *mi compadre,* I say, sure. What's the tradition about?"

You shrug.

He says, "Power. If students have teachers, they're taught it's good to teach. If they have masters, they're taught it's good to rule." He nods smugly, and you see two people, a cool older kid and a lonely teacher's kid. He's trying to impress you. He hopes you'll be a friend.

You laugh. "Man, you are a commie!"

"Sure, if you're talking about Jesus."

You glance at Elverado and hear a distant voice: *My work here is done.* You say, "Jesus wasn't a commie."

Elverado says, "Woe to the rich? If you want to be perfect, give all you have to the poor? Loving money is the root of all evil? Or John the Baptist saying if you have two coats, give one to somebody with none?"

"That's idealism."

"Everything good starts as idealism. What's wrong with what Jesus says?"

"Well, if you give things to people, they won't take care of them, and everything will fall apart."

Elverado grins. "So you don't believe in inheritance?"

You've inherited the world. Don't you deserve it? You must, because you inherited it. Right?

"Inheritance is different."

"How? Do babies earn their parents?"

"Maybe in a past life—"

"You believe in past lives?"

"You can't rule it out."

"You can't rule out a bale of reefer falling out of a plane right now—" Elverado looks up, and so do you. Then he laughs, and you join him as he says, "But you might not want to count on it."

"Still, if you had a past life and forgot it—"

"Being punished or rewarded for something you forgot is bullshit, man. What's the point of being punished if you don't know what you did?"

"Maybe that's just how it works."

"Then life is bullshit and God's an asshole."

"Isn't that what transcending the world is about? Escaping the bullshit?"

"Sure. You'll find bullshitters who say life's an illusion, so what's it matter if they're rich? That's their excuse to feel good about not sharing their toys." He grins. "That's all being rich is, man. Not sharing your toys."

You grin back. Elverado may be a conceited fool, but he's fun to be around. What more can you ask for in a friend?

You like the town. There's a river with a stone bridge, small brick stores and little restaurants, a bakery that smells like doughnuts, and a drugstore with a magazine rack and a spinner full of comics. You would stop, but Elverado would think you were a kid.

He says, "Do you think Heller likes me?"

"Man, she wasn't making out with me on the train."

"That was just fooling around. Once doesn't mean a thing."

You were only with CC once, and it means everything. But maybe he's right. Maybe it didn't mean anything to CC. You shrug. "Thought you didn't like rich people."

"It's not Heller's fault she's rich. People can overcome their past. Her brother was cool."

"You knew Josh?"

"We were on the fencing team. He wasn't exactly enlightened, but he thought things should be a little more fair."

You shake your head. "I don't think Heller's going to overcome her past."

Elverado sighs. "Well, I can be Lady Chatterley's lover."

You want to say that's your job, but it's not. Your job is to become El Elyon someday. If you could do that and be with CC, you wouldn't want anyone else. But since you have to be with Heller, you'll want other lovers. So Heller should be able to have others, too.

You say, "Love is weird."

Elverado says, "No shit, Sherlock."

As you walk, stores give way to large, old houses with bright paint and nice lawns. The houses and lawns grow larger. More and more of the buildings are red brick, and you're approaching a cluster of ivy-covered buildings that look exactly like the pictures in the Academy's brochure.

Elverado points away. "My house is a couple of blocks that way. 1822 Elm. Come by anytime."

"Aren't fourth-formers only allowed off-campus once a week?"

"That's the rule. But if you decide to escape, come on by."

"Thanks, man."

He hesitates, then laughs nervously. "Tell Heller I think she's cool."

"Sure thing."

He holds his hand up, makes a "V," then a fist. "Peace and power to the people, man."

You feel a little silly as you repeat the gesture. "Peace and power, man."

As he starts away, you admire his hair streaming behind him. You call, "Hey, Elverado! How'd you get around the haircut rules?"

He grins, reaches into his pocket, and pulls out something like a dead hedgehog. He twists his hair on top of his head and pulls the thing over it. He looks like a kid wearing a dead hedgehog. "It's a Beatle wig. It was for straights who wanted to look cool. Now it's for freaks who want to look straight. Recycle and reuse, man!"

You laugh. "They think that's real hair?"

"No, man. They think I look like a clown. But the joke is their rule, and I get to keep my hair. So who's the clown?" He yanks off the wig, shakes his hair free, waves again, and walks on.

You head into the campus. Have you made your first friend here? It'd be nice to hang out with someone who wasn't rich all his life. But is that like going to Mexico and hanging with gringos? You're in a new place. Shouldn't you experience it before you judge it?

F. Scott Fitzgerald said the rich are different than you and me. Ernest Hemingway said yes, they have more money. F. Scott and Ernest both wanted to be rich. F. Scott drank himself to death. Ernest shot himself. Maybe neither of them knew what they were talking about.

A sign welcomes you to the Academy. You stare at it. This is the here you have come to, the now you have found. You'll be a savage among civilized people. You should walk to the ocean, get a job on a freighter, build a hut on a tropical island. You should go to any here and now but this one.

You need to learn to be the world's lord. This is where you'll learn to rule.

Boys and families are all around you. Not everyone took the train. Gabriel and Jonathan did a good job disguising you as one of them: They wear blazers, blue button-down shirts and ties, tan trousers, and Top-Siders. Some wear polo shirts. Some wear trousers in navy blue, brown, or green. You see no T-shirts or bell-bottoms, no bright colors or bold patterns, no tie-dyes or cutoffs, no frayed and faded jeans.

Boys look strange in sports coats and ties. Sports coats make sense. They tell people you don't work with your hands. Why ties? To remind you that failed rulers have been hanged?

In the yard before the largest building, two boys use long sticks to throw a ball back and forth. That's lacrosse. Rich people really do throw a ball around with sticks. That's a point for F. Scott.

A boy says, "Hi. Can I help you?" He sounds suspicious, and you wonder if you should've put on a tie. You say, "I'm looking for Rider House."

He points across the lawn at the smallest and farthest brick building in a row of two-story dormitories. "Check in with Mr. Fitzgerald. Then you can go to High House for your schedule." He points at a large four-story building that dominates the lawn.

"Thanks."

You walk past families, masters, and boys. You're relieved when you spot a girl in a blazer visiting from the girl's campus. If rich boys and girls are always kept apart, no wonder F. Scott thought they were different.

Over the door of Rider House is a frieze of two knights mounted on one horse. You're staring at it when a boy comes out, looks at you, then says, "It either means they share everything or they could only steal one horse."

"Uh-huh," you say. "I'm supposed to be staying here."

"Oh?" The boy squints at you. He's black-haired and smaller than most of the boys you've seen. "Mr. Fitzgerald's upstairs."

The house smells of soap and boys and age. Its stone steps are worn. The wainscoting on the hall has gouges, some dark enough to have been made by boys who died in World War I. The whorls of the wood are like ripples on a pond. You walk down the hall with the sense that if you fell against the wall, you would fall through it into another age.

Someone tall in a gray sports coat bumps you. You think he must be one of the masters until he says, "Hey, jack-off, watch where you're going!"

You glance at him to apologize, then stop. He's handsome and wide-shouldered, undoubtedly able to drink at any bar without being asked for ID.

He has the blood.

He says, "What's your problem, kid?"

"Sorry," you say, taking the stairs two at a time, afraid he'll recognize what you are. Or maybe you're just afraid because he's big. It's stupid to be afraid when you have the blood, but he has it, too. He's older. He grew up knowing what he is. He must understand his power better than you understand yours. Even if he doesn't, even if he was just a big human kid, what could you do if he got mad at you? You can't kill him and heal him to teach him to fear you. Power you can't show is worse than no power at all.

In the upper hall, Fitzgerald is checking two boys into their rooms. They look like jocks: The redhead is lean and crew-cut, and the black guy is broad like a weight lifter.

Fitzgerald spots you and says, "Welcome to the Academy, Chris. You're in seven, next to my quarters. If you planned to play loud music, you're in the wrong house, mister. Have you met the headmaster yet?"

"No, sir."

"He'd like you to stop by his office in High House. Better hustle. You need to sign up for classes, too. Dinner's at six. Mandatory. Anyone out of the house after seven twenty has to sign out. The book's by the door. Everyone has to be in their room and quiet by ten. You have read the handbook?"

The handbook turned your mind into mush. All you remember is that if you want to do something, you probably can't. It had one line that you want to use as a caption for a cartoon: "No boy may go anywhere outside of a building above the first floor." In the drawing, Superboy would look at the top floor of High House and think, "Darn it!"

You say, "Yes, sir."

"I like your attitude, mister." His smile softens subtly. "If you need to talk, knock on my door anytime. That's my policy with all of the boys."

"I'll keep that in mind, sir."

He laughs. "I want to tell you not to 'sir' people so much, but the rest of the masters will love you if you keep it up."

You grin. "Got it, sir."

You head downstairs, taking care around the landing. You make it to number seven without bumping anyone else.

The room seems plain for a rich kids' school: white plaster walls, wooden floor. The surprise is that you have a roommate. He's not here, and that seems good. He has a picture of President Nixon over his bed and one of his family on his desk: mother, father, older sister, and dog. You think they look Italian, including the dog, a greyhound.

You didn't bring a picture of your family. Mom asked if you wanted one. You said you could remember what everyone looked like.

You hang your clothes in the empty wardrobe, then find the bathroom. Like your room, it's disappointing: You expected brass fixtures and stained-glass windows, something from a nineteenth century gentlemen's club. The bathroom was remodeled in the last ten years: it's concrete, tile, porcelain, and chrome. On one toilet wall, someone wrote, "Joey sucks." Someone else added, "Best." That's a point for Ernest.

Seven

High House reminds you of the old lodge at Yellowstone Park, not because it's rustic, but because it's huge. You go up steps and a porch large enough for the whole school to assemble on for photographs, then enter the front room. It's crowded with boys lined before registration tables. You hear someone complain that all his first-choice classes are taken. What will be left for you after you're done with the head?

A door to the left leads to the school offices. A pretty woman in a tight white sweater is at the front desk. You say, "Uh, hi, I'm Chris Nix, and, uh—"

She smiles. "Chris, welcome to the Academy! Go right in. Mr. Mather's expecting you."

You step into a room that looks like the office of a tycoon in an old movie: a big oak desk with nothing on it, landscape paintings on dark paneled walls, a Persian rug on the wooden floor. There's a knight's sword and shield on the wall that you would love to hold, and a crucifix with a dead Jesus.

A small, muscular man smiles as he walks toward you. His gray hair is combed back from his forehead. The cut of his clothes say he's hip: wide lapels, a wide tie, a wide button-down collar. The colors say he's not: dark blue suit, white shirt, a tie striped in burgundy and royal blue.

When he shakes your hand, you feel the blood, weaker than a

nef, stronger than any worshipper you've met. You know its source. It's as if Mather is a shadow cast by Jay Dumont.

"Christopher Nix! Welcome to the Academy! Come in, sit down!"

He closes the door, drops to one knee, and bows his head. "My lord."

His bald spot makes you think of drawings of medieval monks. He stays kneeling until you realize he's waiting for you. Will you ever be able to be the world-prince without feeling mortified?

"Uh, Mr. Mather?"

"Yes, my lord?"

"Uh, please rise."

He stands. "Forgive this indulgence. You're my lord and the heir of my lord. As I've served him well, I hope someday to serve you." He gestures at a seat. "Please, sit. From now on, we'll play our parts properly."

You sit as he continues, "With few exceptions, you'll be like any other student. The only ones here who know your identity are Miss Huntington of the girls' school and me. And, of course, Heller Dumont."

"Uh, of course."

"Boys and girls have little opportunity to be together privately at the Academy. We've had to be creative. You'll have study leave three evenings a week. Miss Huntington has a guest room in her house for you and Heller."

You frown. "What'll we study? Oh."

He smiles, and your embarrassment grows. You say quickly, "That's not necessary. The plan's not to marry until after college, so we can wait for— I mean, there's a guy she likes, and that's okay for now—"

Mather's face loses every hint of expression. "What boy?"

"It's nothing serious. I mean, not yet, anyway, and maybe it won't be, and if she and I aren't marrying for years—"

"Do you know the boy's name, my lord?"

"Elverado. That's what they call him."

Mather looks at the crucifix. "Peter Sanchez."

"He seems like a nice guy."

"Peter's naïve, my lord. He's not part of the circle, and there's no reason for him to be."

"Mr. Dumont said I can tell people who I am. I mean, once Josh's killer has been found and it's safe."

Mather studies you, then says cautiously, "I'm sure he means people who're known to be worthy. Discretion is the elohim way. They've ruled through intermediaries for three thousand years. I'm afraid you'll have to separate yourself from the Sanchez boy. There are more fitting companions—"

You think you should be quiet, but if you don't speak, Mather will believe he can tell the world-prince what to do. Speaking up may not change that, but at least you'll learn if you have any influence at all as the elohim's prince, or prince-to-be, or whatever you are. You say, "Maybe he won't become a friend. Even if he does, I won't tell him anything without getting an okay first from Mr. Dumont."

"You say Miss Dumont likes him? Romantically?"

You think of them kissing between train cars. "A little."

"He has wormed his way into a place he shouldn't be."

"It's not like he planned it. It just happened." As you speak, you hide a memory: *My work here is done.*

Mather taps his fingers on the desk like a pianist doing exercises. "This is awkward."

"You can't control who you like."

He frowns as if you spoke in Aztec, then smiles. "I suppose not. Well, we'll put off your visits with Miss Dumont for now. Whenever you wish to change that, tell me."

"Okay." You look at the photos on the wall of people with

Mather. The older ones are black-and-white. Mather has a pale crew cut in most of them. The people look important, not like movie stars or presidents, but like people who sometimes appear in photos with movie stars or presidents. Off in the corner, as if it's not as important as the rest, is a picture of Mather standing in a living room talking to a seated Jay Dumont. "Uh, may I ask some questions?"

"Certainly, my lord."

"I can tell you're not a nef. Uh, of the nefilim. But you don't seem like a, um, steward, either."

"That may be because I'm among the oldest stewards. I've served our lord for four centuries. His generosity is boundless."

You want to ask Mather if he met George Washington or fought in the Civil War. But you have more important things to learn: "There's a guy in my dorm with the blood."

"Chad Vaughn. Yes. Sixth-former, eldest son of a former senator. The Vaughns are an ambitious family. Among the lines of the nefilim, they're second only to, well, the first line."

"Excuse me?"

"The line that's adopted you. The Vaughns will see that as a setback. After Josh's accident, there was talk that Chad should be anointed. The other lines would've supported it."

"Is there anyone else here who could've been anointed?"

"At the Academy?" He shakes his head. "Our only other student of the blood is a Canadian girl, Blaise Selby. There's a young man at Oxford who might have a claim, and a four-year-old in São Paulo. But Chad's claim is strongest."

You missed Selby's blood because you were high or worried about hiding the joint or, most likely, simply new to recognizing the blood. Her line must be weaker than Heller's, or Heller couldn't have made her forget what she saw. Heller is of the first line, but does that mean her line is more powerful than the others? Could

Chad Vaughn's power have been greater than Josh Dumont's? Would Chad need to be more powerful than an elah to kill one?

Mather waits patiently. You say, "What happened to Josh Dumont?"

"His scull was found on the riverbank last fall. His body was found by divers a day later."

"Someone cut off his head?"

Mather blinks, starts to smile, then stops himself. "Forgive me. 'Scull' with a 'c.' A one-man rowboat. Josh won many races for us."

"He drowned?"

"Apparently. There was no autopsy. Our lord said an autopsy wouldn't help us learn the truth, and it's best to keep nefilim affairs from human eyes."

You realize you're stroking your throat. You lower your hand. "Did Josh and Chad get along?"

"Very well. They were nearly inseparable. Chad was depressed for months after. His grades fell. But people told him he could be the next consort, if he rallied. He seems to have taken that to heart."

Which means that even if Chad Vaughn had nothing to do with Josh Dumont's death, he wouldn't mind if you disappeared. "What if it keeps looking like Josh's death was an accident?"

"Forgive me, my lord. I don't follow."

"Uh, you know. You can't prove a negative. How long do I have to hide what I am if nothing suspicious turns up?"

Mather smiles. "In one sense, you'll always hide. People overthrow lords whose rule becomes too obvious. But the time will come when all the lords of the earth will call you 'lord.' "

Mark Christopher Nix, Lord of Lords. You want to ask if you can rule from your own Fortress of Solitude or Elah-cave. But who wants a secret hideout when you can have palaces and penthouses around the world? By day, you'll be the Mysterious

Mr. Nix, but at night, you'll be the Spectacular Party Man. Rock stars will befriend you, and the most beautiful women in the world will love you.

If no one kills you.

Mather rises. "Dinner is approaching, my lord. From now on, I shall call you 'Christopher.' When I do, know that I'm saying, 'my lord.'" He hands you a registration packet. "No need for you to go through the line."

"I heard some classes are already filled."

"There's a place for you in any you'd like."

You glance at him, wanting to say that doesn't seem fair. But then, private schools exist to give rich kids an advantage over poor ones. Take what you can get.

You look over the list. After public school, the number of choices are overwhelming. You pick Imperial Rome, Marlowe and Shakespeare, Biology, Algebra 2, Introduction to Art, and Crew.

Mather smiles at the sheet. "Fine choices. You'll do admirably at the Academy. If you need me again, tell Fitzgerald."

"Got it, sir." You shake hands and go.

The information in the registration packet is boring, with one exception: There's the number and combination of your mailbox, so you head downstairs to the mail room. Mom might've sent you something, or there might be something more from the school office.

There's a postcard and an envelope. The card is from Mom. She says everyone misses you. You know that's not true, but it's nice that she believes it.

You tear open the envelope and find a sheet of typing paper. It says:

> sweet thing,
>
> i can't call you mark or chris if i don't know who you decided to be, can i? (a rose by any etc.) (i would

call you rose which is a fine name for a boy because of the thorns but i fancy you would rather be my eagle or my wildcat and i want you to be my anything you want to be.)

i miss you more than the most. i want to tell you all about the place where i am but all i can say now is i'm fine.

but i worry about you!!! i'm sure you can find good people at that school because there are good people everywhere. only sometimes good people are hard to find. if that's so, remember it's okay to trust nobody.

i will write again when i can. actually, i will write every day, but i will only send mail when i can.

with love and love and more love,

cc

p.s. this page is covered with kisses for you.

You read it three times, then look at the envelope. The Academy's address is printed in the corner. No name is written above that. The address consists of your name and box number. There's no stamp. It was sent through the Academy's mail system.

You stuff the letter and envelope into your coat pocket. Your heart beats fast. You look around, expecting Rod Serling to step from the shadows as the *Twilight Zone* theme song begins to play. You see no one. You're alone among the long rows of mailboxes.

The letter only tells you one thing: CC's fine.

No, two things: She's found you, but she's afraid to say anything that would help you find her. It would've been easy for her to find you. All of your friends in Florida know you're here.

No, three things: Someone is helping her who can use the campus mail.

You look around again, half expecting CC to step into the light. But if she's afraid of being found, she must be thousands of miles away.

There's a fourth thing the letter says: She still likes you.

You smile and read it again. "Trust nobody" makes your smile go away. Was trust a factor in Josh's death? Who would dare kill an elah? Or did someone kill Josh without knowing he was the world-prince?

You need to think like a spy. You tear CC's letter into tiny bits and eat it. The idea is romantic. The taste is disgusting. You wash it down with water and think you've done one thing right. Can you do more?

Eight

As you walk up to Rider House, Fitzgerald and thirteen boys come out in jackets and ties. The tall nef, Chad Vaughn, is one of them. So is the small boy you met on your way in earlier. Fitzgerald says, "Mr. Nix!"

You say quickly, "Sorry, sir, I'll be ready—"

"Either you're ready or you're not, mister. Take that to heart."

"Uh, yes, sir—"

Fitzgerald smiles. "Relax. We're going up a little early. You want to be a winner in life, remember Confederate General Nathan Bedford Forrest's advice. 'Git thar fustest with the mostest.'"

The small boy says, "So we should follow the advice of the losers?"

As Fitzgerald frowns, Vaughn says, "They hardly ever had the mostest."

"True," Fitzgerald tells Vaughn with approval, and turns back to you. "Christopher Nix, your housemates. I expect us to be one big happy family." He names the others quickly.

No one looks at you like they think you're a brother. The only new name that sticks is David Levitz, the small boy; he's your roommate.

Vaughn studies you, long enough to say he remembers being bumped in the stairwell. Then he smiles broadly, saying, "Welcome to the Academy, lad."

Fitzgerald adds, "Mr. Vaughn's the senior resident. When I'm not around, he's in charge. He'll do morning inspection and assign demerits to anyone whose room isn't up to snuff. If you have questions about any aspect of Academy life, take them to him first."

Vaughn looks at you and says dryly, "There's nothing I enjoy more than setting wayward scholars straight."

Fitzgerald tells you, "Better hustle, Mr. Nix." He starts toward High House, and the boys follow.

Levitz lingers. "Nix?"

"Yeah?"

"I'm Jewish."

You shrug. "That's cool."

"You can ask for another room if you don't like Jews."

"How do you know I'm not Jewish?"

He looks at you, taps his forehead, and says, "I have amazing psychic powers."

You think you didn't feel the blood in him, then realize you're taking all this a little too seriously. You say, "Hey, I'll always be grateful to the Jews. They invented superhero comics."

"Fuck." Levitz shakes his head and heads after the others. "I could've had the biggest single at school."

As you yank open the front door, Levitz calls, "Nix! *Superman* or *Spider-Man*?"

You glance back. "Neither. Give me *Batman, Dr. Strange,* or *Captain America.*"

Levitz nods. "That's cool. Totally fuckheaded, but cool."

You nod back, run inside, grab a blazer, then the first tie you see. You lose three minutes trying to make it look like it was knotted by someone with opposable thumbs, then run out.

The dining hall is enormous. Dozens of round tables are covered with white linen. Platters of food are brought out by students. Each table is supervised by a master. You might like this if boys and girls ate together, but girls eat most meals on their campus.

Fitzgerald stands by a table. As you come up, he says, "A place opened up at the headmaster's. Since you're new, he thought you might want to join him."

You cross the dining hall, feeling conspicuous. Mather may think boys will respect you if you sit at his table. That's only true for brownnosers. Everyone else will think you're a suck-up.

As you come closer to Mather's table, you're glad you were chosen. You barely notice the boys there. Your eyes are on the woman standing across the table from Mr. Mather. She's pretty, young, slender, green-eyed, red-haired, and as tall as you. You decide you could sit at the head's table for every meal. Given his age, she could be his great-great-great granddaughter. But as you come near, you know she's not a nef or a worshipper.

Mather turns to her. "Miss Chabot, Christopher Nix is a new student from Florida. Chris, Miss Chabot is our librarian."

You wonder if she's seen *Tea and Sympathy,* a movie that had seemed stupid until this moment. She takes your hand and says in a pleasant midwestern accent, "Chris? I'm Christine. We could start the League of Chrises."

You grin like an idiot as your brain shuts down. Mather spares you from having to answer by pulling out a chair for Miss Chabot. He goes to his own seat, and everyone sits. Mather bows his head for thirty seconds, and the hall is silent. When he lifts his head, the room rumbles as diners talk and servers clatter about with steel pitchers and platters.

No one says anything nice about the food, so you don't, either. But you see a feast: crusty rolls, salad, baked potatoes, string beans, gravy, and little birds that you learn are Cornish game hens. The conversation moves from sports you don't know, like tennis and skiing, to places you don't know, like Martha's Vineyard and Gstaad. You decide Ernest was an idiot and should have shot himself sooner.

Miss Chabot is telling Mather, "I have trouble understanding how a minister can support what we're doing in Vietnam."

He smiles. "Many great soldiers have been Christians. You mustn't overlook the difference between fighting for conquest and fighting for freedom."

"If Jesus was alive today, do you think he would fight?"

"In a just war, he would be on the front lines."

"Is this a just war?"

Mather shrugs. "As St. Paul said, we must trust the rulers God gives us."

"Didn't Germans in the World Wars say the same thing?"

"Which only shows how very wrong they were. God put us here to test us. There's no greater test than war."

"Maybe we pass the test by rejecting it."

"And let evil triumph? No, Miss Chabot. I'll never believe that." He glances at the boy bringing dessert. "Would we have ice-cream sundaes if communism wins? I very much doubt it."

Most of the boys laugh, and Miss Chabot smiles politely.

"But war's bad," you say, and immediately wish you'd stayed silent.

Mather looks at you. "Of course. As General Sherman said so indelicately, it's hell. On the other side of that conflict, General Lee said it's good that war is terrible, or we would grow too fond of it. Sometimes a man must do terrible things for a greater good. The Romans had a saying: If you want peace, prepare for war."

Mather waits for you to nod or say you see his point. You think you know where Fitzgerald learned to quote a Civil War general. You should say something politely vague, but isn't that lying? The entire table's watching, and all you can think is what the Beastman would say: Fuck that bullshit. Wrong is wrong.

Miss Chabot says lightly, "And look where the Romans are today."

The boys laugh. Mather says, "Touché," and laughs, too, then asks, "Tell me, Christopher, what do you believe is worth fighting for?"

You say, "Peace."

"Then we agree in principle, if not in this instance."

You don't agree in principle. There's something wrong with your answer because there's something wrong with his question. But it's your chance to escape, so you say, "I guess," and hope Miss Chabot doesn't think less of you.

When you return to Rider House, you want to talk with Levitz about life at the Academy or comic books or girls or anything that doesn't matter. He's reading books from the school's recommended summer reading list. He wants a 4.0 average this year, not another 3.9. He does not want to be disturbed. You tell him that's too bad, since anyone with his work habits is clearly disturbed. When he looks at you, you apologize and leave him in peace.

So you look at his library. You flip through the indexes of the history books. They tell about individuals, economies, and wars. They have almost nothing about gods.

But he has *Bullfinch's Mythology*. You find stories about families of gods and half-gods in Greece, Rome, Persia, India, and Scandinavia. You can't find anything about nefilim or elohim.

You're beginning to think the names are only known to Dumont and his people when you hear a light knock as the door opens.

It's the big blond jock from upstairs. Levitz says, "O'Reilly, it's still study hour."

O'Reilly says, "Levitz, are you a brownnosing grind or a grinding brownnose? Never mind. Want to do something amazing?"

"No."

"You don't want to hear about it?"

"I've got a lot of reading."

"I should've known. You're such a dickweed." O'Reilly turns to you. "How about it, Nix?"

Dad said the way to survive at prisons and schools is to find the biggest, baddest guy and make him your friend. O'Reilly fits. "What is it?"

"A major mindfuck. See, your brain can get convinced of things even if you know they're not true. Like if you try to do a sit-up and someone holds you down for a minute, you can't sit up when they let go."

You look at Levitz. He stays at his desk, his back to you. You say, "Really?"

"No shit, man. It's like psychology. You got to try it. Come on."

"Where?"

"Vaughn's room. We all tried it. It's freaky. Come on."

Levitz continues to ignore you both. O'Reilly's proposal sounds odd, but preppies are odd. It's a chance to meet some of your housemates without any masters around. And it's a chance to learn more about Vaughn.

You shrug. "Sure."

O'Reilly opens the door enough to see if the way is clear. Fitzgerald's door is closed. O'Reilly goes out quietly, and you follow him to the door at the end of the hall.

Vaughn's tiny single is full: maybe half of the boys in the house are in a room barely wide enough to stretch out your arms. They're sitting on Vaughn's bed, in his chair, on his desk. A stereo plays the first Creedence Clearwater Revival album. The room's a strange mix of jock and hippie: an oar hangs on the wall near a black-light poster of Jimi Hendrix.

Vaughn grins at you. "Nix! Good man! I'm taking bets you can do it!"

A tall, skinny kid says, "Hell, Vaughn, nobody can."

"Five bucks says the new boy can," Vaughn says. "He hasn't been polluted by watching you lame-asses fuck up."

The other kid says, "Ten bucks says no fucking way."

Vaughn nods. "Ten bucks it is."

You say, "Hey, I don't want you to lose money on me."

The other kid says, "Fine." He holds his hand out to Vaughn. "Pay up."

Vaughn puts his arm around you. "Don't sweat it, Nix. We let ourselves get psyched out. Big mistake. All you need to do is keep remembering it's all in your head. Keep thinking yourself through to the other side, and you and me'll be splitting easy money."

You say, "I don't know—"

"Sure, you can. Lie down here." Vaughn indicates a braided rug. "Banner'll put a towel over your head to hold you down. Can't weasel out on me if you're doing the holding, can you, Banner?"

The tall kid shakes his head.

"Okay," Vaughn tells you. "Make us some money!"

You say, "Well, I'll try—" and lie back. The rug is a poor cushion, but you won't lie there long.

Vaughn says, "That's the old school spirit! Arms at your side. No cheating! Maestro, the towel!"

Banner has a white towel twisted in a roll. He says, "I'm going to put this over your face to hold you down. It'll be over your eyes until I pull it free. And you won't be able to sit up."

"Of course he will," says Vaughn. "Let's do it!"

As Banner puts the towel across your eyes, the boys begin to chant softly, "Nix, Nix, Nix, Nix!"

Vaughn says, "Gentleman, start your sit-up!"

As you press forward against the towel, O'Reilly begins counting: "Thirty, twenty-nine, twenty-eight—"

Banner says, "Come on! Everything you got!"

Vaughn says, "You can do it, Nix! I know you can!"

You know you can, too. The towel is tight against your head. You can't see, and you hear little more than the stereo. You strain, certain that when the towel is pulled away, you'll snap upward and finish with ease. It's odd the other boys couldn't do it. Their failure will make your success sweeter.

Thirty seconds of trying with all your might to sit up is tougher than you thought, but you won't slack off with people watching. Your stomach's tight and your back's sore and O'Reilly's count goes lower and lower. You want to laugh because this'll be so easy.

O'Reilly says, "Two," and the towel is jerked away. You lurch upward.

Something pale is just in front of you. You can't stop from rocketing forward. The pale thing and your face will collide.

Karate practice brings the response: Your right arm drives up and turns to deflect the threat.

You see it as your arm begins to turn. Someone straddles you, turned away, leaning forward, pants and underwear down around his knees, his pale hairy ass just in front of your face.

Your forearm hits his buttocks hard, throwing the kid across the room and into the laps of the boys on the bed.

You scramble to your feet. Vaughn, rubbing his ass, stands. He yanks up his pants and buttons them while he glowers at you. You look at the door. Several boys block your way, but not deliberately. First they gawk at Vaughn, and then they wait for his decision.

He's quiet for a long moment. Then he grins. "Good one, Nix. Let's see how the next one goes."

O'Reilly opens the door. You leave wishing you'd decided to be a grind tonight, too.

Levitz looks up as you enter, then turns back to his reading. You say, "Did you know?"

"It's an old trick."

"You could've warned me."

"They'd just make it worse for me."

"So you helped them."

He glances at you. "I didn't take sides!"

"And who did that help?"

He shakes his head. "You can't beat them, Nix. People with power do what they want. People who don't—" He shrugs. "They're jerks. Stay out of their way, and you'll be fine."

You watch him go back to his reading. You want to despise him, but he's smaller than you and just as much an outsider. He came to the Academy because he wants to be as rich as any of them, if not richer. How could he have done anything else?

What should you have done? Zeus would've fried Vaughn's ass. Jesus would've kissed it. Or would he? You never thought you would wish you'd paid more attention in Sunday school.

You say, "Levitz, do you have a Bible?"

"Do you read Hebrew?"

"No."

He shrugs and keeps working.

You stare at the wall and think you want to do anything but think. You take out paper and a pen from the things Dumont gave you and draw a boy burning in hell. He's supposed to look like Chad Vaughn. He looks a lot more like you.

Nine

You wake when Levitz's alarm goes off. In the bathroom, sleepy boys rush through showers, shaving, and brushing teeth. Everyone ignores you. You hope that's good. You dress, wishing you could wear jeans and a T-shirt, glad you don't have to wear a tie until dinner.

You make your bed and hang up your clothes. When you're done, you take a last look at the room. You should make a cartoon for Mom showing the Kid cleaning a room at super-speed and a caption: "After he graduates from the Academy, he can go anywhere in the world . . . and clean rooms."

On your way into the hallway, you hear Vaughn call, "A moment of your time, Mr. Nix."

You glance back. You can't tell what he's thinking. He says, "The wombat's here. Is everything shipshape?"

You say, "The wombat?"

"Mrs. Medeiros. The maid."

"Oh. Yeah, it's ready to sweep."

"Well, it's just a formality, but I should inspect."

You open the door. He walks into the middle of the room and glances at the beds. Levitz's is as perfect as an illustration in a magazine, but yours is wrinkle-free and tightly tucked. He points at it and says, "You have that one?"

You nod.

He steps over to the wardrobes and looks in both. "And this is yours?"

Unlike Levitz, you don't have your clothes organized by color and purpose, but everything's in drawers or on hangers. You nod again.

Vaughn touches one of your new wool sweaters. "Nice."

You shrug.

He says, "The Academy's rules are simple. Nothing on the floor." He pulls out the underwear drawer and shakes the contents onto Levitz's rug.

"Hey!" you say as he steps over to your bed.

He yanks the covers down. "And always make your bed before breakfast."

You stare at him. His expression stays pleasantly bland. "Good thing I caught you before you left. Be a shame to start the school year with a demerit."

He walks out. You're still glaring at his back when a short gray-haired woman in a baggy blue dress steps into the doorway carrying a dust mop. She jerks her head back in surprise and says, "Oh, you spoiled boys!"

You say, "I'm sorry," as you snatch up your underwear and begin making the bed.

She taps her foot. She reminds you of your grandmothers, meaning she terrifies you. She says, "So, you think I'm nobody? Fine. I'm nobody. But expect me to clean up after you, that's not treating me like nobody. That's treating me like Mrs. Not Even as Good as Nobody. I'm the housemaid, not *your* maid, you got it? Remember what I said, we'll get along fine."

"Yes, ma'am. Sorry, ma'am. You're Mrs. Medeiros? I'm Chris Nix. It was just—"

"I don't need excuses, young man. I just need you to do what you should. I'll do the same, and all will be right in God's world."

You nod and hurry out. As you cross the green, you wish the Academy let boys lock their doors. Will Vaughn mess up your room every morning? Will his buddies get more inventive? You'll have to look in your sheets before you get in bed. And in your clothes before you put them on. Vaughn doesn't have to do one more thing to make you expect trouble for the rest of your days at the Academy.

It seems stupidly petty of him. But then, it's easy for him to be stupidly petty. He must think you're an amusing distraction in his busy life.

If your first act as elohim-prince was to punish Vaughn for being a jerk, what would the other nefs think? Would you look as petty as him? You don't want to look as petty; you just want to be as petty. No. You want to be pettier. Is it wrong to hope he killed Josh so you can enjoy his punishment?

What will his punishment be if he killed Josh?

It doesn't matter. Killers should be found so they can't kill again. If you find Josh's killer, you'll tell Jay Dumont, no matter who the killer is.

Breakfast in the meal hall is cafeteria-style. There's raisin bread, scrambled eggs, potatoes, sausages, milk, and orange juice. You want to fill your tray, but thanks to Chad Vaughn, you only have a couple of minutes before your first class. You think, I want to go five minutes back in time.

The clock doesn't change. Elahs need better powers. You didn't expect it to work, but you should've known it wouldn't. If elahs could change time, Josh would be eating breakfast and you would be riding the bus to a Florida public school. You cram a peanut butter and jelly sandwich in your mouth, chug a glass of OJ, and trot across campus.

The Roman history master, Al Collins, is young, British, and enthusiastic. The class is small, about fifteen students, half the size of classes in Florida public schools. You feel nef blood and look around the room. Blaise Selby glances at you without a hint of recognizing you from the train.

Collins devotes the first class to myths about the Roman Empire.

Myth: Rome stopped expanding because it chose to.

Truth: Every army that Rome sent east was defeated by the Parthian Empire.

Myth. The empire fell in the fourth century when Goths invaded Rome.

Truth. Long before Rome was invaded, Constantine moved the empire's capital to Byzantium, which became Constantinople after Constantine's death. The empire lasted until 1204, when Crusaders decided it was easier to take Christian Constantinople by treachery than any Muslim city by siege.

When Blaise Selby asks about Roman religion, Collins adds one more:

Myth. Romans worshipped Greek gods under Roman names.

Truth. Romans worshipped many gods from many lands, including Mithra, Parthia's sun god. The Romans called him Sol Invictus, the Invincible Sun.

You like listening to ancient events that have nothing to do with anyone. Then you wonder if these events seem ancient to Jay Dumont.

After class, you go to the post office. There's nothing from anyone, but you only notice there's nothing from CC. You tell yourself that's good. But what if silence means someone found her? Her aunt could be crying over CC's body at this moment. You would never know.

Math is taught by Jarred McGinnis, who seems kind, but math is always a subject you merely endure. You're only interested when McGinnis talks about the history of algebra. Though the name is Arabic, it was developed by Babylonians during the Persian

Empire, when priests called magi were masters of math and astronomy.

The lunch choices make you a little homesick: grilled cheese sandwiches, French fries, milk, and chocolate cake. You see Levitz studying at a table. You carry your tray in the opposite direction and hear, "Chris! Hey! Chris! Over here, my man!"

Elverado sits alone with schoolbooks beside him and a booklet called *Fuck the System* in front of him. His wig doesn't look as silly when he's had time to put it on properly. It only looks like a haircut that's out of date. His clothes are as sedate as any student's.

You say, "Your secret's safe."

"What secret?"

You whisper, "The Amazing Freak Man is really Peter Prep."

He grins, says, "Don't let the masters of evil know," and shows you the booklet. "Have you read this? I forgot how fucking amazing it is, man. Tells how to hustle free food, find places to crash, all kinds of shit. It's the guide to gaming the system."

You sit and start eating. "I dunno. I like that Dylan line. To live outside the law, you must be honest."

"It's not called 'Fuck the People,' Chris. The earth belongs to everyone, but the Man keeps grabbing all he can. This is just a way to survive in a world full of price tags."

Is he about to leave school for life on the street? You simultaneously think that would be cool and you'd hate to lose the only person here who might be a friend. "Why're you reading it?"

"It tells how to fake credit card numbers to make long distance calls." Elverado looks embarrassed. "Heller spends most weekends in New York. I got to be able to call her."

You smile. "Man, you work fast!"

He's still embarrassed. "I don't know if anything'll happen. I slipped her a note in International Relations, and she sent me one back."

"Good luck on those international relations, man."

"Thanks, Chris. I caught the right train this weekend." His grin says he's including you in that. Now you're the one who's a little embarrassed.

You say, "Hey, Elverado, how come you don't use people's last names like the rest of the guys here?"

"'Cause they're into dynasties, and I'm into people. That's what Jesus meant when he said you should hate your family. Families are just a way to hide the fact we're all family." From that, Elverado segues into a rant about another military operation starting in Vietnam, and how he wishes he could've been at last weekend's peace rally in Pennsylvania, and how he hopes Lieutenant Calley will be convicted for the My Lai Massacre even though the politicians are really responsible, because no one has ever had a tidy war in which everyone behaved properly and only the bad people were hurt.

In the afternoon, when classes end, sports begin. As you head to crew, you think you should've picked something on campus that you could get to, get done, and get away from fast. But it's nice to be away from the Academy. You like walking through the edge of town and passing houses built before the Revolutionary War. You love watching the river and seeing the boathouse with its gleaming one-man sculls and sleek racing boats. You wish you were coming to paint, not sweat.

You're assigned to row stroke. You would rather be the coxswain and sit looking ahead, calling out the tempo and steering. But there's honor in rowing stroke. Your job is to pull hard and keep a steady rhythm that the other rowers can follow.

You like being on the water. You would happily row up and down the river, watching the countryside slip by. But the coach has seen too many movies about Roman slave ships. He only wants two things: your best effort, and a little more.

At first, you hate rowing fast. Your muscles ache almost immediately. When your timing and the depth of your stroke aren't perfect, you throw off the crew. But when you all work together, the boat skims over the water like a gull.

To row well, you can't think of anything else, not home or dead boys or homework or how much you hate sports. You just row, and your whole body is in agony, and you love this.

You think you must have had Viking ancestors. You think Josh Dumont must have loved this, too. You hope he was rowing perfectly in the moment before he died.

Ten

The next day, going back to Rider House to drop off books and grab art supplies, you rush in the front door, thinking you'll have to write home soon and wondering if you can get away with, "Dear Mom and Dad, I'm fine and hope you are, too. Love, Chris. P.S. Being prince of the world sucks."

Vaughn and O'Reilly come from the hall. O'Reilly grins at you. "What do you know? It's Levitz's little butt buddy."

You stop, look at him, and consider your choices.

If O'Reilly tries anything, you could make him fall down. You could make him run to the girls' campus, strip naked, and imitate a duck. You could make him forget he saw you.

O'Reilly frowns. You're supposed to be afraid.

Then you are. If you do something odd, Vaughn will know what you are. Can you make him forget what he sees? It's too risky to try.

If you run, you're a coward. If you stay, O'Reilly gets to hurt or humiliate you. Why is it when you only have two choices, they're usually both bad?

Vaughn watches with a small smile as O'Reilly says, "The point of going to a good school is to learn good lessons. Here's one for you, Nix. There are somebodies, and there are nobodies. You, Levitz, and Sanchez, you're nobodies. So long as you act like what you are, life is good for you." He grins. "Well, good enough for nobodies. But when you try to act like a somebody, why, the real somebodies have to test you. Because we don't want to misjudge anyone. But I don't think you're ready to be tested. So, tell me, Nix. What are you? Somebody? Or nobody?"

It should be easy to lie and say what he wants.

O'Reilly says, "I'm waiting."

The lie won't come. Why? Because you're afraid it might be true? That Dumont chose the wrong heir? You say, "I don't want trouble."

O'Reilly nods. "Who does? Terrible thing, trouble. So all you have to do is give a simple answer to a simple question. Somebody? Or nobody? Time to decide."

You say, "Fuck you," and start to walk past him.

He laughs and grabs your arm. "Why, that's a 'somebody' answer, Nix! Want to take it back?" His voice is light, but his fingers dig deep into your muscles. As you wince, he says, "Looking like a nobody. Is that it?"

Metal wheels rattle across the floor. Vaughn and O'Reilly look back. Mrs. Medeiros comes down the hallway pushing a mop in a bucket. "Don't you mind me, boys. Go right on with your talking."

O'Reilly laughs. "It's the wombat!"

She lifts her wet mop as if to hit him. "I'll wombat you, you heathen!"

Vaughn catches her arms, gives her a quick kiss on the cheek, and says, "Mrs. M, will you marry me?"

She raises her shoulders and her chin high. "You should be so lucky, Chad Vaughn!" She looks at you. "Now, this polite lad I might consider. If he ever learns to tidy his room."

O'Reilly laughs. "Hey, Nix, you're moving up in the world!"

Vaughn tells him, "More than you can say, O'Reilly."

O'Reilly scowls at Vaughn, and the boys go. You wish you were more like Vaughn; you want to kiss Mrs. Medeiros for arriving when she did. You say, "Thanks, ma'am."

She dunks her mop and starts swabbing the floor. "Don't you got a class coming up?"

"Yes, ma'am." You drop off your books, grab your art supplies, and run to the Joshua Dumont Art Center.

You rush into the studio and go to an empty easel as the master, Hans Janowitz, walks to the center of the room.

You feel the blood and look around. Heller is at an easel. You ignore her as the class begins. For the next fifty minutes, you draw. You think about light and dark, negative space, the difference between what you see and what you feel. The students around you draw quickly and confidently. Your hand is so much stupider than your eye. You will never be an artist. You should walk out before anyone sees how bad you are.

But at the end of the class, Janowitz says, "Keep it up, Nix. You could be an artist someday."

"It's not all, uh, crap?"

"That depends. Are you serious about art?"

You nod.

"Then you're right. It's shit, and you should be glad, because artists need to produce all the shit they can. Stupid shit, derivative shit, technically interesting and conceptually flawed shit, conceptually interesting and technically flawed shit, any kind of shit you can think of and shit that happens without thinking about it. Any shit that teaches you something about your art is good shit. But if you're afraid to produce shit, you'll quit trying to be an artist, and instead of going through life producing shit, you'll go through life full of shit. So promise me two things."

"Uh, what?"

"One. Produce honest shit. Not shit that looks like the shit of artists you like. Your own shit. If you do, eventually you'll get all the shit out of you, and you'll be an artist."

"Okay. What's two?"

"If you tell anyone about this, say I said 'junk.' "

You grin. "Deal."

You can take a few minutes before going to crew, so you walk among the paintings and sculptures in the art center's atrium. The show is called "The Divine Impulse." The oldest piece is a thirteenth century French Madonna with dark skin, but most of the work is recent: a Christ crucified on a U.S. missile being fired into space, a Muhammad with a glowing lightbulb instead of a head, a fat Buddha who looks like a melting candle, a Moses parting a sea of money, a gang of Hindu gods in bikinis and speedos at a beach party with Marilyn Monroe, James Dean, and John F. Kennedy.

Most of the pieces are clearly the work of experienced artists, but one looks like the work of a promising beginner. It shows angels with flaming swords flying to battle.

A card identifies it as "The Last War" by Joshua Dumont. The main figure has his father's face. The angels around him look like people you've met: Mrs. Dumont, Gabriel, Jonathan, Mather. You study the other faces. Heller isn't among them. None of them looks young enough to be Josh.

You look up, feeling the blood. Heller is across the room, watching you. You don't know what to make of her expression. Does she hate seeing you next to her brother's work? You say, "He was good."

"Better than—" She catches herself, turns her head as if to shake off something, and says gently, "Anyone."

You want to say or do something to comfort her. You try, "Elverado likes you."

"He's a fool," she says, then smiles slightly. "But he's sweet."

Eleven

The Academy's week is scheduled to keep students busy. It works twice as well with you because you know even less than the third-formers. They're also new to the Academy, but they've heard about boarding schools from parents and siblings and friends who went before them. You don't have time to look for clues about Josh's death. Every night, you fall into bed exhausted. Sometimes you wake thinking your dreams were strange, but you don't remember them.

On Friday, shortly before dinner, you run across the green to the Academy's stone church. Boys and girls are gathering already. Their jackets and ties make you think of a funeral. The mood makes you think of a funeral, too. People are glad to see each other, but they show it by bitching about mandatory chapel.

Heller is with the girls from the train station. You know they think they look hopelessly straight in blazers, long plaid skirts, and knee socks, and they do, but they still look hot. So you're younger, shorter, and pimply. Why are hot girls so superficial? Why haven't you told Mather to set up the love pad with Heller? Being honorable sucks.

You don't expect Heller to acknowledge you. When she says, "Hey, Chris," you're so surprised you stop, then realize she expected you to say "Hi" and keep walking. But she just shrugs, looks at the girls, and says, "Chris Nix, Marrije Schaake, Geminem

Urdaneta, Xochi Sprinkle, and Gigi Rose. Chris is in my art class."

Girls in Florida have names like Pam, Cindy, Susan, and Mary. F. Scott is kicking Ernest's ass. Except for the names, these girls seem like the ones you knew in Florida: They nod and smile and say hello and laugh a little and make you sure that anything you say will be wrong. You say, "Uh, hi, uh, good to meet you. I'll, uh, catch you, uh, later."

You walk away quickly, hoping you look like you have somewhere to go and not like you're fleeing. The good thing about being forgettable is people don't remember when you act like a dweeb.

You're relieved when you hear, "Hey, Chris, my main man!" You're less relieved when you see Elverado in the Beatle wig with an olive green U.S. Army dress jacket, a purple paisley tie, a yellow shirt, and lime-green bell-bottoms that make his legs look like they grow from the earth.

People turn to see who he's calling. You could pretend you didn't hear him. Then you're ashamed of considering that. Whatever Elverado is, he doesn't care what others think, which makes him braver than you. You walk up to him, saying, "Elverado! Day students have to come to chapel, too?"

"Yeah. Major bummer, man. But afterward, you know nothing worse can happen for seven whole days."

"You could die."

"Sure. Smiling 'cause you'd never have to hear one of Mather's sermons again."

You grin, then see Heller glance at Elverado. Why are you jealous? You want CC. But Heller reminds you of rock god wisdom: "Love the one you're with."

Elverado flashes her a peace sign. She looks away fast, laughing with the other girls.

That's why you told Mather you don't want private meetings

with Heller. CC would come over and kiss a boy she liked, no matter who was watching.

You say, "Things not going so good?"

Elverado says quietly, "*Au contraire, mon frère.* She's afraid her folks would freak if they heard she had a boyfriend. So we're playing it cool in public." The chapel bell begins to ring. Elverado adds, "Showtime. When you get bored, read the lord's prayer backward under your breath. Deconsecrates a church. I bet this one's been deconsecrated weekly for decades."

Fitzgerald calls, "Mr. Nix!"

"Later," you tell Elverado and head over to Fitzgerald and your housemates.

You all shuffle in without talking. The chapel is large, beautiful, and old, by Florida standards, anyway. A plain wooden cross hangs on the wall. Stained glass shows creatures of the earth, not scenes from the Bible. The pews are wooden, dark and handsome and uncomfortable, despite or because of hard thin pads. If anyone wanted to be here, it might feel religious.

When you sit, Levitz whispers, "Is Superman Jewish?"

"Because his creators were?"

"Because he's got a Jewish name. Kal-El. Like Michael, Rafael, Joel, Nathaniel, you know."

O'Reilly, a few seats away, whispers loudly, "Hey, keep it down, you lovebugs!"

Several boys laugh, including Vaughn. Levitz shrinks into his seat, and you feel your ears redden. As Fitzgerald looks over, Vaughn says, "Gentlemen, please! We're in church!"

An organ starts playing something that's religious or martial or both. Mather comes out in a minister's robe. Everyone stands, and a few people sing with the choir. You mouth the words. Could you make yourself sing on key? You hate Mather's taste in music too much to try.

The song has something to do with praising God and serving God and being grateful for being able to praise and serve God. If it was faster, it would be better because it would be over sooner.

Mather welcomes everyone, then says that some students fail to see the importance of chapel, but it's the soul of the Academy. He says it's not denominational, that there are students here who are Jewish, Muslim, Hindu, Buddhist, and even atheist, but the services are based on Christianity, and he's sure that will be good for everyone, because even if you think Jesus's story is only a story, it's a good story, and there's truth in all religions.

He has everyone read the Apostles' Creed: "I believe in God the Father Almighty, maker of heaven and earth, and in Jesus Christ his only Son, our Lord, who was conceived by the Holy Ghost, born of the Virgin Mary, suffered under Pontius Pilate, was crucified, dead, and buried. He descended into hell. The third day he rose again from the dead. He ascended into heaven and sitteth on the right hand of God the Father Almighty. From thence he shall come to judge the quick and the dead. I believe in the Holy Ghost, the holy catholic Church, the communion of saints, the forgiveness of sins, the resurrection of the body, and the life everlasting. Amen."

You mumble along with the others. What do words matter?

When everyone sits, Mather talks about God's truth. There's the truth that people should serve the masters God gives them, and the truth that masters should rule wisely, and the truth that we all must trust our masters to be wiser than we are, for God is the greatest master, and God's wisdom is greater than ours, and God gives us everything, so we should give everything to God.

You decide you know why chapel is mandatory. Mather wants an audience. If this was optional, like the Sunday service, he would only get a few brownnosers.

After a final song about how great God is, you go out into the sunlight. You see a bluebird fly by. A breeze carries the smell of the forest. Elverado's right. Leaving chapel feels great.

Saturdays are half-days: morning classes only, no sports. Many kids from New York and New England head home for the night. Nearly a third of Rider House goes, including Levitz. Elverado has a sister in Boston; he goes up there most Saturdays to hit the folk clubs with her.

So you're alone. You have enough homework that you don't want to read an extra word, but you head to the school library.

It's the opposite of the art center. It feels as old as the Academy. Everything's varnished wood or polished brass. Sherlock Holmes should be reading in a corner. Its effect is the same as the art center's. You would happily spend all of your time here if you could chase any idea that interested you.

Miss Chabot smiles when she spots you. It's much better seeing her than Sherlock Holmes. She asks if she can help you. You say yes to spend a few extra minutes with her. The price is that you leave with three times as many books as you planned to get. You don't have the heart to reject anything she suggests.

You spend the afternoon reading about genetics and mutations. One word fascinates you: "mutagenesis," the creation of a mutation. So does a fact you must have learned in fifth grade and forgotten: Mutations tend to be neutral, meaning they have no practical effect on a new creation, or harmful, meaning they hurt its chance of survival. Only useful mutations thrive. Are nefelim some form of human mutation? Or are humans the mutant children of nefs? If either or both races were made, who made them and why?

After dinner, you return to Rider House, ditch your coat and tie, and sign out. Boys are allowed on the girls' campus until 8:30 P.M. Maybe you'll see Heller or one of the girls that she introduced you to. Maybe you'll be able to say something besides "hi." Saying hi to a girl would be nice. If nothing else, you can see if the girls have the nicer campus. Sometimes anything is better than a book.

But as you cross the street to go to the new campus, you look toward the woods. It would be nice to escape the Academy completely, if only for a few minutes.

And you might feel the call of the blood. It's barely a whim, a hint that you could walk in that direction. Was this what Grandpa Abner felt in France before he found Jay Dumont?

That thought stops you. Grandpa was a medic with the American army. What was Jay Dumont doing when he was hurt? Why would the world's king be on a battlefield?

The woods are full of paths. Boys have hunted privacy here for decades. The land belongs to the school, but it's not part of the campus. You can be punished if you're caught here.

You look back at the Academy. A few students cross between the campuses. No one is watching. You walk casually into the trees. If anyone comes after you, you can say you thought you saw something interesting.

But these woods aren't interesting. They're just pleasant. New England forests were tamed centuries ago. In Florida, you would watch for rattlesnakes and boar. Here, you expect nothing worse than crows and squirrels.

No one shouts at you, so you stroll deeper into the woods. You like being under the trees and walking on grass and dirt. As the shadows grow longer and darker, you think these woods could be scary, not because you would expect wolves or bears, but because the growing darkness reminds you that old is not the same as tame. This is the land of the Headless Horseman and the wendigo. Were witches burnt near here? What tribes lived here before the Europeans drove them off? Did Vikings come here before Columbus? What gods were worshipped here, before people built churches to Jesus?

It would be nice to walk here with CC. But then, if you were alone with CC, you wouldn't be walking.

You stop still. About fifty feet away, almost hidden by trees and twilight, a woman lies in a small clearing like a corpse. She's on her back, looking up at the sky. Her arms are at her side. She seems to have been left for nature to consume.

You stare because you doubt what you see. Then you breathe. She's a girl in a blazer and plaid skirt, and her chest rises and falls normally. You want to tiptoe away without disturbing her, and you want to paint her, lying still in a grove. You understand the desire to feel the earth under you when you've spent a day surrounded by buildings and people and rules that serve the Academy's masters, but not its students.

Then you recognize Blaise Selby. Is she waiting for Vaughn? Has he been here and gone, and she stayed, wanting time alone before returning to the Academy?

She's the source of the call. You don't feel any other nef nearby. How do you know that? You just do.

As you wonder about nefelim, you feel a faint call from the boys' school, then another from the girls': Vaughn and Heller.

And then you can feel a farther, diffuse call, like noise in a radio signal. Those must be distant nef, in New Haven or Shanghai. While you focus on them, your blood resonates with theirs.

Then you recognize other calls like noise at a new pitch. There are fewer of them, but the call is distinct. They're the people who drank from you.

And last, as you stand in that quiet place, you feel something you can't identify, something that pleases and strengthens you. It comes from all around you. It's power beyond understanding, power so great that it can't contain itself. It spills into the world for you to tap.

That's what Blaise Selby is doing. She's found a quiet place to bathe in power.

You should go. The woods are big enough for you both to be

alone in them. You were told to keep other nefs from knowing who you are. It's good advice.

You call, "Blaise Selby?" and walk toward her.

She sits up and frowns, saying, "Do I know you?"

"I was with Heller on the train."

"Heller was on the train?" Her frown deepens. "I don't remember you."

"I'm Chris Nix."

"Oh. Hi." There's no happiness in her voice. She wants you to figure out you interrupted her and go away.

"I'm the prince."

"Excuse me?"

"Of the elohim."

She stares at you. "You're not—"

How did Dumont show his power? Feeling a little silly, you say, "I am who I am."

She glances around the woods. "If I scream, people will hear."

She's right. There must be other kids out here, bored or making out or getting high. People would hear her by the school buildings. They would find you, and no matter what you said, they would think you were out here being some kind of creep who bothered girls. You say desperately, "Don't!"

She drops to the ground so quickly you think she was shot. Covering her face with her hands, she says, "No, lord, please! I'm sorry, I didn't know you, forgive me, I won't, I would never do anything to make you unhappy, never!"

You feel like you meant to move a kitten out of the way and kicked it across the room instead. Begging, not commanding, you say, "Stop it, please! And call me Chris."

She doesn't look up. "But you're an eloah—"

"Being called 'lord' is weird. I think it's okay to look at me now. If I hurt you, I'm sorry. I didn't mean to do anything, honest."

She raises her eyes cautiously. “You didn’t hurt me. I just—I just knew you’re one of the elohim.”

“You know the others?”

She nods. “Of course.”

“And you’re cool around Heller.”

“When she’s not drawing on the glory, sure. But you—I didn’t have any warning, and then you were so much more than I can ever be—”

“It’s just power.” That sounds stupid, so you try, “I mean, if I had an H-bomb, I’d still be me.”

She shakes her head. “Elohim don’t have the glory. Elohim are the glory.”

“That’s what elohim do? Call up power?”

“You don’t—” Disbelief is strong on her face until she hides it. “Yes.”

“What do nef do?”

“Excuse me?”

“What makes a nef different from a human?” She hesitates again, and you say, making sure it’s not an order, “Please. I’m new to this.”

“Well.” You see her weighing answers, and you think the truth wins. “Humans don’t live long. Maybe a century at best. And they’re awfully weak.”

“Physically?”

She nods. “Plus it’s easy to make them think things. I guess that’s it.”

“Can nef walk on water?”

She smiles slightly. “If they water ski.”

So what does it mean that you rode on water ten months before Dumont anointed you? Is it just that the blood is strong in you? “What about healing?”

“Well, nef blood or sweat helps humans. But if you mean heal at a distance—”

"Yeah."

"That's only for elohim."

"Why are elohim different?"

She shrugs. "They just are. They've got the glory."

"Okay. Did you know Josh well?"

She smiles, reminding you that she's older than you. "Very."

"Oh." You hope you don't look embarrassed. "Do you think he was killed?"

She squints at you. "Who would want to kill him?"

"Chad Vaughn?"

"No way. Chad and Josh were like Batman and Robin."

"Maybe Robin wanted to be Batman."

"You didn't know them."

"So who else might've killed him?"

She shrugs. "It had to be an accident. It's tragic, but that's life sometimes."

The light is growing dim. You nod and say, "I've got to make you forget we talked."

"I wouldn't tell anyone."

You want to believe her. But if Vaughn didn't kill Josh Dumont to become the next world-prince, Blaise Selby might've killed him for Vaughn's sake. So you feel the power—the glory—growing, and you say, "Forget everything we said since I called your name."

She squints, shakes her head, and says, "Do I know you?"

You nod. "Heller Dumont pointed you out on the train." And you walk her back to the campus, talking about teachers and classes and life in private schools.

September passes, not slowly, not quickly. You decide Josh's death must have been accidental. You're glad to let your worry fade. You begin to like keeping your secret identity from Blaise and Vaughn. The longer the secret lasts, the worse they'll feel when they learn that they should have been nicer to you.

You don't get any more mail from CC. You know you have to accept that you may never see her again. You like Heller's friends. Maybe one of them will like you, or will have a younger sister who will like you. But at night before you sleep, you don't think about Marrije or Gigi or Geminem or Xochi. You wonder where CC is and hope she's thinking about you.

Elverado and Heller keep their flirtation a secret from everyone except you, which you hate. You're the one who has to keep watch when they want a quick kiss in a quiet classroom or behind a tree when you're all walking through the woods.

The world seems far away from the Academy. There's no TV. When you study, you listen to tapes, not radio. The library gets newspapers from New York, Washington, Boston, and London, but you're always behind on your homework. Why waste time reading news that you can't affect and doesn't affect you? What you overhear doesn't make you happy. The Vietnam War continues. There's fighting in Jordan and Israel. Jimi Hendrix OD's on barbiturates.

October starts just as badly. Janis Joplin OD's on heroin. Nixon offers a peace proposal with terms that no one expects the Vietnamese to accept, and they don't.

At the Academy, to your amazement, crew becomes your favorite part of the day. The coach thinks you're good enough to keep rowing stroke. Your boat usually wins when you race the junior varsity boats. Your team is good, and while all of them are too obsessed with sports to be your friends, you respect them. You work as hard as you can to be as good as they think you are.

You have one fear when you row. "Catching a crab" is putting your blade in too deep. Then water will grab your oar as if the river has a hand, and you'll throw off everyone's rhythm. Oars tend to smash together if someone catches a crab. Sometimes boats are turned over. Catching a crab is a sin for any rower. It's worst for the stroke.

But you almost never think of that when you're rowing. You think only of what you're doing. You don't think about winning or losing. You just think about rowing as hard and as well as you can with each stroke. You've read about people meditating. You think crew must be better.

On a gray day in October on a practice sprint, the coxswain turns the rudder to change course. Each time you come forward for another pull on the oar, you see a different part of the shore behind him. You've seen it five days a week, but something looks different.

As you reach for the next stroke, you see what it is. Someone sits on shore, watching your boat. Someone you know.

Your crab must be a record. The boat lurches like a wounded gull. It nearly tips. You don't care.

The person on shore is CC.

The coach yells something extremely unhappy through his megaphone from his boat. Your coxswain keeps calling the beat. You're back in the pace before you're sure what happened.

The coxswain turns the rudder again. The shore disappears, but you think CC was beginning to stand when the boat lurched. The prow comes around after five or ten centuries pass, and your suspicion is confirmed. CC is gone.

So is your joy of rowing. Every second is sandpaper on your heart. When the coach finally lets you dock, you shower, dress, and run out before anyone else.

CC's nowhere around. Is she in town? Was she passing through and stopped by the river? Why are you sure it was CC? Someone with dark skin sat by the river. You must have imagined it was CC.

But you know you saw her.

You walk toward campus studying every house and bush that might hide her. You expect to see her running toward you. Why didn't she wave? Why didn't she wait? Why didn't she send you another note? Was the one you got her idea of a Dear John letter? Does "trust nobody" include her?

You're Chris Nix the Elah Prince. What good are powers that you can't use?

Your eyes are wet. Your throat is thick. You sob and think, CC, I miss you. CC! Come here! CC, I don't want to be alone! CC! Come be with me! CC! CC! CC!

But you are alone. You rub away tears and snot, you take several deep breaths, and you walk on. You try to think of other things, homework and elah powers and Heller. Every line of thought takes you back to CC.

Someone comes running behind you. You turn without thinking what you might see.

She wears a green T-shirt, white jeans, and black tennis shoes. Her hair is longer than you remember, down to her shoulders. She's crying and mumbling something. You think she misses you as much as you miss her. You open your arms and say, "CC!" You're hugging her, and there's nothing bad in the world.

No.

Something's very bad.

Her skin is hot and slick. She's drenched in sweat. She's not hugging you back. She's rigid in your arms and saying softly, "Don't do this, I thought you wouldn't do this, you goddamn motherfucker, let me go, please, dear God, stop it, please!"

You open your arms. "CC?"

She gasps and staggers away, gulping air desperately. She looks like she'll fall over. When you reach out to steady her, she scrambles back farther. "Don't touch me!"

Terrified you know why, you say, "What's wrong?"

She glares at you. "I thought you liked me."

"I do!"

"Then how could you do that! To anyone?"

"I didn't do anything!"

"You know how far I ran?"

"No."

"Good." She gasps again. "I couldn't stop, not for cars, not to breathe—"

"I didn't know!" You don't say more because you're not sure what you didn't know. That you were doing anything? Or that it would work?

"Now you do."

"I'm sorry."

"Then don't do it again! To anyone!" She shakes her head and staggers back the way she came.

"CC!"

She stops. You're afraid you made her stop, but you don't think you did. She turns and says, "What are you going to be?"

The question doesn't make sense. But since that's what she wants to know, you say, "I don't care. You can call me Chris or Mark or anything—"

"No. What are you?"

Oh. You say, a little proudly, certain this will convince her to give you the chance to make things right, "Prince of the elohim. That's—"

She says, "I know what that is. Do you like me? At all?"

"Yeah." The pain you feel strongest is knowing she doesn't trust you. So you don't say you like her more than anything you can think of.

She says, "Then forget me."

She runs off. You could follow. You could command her to come back. You're the world-prince. You could make her do anything.

But she thinks you would hurt her. She wants you to forget her.

You let her go. Soon, you'll show everyone what you are. She'll be sorry then.

Twelve

That Friday, before chapel, Elverado whispers, "Heller told the school she's spending Saturday night at home. She told her folks she's spending it with Blaise Selby."

As you connect the dots, he nods. "Life is sweet for a backdoor man."

You should warn him. You say, "Elverado–"

"Yeah?"

What can you say? He knows Heller's the daughter of a rich man who wouldn't like the idea that she's dating a hippie weirdo. That's the essence of what he needs to know, right? And love is love, right? At least he wants to be with someone who wants to be with him.

And maybe you're imagining too much. Maybe they both just want some fun. When it comes to love or sex, Elverado and Heller and everyone who has ever lived know more than you. You're jealous, not because he'll be with Heller, but because you can't be with CC. You say, "Have a far out time, man."

He smiles. "With Heller, what else can it be?"

Chapel seems as boring as always until everyone begins reciting the Apostles' Creed. It says the one God, Father and Son, came from heaven thanks to the Holy Ghost and the Virgin Mary. Isn't that four gods? It says Jesus was killed by Pontius Pilate for humanity's sake. Doesn't that mean Pontius Pilate saved us?

You look up at Mather, then at the cross behind him. Why do

Christians use crosses? Wouldn't that be like using guns to remember John F. Kennedy, Robert Kennedy, and Martin Luther King?

Mather's sermon follows its usual pattern. He says God's rulers serve God, so we must serve them. Most people are born to serve; they should serve joyfully. A few are born to rule; they should rule wisely. Those who are given more should enjoy all that God gives them. Those who are given less should accept God's wisdom. What is, is. Don't question God. Why should you? God has chosen you to lead the world. When your turn comes, rule with wisdom and joy, and give thanks to God.

You think something is different, then know that something is the same, only you never noticed it. A strangeness is at work in this room. Mather is using the blood.

When he finishes, you bow your head and listen as the others mumble the Lord's Prayer: "Our Father which art in heaven, hallowed be thy name. Thy kingdom come. Thy will be done in earth, as it is in heaven. Give us this day our daily bread. And forgive us our debts, as we forgive our debtors. And lead us not into temptation, but deliver us from evil. For thine is the kingdom, and the power, and the glory, for ever. Amen."

Their words are directed toward Mather. The blood within him, the blood from Dumont, grows stronger as prayer fills the chapel. The power of the worship is being directed to Jay Dumont.

It extends beyond the chapel. It's a web, one place of worship linked to the next. It lies across the land, across the oceans, around the world, wherever people gather and pray to the ruler of the world.

Is this why religious leaders hate atheists? Because they don't do their part to feed the world's lord?

There's a last song, then freedom. As you shuffle into the sunlight, Elverado calls, "Hey, Chris! What should we organize, a walkout for migrant workers or a march against the war?"

Levitz says, "They'll kick you out for either."

Elverado says, "Not if there's a lot of us."

Vaughn, a few steps ahead, looks back. Your stomach tightens as you prepare for an insult. He says, "Go for the war. Most of these nimrods think unions are commie fronts, but just about all of them agree the war's wrong." Before anyone can answer, he walks ahead to talk with Blaise Selby.

Elverado looks at you in surprise, then shrugs and nods. "March against the war. Cool. Catch me at lunch Monday. We'll plot the end of the military-industrial complex."

"What'll we do Tuesday?"

He grins. "Plot the victory party!"

He cuts off the path, heading across the lawn away from school. He yanks off his tie and his wig, waves them high as he shakes out his hair, and wanders away singing loudly like Richie Havens at Woodstock, "Freedom! Freedom! Freedom! Freedom!"

O'Reilly, following Vaughn, says, "What a douchebag!"

But several girls laugh, telling you they think Elverado is both silly and cute. Heller watches him, then turns her head away quickly.

You look back at Elverado. He's swaying in time with his song as he walks. He'll eat with his mother, then have the night free for TV or a movie or cruising with one of his townie friends. You'll stay on campus and be in your room by ten. Tomorrow, he'll be with Heller. You'll be with your memories of CC and your fantasies of how things might have gone.

You would be as free as Elverado if you had stayed in Florida. What are George and Tish doing now? Do Mom or Dad miss you? To your amazement, you miss them all. What'll they say when you tell them you're the prince of the world? George will probably say you always acted like you thought you were.

The girls head for their campus to eat far from the corrupting influence of boys. As you enter High House with Levitz, he says, "You're not really going to be part of a protest."

You remember the National Guard shooting unarmed students at Kent State and Jackson State. Six killed, twenty-one wounded. You say, "Why not? They won't shoot preppies."

"Yeah, but it'll go on your permanent record."

"So?"

"So you might not get into an Ivy League school when you graduate. You might get kicked out of the Academy and have to go to a public school."

You smile, thinking of what's to come. Jay Dumont may tolerate war, but you'll rule a world of peace. You say, "Hey, if a school rejects me because I don't believe in war, I'll send them a thank-you letter."

He shakes his head. "The war won't end any sooner if some boys protest."

You shrug. "It would if every boy did."

You spend the weekend working on an essay about slavery in Rome. When you read it over Monday morning, you decide it sucks, but the master might not notice if you add illustrations. So, at breakfast, you take an empty table where you can eat and draw. Your favorite part is about Spartacus, who led a slave revolt, then died on a cross, the traditional punishment for Rome's traitors. You don't want him to look like Jesus, so you make him clean-shaven and give him shorter hair.

And you realize you've drawn yourself nailed to a cross. Why? You're going to rule the world, not die for it.

As you try to decide whether to start over, you notice a couple of kids talking at the next table. They seem excited. You say, "Excuse me. Did something happen?"

One says, "You know Peter Sanchez?"

You start to smile, thinking that word of Elverado's peace protest is spreading and wondering what he'll tell you about his night with Heller. "Yeah?"

"He OD'd."

You know what you heard, and you still say, "He what?"

The other boy tells the first, "No, he didn't. He hung himself."

The first says, "I heard there were drugs involved."

The second says, "With that guy, there'd have to be."

You say, "You're talking about Elverado?"

The second says, "Yeah, Pete Sanchez. He was always high. He supplied this school."

The first says, "No, he didn't deal. But he died high. Everyone says so."

You return your tray with breakfast half-finished and go straight to Mather's office. The secretary says, "The headmaster's busy now." Then she looks closer at your face. "Were you a friend of Peter's?"

"I have to see Mr. Mather. It's important. Tell him it's Christopher Nix, please."

"I'll see if he's available." She goes in, and a moment later, she's saying, "He'll see you now."

Mather meets you at the door. "You heard."

"I've got to see him."

"I'm afraid there's nothing you can do."

"There is!"

The secretary looks up from her typing. Mather frowns, gestures for you to come into his office, and closes the door. "You shouldn't disturb his family."

"But I can save him!"

"You don't know that."

"I brought back a man at the Dumonts'."

"A man who had just died, and whose damage was comparatively simple."

"What do you mean, comparatively?"

"Sometime Saturday night, Peter dove from the roof of his three-story house onto a brick patio in their backyard. His mother was in Boston for the weekend, seeing his sister. His body lay there until she returned Sunday night. Dogs had found him. If there's a service for him, it'll be closed casket."

Your stomach turns. You swallow and say, "Couldn't I heal him?"

"Even if you did, how would you explain it?"

"It could be a miracle. No one would have to know it was me."

He smiles. "We all must be discreet, my lord."

"I can't let him die!"

"He's already died."

"But his family—"

"They'll mourn. The Academy will help them with the funeral. Mrs. Sanchez is taking leave and going to stay with her daughter."

"I have to bring him back."

"No, my lord. You do not."

Thinking, I'm the world-prince, you say, "I have to try."

Mather flinches like a man with a headache, then squints at you. "So long as I serve our lord, you mustn't seek to compel me. When you're El Elyon, I'll obey you as faithfully, and as gladly."

"How does this serve Mr. Dumont?"

Rubbing his forehead, Mather says, "Peter wasn't part of the plan." His eyes go wide, and he says, "Stop, my lord! What I do, I do for the greater good. This benefits our lord. What benefits him, benefits the whole elohim."

"How?"

Mather holds your gaze with effort. "I'm old and determined, and I know what you're doing, my lord. Break me if you will, but you'll learn nothing more from me. Let me live to serve you in your day."

He thinks you might kill him. The idea's so shocking you stop trying to make him answer. You don't have the skill to trick him into revealing more. You nod and turn to leave.

He says, "If you go to the dead boy, you'll be a rebel. The punishment for rebellion is death."

You look back. He says, "Be wise, my lord. Let this pass. Let our lord know he was right to choose you. Think of your earthly family. Think of Heller. The boy is dead. I speak the truth when I say I doubt you can call him back now. Don't show a rebellious spirit. Let the rest of the elohim know you can obey, and you'll be El Elyon someday."

You hesitate. Elverado is dead. What can you do? Go to the police and say the world-king decided a boy was a nuisance, so one of his servants made him get stoned and dive from a roof?

Then you see there's more to Elverado's death than removing a nuisance. It's a message. You may be prince, but Dumont rules. The lives of everyone you know hang on pleasing him.

You say, "I don't know what to do."

"Of course not. Trust that we do. Time teaches. Learn, and you'll know we're right."

"I liked Elverado."

"And I admired his spirit. But power demands hard choices sometimes."

You look at Mather and don't know what you're trying to see. He says gently, "First period begins soon."

You nod and go. Who should you blame for Elverado's death? Mather as much as admitted that Dumont had him killed, but Elverado was put in Dumont's path earlier: *My work here is done.* Was this part of that work? Has that work gone horribly wrong? If there's a god who is all powerful and all knowing, shouldn't that god be blamed for every bad thing that happens?

The day goes in fits and starts. You can work hard in class for five or ten minutes, but then you think, Elverado is dead. I could've done something. I don't know what, but something.

In the afternoon, you spot Heller going down the art center steps with Marrije and Gigi. You run after her, calling her name. She frowns, and you know she's heard about Elverado.

You say, "Uh, I don't want to bother you, but—"

She tells the girls, "I'll see you at field hockey!" and leads you a few steps away. "Well?"

"Were you there?"

"Was I—" She figures out what you can't ask. "No! My God, Chris, do you think I would just watch—"

You don't know what you think. You say, "You were going to spend the night—"

She nods. "That was the plan. Only Daddy was there when I walked up to Elverado's house, so I had to go to New York instead. I should've known he would have someone spying on me."

"Who knew about you?"

"Just you." Before you can ask if she thinks you told her father, she adds, "And my girlfriends."

"Did he—" You can't ask a girl if her father killed her boyfriend to keep them from sleeping together. "What do you think happened?"

"I've been trying to figure it out. I think Elverado must've been disappointed, so he got high, and then he fell." She looks away. "We'll be late for sports."

"We need to talk. I mean, undisturbed. I was thinking I would tell Mather I want to see you tonight."

She shrugs. "You're the prince."

"Just to talk. They'll assume it's, uh—"

"Sex?"

"Yeah. Are you cool with that?"

She shrugs again. "If it's what you want."

A year ago, if someone said a pretty girl would do whatever you want, you would've thought life could get no better. If you're ever offered this deal again, you'll make sure the wording is "would *want* to do whatever you want."

You run to find Mather. You say you want to see Heller that night. He says it'll be arranged. You thank him and hurry off to crew. You row perfectly, but there's no joy in it. When you're done, you rush to the library.

Miss Chabot sees you and says, "Chris! You heard about poor Peter Sanchez?"

You nod.

"The masters say he could be a problem, but I liked him. With most boys, I can guess the sort of thing they'll check out next. I never knew with Peter. He would've gone on to great things." She smiles again. "If not great things, definitely interesting ones."

You say, "Yeah," and think, He's not even going to go on to boring things now.

Miss Chabot says, "You knew him?"

You nod. Miss Chabot waits, not impatiently, just sharing a moment of silence. You say, "I'm researching God."

She laughs. "That's ambitious!"

"Well, how religious stories started? How people saw gods and how that changed. Does that make sense?"

"Sure. Which people?"

"Uh, everyone?"

"Okay. How many books do you want to start, and how many languages do you read?"

"Uh, one book in English?" You hold up two fingers close together. "One little book?"

She laughs. "Dream on, Chris." She leads you to the religion section and begins handing you books. "Let's see. Greco-Romans, Egyptians, Norse, Zoroastrians—"

"Zorro what?"

"Zoroastrianism. The first monotheism."

"Wasn't that Judaism?"

"Jewish and Christian literalists say so. It's not supported by archeology or textual analysis." She keeps giving you books. "Judaism,

Christianity, Islam, Hinduism, Buddhism, African religions, American Indian ones—"

You stagger back to Rider House with a stack of books so tall you can barely see over it. You're tempted to make them lighter, but you don't like the idea of wasting your strength. How do elahs recharge?

You're reading about Jupiter killing his father, Saturn, to become Dies Pater, a name that means Sky Father, when you hear a knock. Fitzgerald leans in, nods to Levitz, and hands you a slip of paper. "Your pass. The head says you may spend your evenings out until your project's done."

As soon as Fitzgerald goes, Levitz says, "What project?"

You glance at the paper and wonder if the answer reveals Mather's sense of humor or Dumont's. "Biology."

You set aside your library books to finish some of your assigned reading, but now that you're looking for information about religion, you find it everywhere:

Your biology book says science began when people tried to understand their gods. How did they want to use that knowledge, for gods or against them?

Your English book says Christopher Marlowe, the first great English playwright, was a member of a secret society called the School of Night, and a spy for Queen Elizabeth. In *Tamburlaine the Great, Part II,* he wrote, "There is a God full of revenging wrath, From whom the thunder and the lightning breaks," and "Come, let us march against the powers of heaven, And set black streamers in the firmament, To signify the slaughter of the gods." Marlowe was killed at the age of twenty-nine in a drunken fight. After his death, Shakespeare began writing his great work. Was Marlowe killed to protect a secret? Did he fake his death and keep writing under Shakespeare's name?

You realize you're in danger of thinking every mystery is connected to elohim. Why did the *Titanic* sink? Elohim. Why did

Amelia Earhart disappear? Elohim. Why is the U.S. at war in Vietnam? Elohim. Why did NBC cancel *Star Trek*? Elohim. Who stole your *Lone Ranger* lunchbox in second grade? Elohim.

Levitz warns you to stop reading and dress for dinner. You want to skip it, because that would be a gesture that Elverado would appreciate, but you don't want anyone to wonder about you. So you grab a jacket and tie and run, promising yourself that someday you'll be early for something.

When you reach Fitzgerald's table, you see a good reason to start being early. There's one seat left. It's on the far side of the table from Fitzgerald. It's between O'Reilly and Vaughn.

Vaughn smiles. "Hey, Nix. How's it hanging?"

"Uh, okay." You sit.

Vaughn holds out his hand. "We got off on the wrong foot. What say we shake hands and start fresh? You seem like a good man. You might've misunderstood that little initiation at the start of the term." He laughs and adds, "You did a lot better than the rest of the tools at this table, I don't mind telling you."

You grin in relief, say, "It's cool," and shake his hand. His grip is strong. You feel yourself liking him. His smile grows.

He's making you trust him. You think, No! and release his hand.

Does something flicker in his eyes? Or are you imagining too much?

He says, "Glad that's cleared up." Only his friends are listening. They're grinning innocently, like boys with nothing to do before dinner.

"Ditto," you say. You eat as quickly as you can and ask if you may be dismissed before dessert.

Heading down from High House, you pull off your tie and unbutton your collar. Maybe people like ties because it feels so good to get rid of them.

The girls' campus is new and shining, all glass and steel and tile. You see a few older boys laughing with older girls. No one stares at you, but you know they're wondering what a fourth-former is doing here. When you pause to look around, a woman asks if she can help you. She checks your pass, then points you toward the headmistress's house.

Miss Huntington's home would amaze you if you hadn't visited the Dumonts. The inside is art deco, from the curved stairway to the statues of dancing women. The air smells of flowers. The living room is all gleaming black and white, except for several crystal vases holding red roses. Does Miss Huntington always have flowers? Or is that stage setting?

She's tall, athletic, and very New England. Her hair is short, mostly black, but speckled with gray. You see her and think she's hot.

That thought disappears when she closes the door behind you. She curtsies and says, "My lord, welcome. Your lady awaits you."

You're not ready to see Heller. Maybe you'll never be ready. You look around and say, "This is nice."

"Thank you." Miss Huntington seems perfectly content with whatever you want. That's the mark of a good servant. You could raid her fridge and read her books and sleep in her bed, and she would be pleased, because she likes thinking you're better than her. You could tell her to strip and have sex with you, and she would. It would be as easy as jerking off. It might be more fun while it was happening, but you suspect it would be less afterward. At least half the reason you want CC is she wants you.

No. You don't want CC. At least half the reason is she doesn't want you anymore.

Now you're ready to see Heller. You say, "Where is she?"

"Upstairs. I'll be out until nine. Your housemates will wonder if you return later than nine fifteen." She goes to the door, then smiles. "I wish you a delightful evening, my lord."

You blush. "Thanks."

You take the stairs slowly. Near the top, without trying, you feel Heller's presence. You start to say her name, but that would be silly. She must know the call of your blood. You take a deep breath and open the door.

She lies on her side on a large bed with white covers, facing you, hands folded behind her head, hair loose on the pillows. She's naked. The artist in you approves: pale girl, pale room, dim lighting, red roses on a dresser and a table, a record playing something sung in French by a woman with a husky voice.

You ignore the artist and turn your back. "I said talk!"

"Of course. Before, after, or during?"

"Now! With clothes on."

"You have clothes on."

"With both of us with clothes on."

"You don't like *The Naked Maja*?" The bed rustles. "Is Marilyn Monroe better? The sheets should be red—"

"It's not the pose."

"I thought you couldn't go wrong with Goya. 'Venus on The Half Shell' isn't sexy, and Klimt needs the right fabrics. *The Naked Maja* is so simple. But this is a fairly good Monroe, don't you think?"

"If I looked, I'm sure I would."

She moves again. "Chris?" Her voice is gentle, so you look, ready to turn back if she has another pose ready. She simply sits on the bed with her feet on the floor. She says, "It's not a big deal, really."

You give a cold laugh. "I'm not that bright, but I've figured out it's a big deal. All your dad wants from me is a grandkid."

"So give him one. Then we'll be free to do what we want."

"You, maybe. What about me? He killed Elverado."

"He didn't! I waved good-bye to Elverado on Saturday. I was with Daddy until Sunday brunch."

"He didn't have to do it. He just ordered it. Maybe he didn't even have to do that. But Mather had Elverado killed for your father's sake."

"He said so?"

"Pretty much."

She glances away, toward the lace curtain and the lights of campus. "Then it was necessary."

"Elverado was a kid! An ordinary human kid! It's not like he killed Josh or something. How could killing him be necessary?"

She shrugs. "I don't know. But sometimes you have to do hard things to keep things as they should be."

"Like fucking you."

As she looks down, you hate yourself for saying that. She's the world-princess, but she's still a seventeen-year-old girl. She says, "I'm sorry you think that'd be so bad." She looks up. "But if it's so disgusting, let's get it over with. I'm supposed to be fertile now. Once should do it, if that's all you can stand."

"Then you bite off my head and eat me?"

She laughs, which is nice, because you hoped she would. "Why, yes, Chris, I'm a mutant praying mantis and you should be terrified of me."

"I'm not terrified of you. Well, not if you're not mad at me. I'm terrified of your father."

"Who isn't? But he has a code. No one would follow him if he didn't. He anointed you. He won't go back on that." She hugs herself. "It's cold."

"So get dressed."

"You could put your arm around me."

"You're not going to seduce me."

"You can pretend I'm whoever you want. I don't care."

"That's a lot of the reason I don't want to."

She glances at you. "I do like you, Chris."

"As a kid brother."

"No." She turns slightly away, then looks back. The light is beautiful on her hip and arms. "If there weren't any expectations, would you make love with me?"

"Sure. But you're only willing because of the whole elohim business."

"Because I wouldn't have gotten to know you. Now that I know you, it could be nice."

It could be very nice. Part of you wants her, or maybe will take her since CC isn't available, or maybe simply thinks: Naked willing girl, pounce!

You turn your back.

"Chris!"

"What do you think of Chad Vaughn?"

"He's cute. A little conceited. Why?"

"Do you think he could've killed Josh?"

"No!" She frowns as she looks away. "Daddy says Chad is too soft to be prince."

You laugh. "So he picked me?"

"You grew up poor. You don't know the families. If you had to kill a nef, it wouldn't be someone you'd known all your life."

"He expects me to kill people?"

"No! He expects you to become like him. You only kill when you must."

"Like with Elverado."

"I guess. He got in the way."

"Which makes it all right?"

"It's like getting in the way of lightning. It's sad, but it happens."

You look at her. She's the most beautiful person you've ever seen, naked or clothed, in life or in art, and the blood is calling for you to join her on the bed, but you know you will never choose to answer that call. "Who would kill Josh for Vaughn's sake? His parents? Blaise Selby?"

"We're not going to do it tonight, are we?"

"No."

Heller goes to a chair where her clothes are piled and begins sorting through them. "Let me know when you change your mind."

"Who else would kill Josh?"

"I don't want to talk about it. It makes me sad."

She puts her bra on first, which seems odd, but watching a girl dress is nice. You had always wondered how to fasten bras that clasp behind the backs.

You look out the window, which is less interesting and more satisfying. "How would finding his killer make you feel?"

"If Daddy can't, no one can."

"Maybe one of his people overlooked something. Maybe one of them did it. If we find who it is, we'll take the information to Daddy. Cool?"

She's quiet. You look back at her. She's put on everything except her plaid skirt. You say, "That's a good look for you."

She smiles and steps into the skirt. "Everyone liked Josh. I know little sisters say that, but they really did."

"Uh, I was wondering, if he had married someone, would she replace you?"

Heller gives you a puzzled look. Her look hardens, and you think she would happily watch you die. "I didn't kill my brother."

"I didn't mean that. If he had married, when it was time for him to become El Elyon, who'd be queen? His wife or you?"

Her lips quirk. Then she says, "What do you know about Egyptian royal families?"

"Well, they marry their— Oh."

She nods.

You say, "So someone could've killed Josh to keep you from having to marry him."

"Chris, we're nef, not humans. Everyone knows I want to rule.

Maybe someone hates me enough to kill Josh to prevent that, but if someone hated me, they'd come after me, not Josh, wouldn't they?"

"What if someone wanted to marry you?"

She looks back at the window, but there's nothing new there. "Chad said he loved me. He said he always wanted to be with me."

"Sherlock? Isn't that a motive?"

"Not among us. Mates and lovers aren't expected to be the same."

"Are you still with Chad?"

"Not since he said that."

"Which was when?"

"A little before Josh died."

"Then—"

"It doesn't mean anything! Chad and Josh loved each other!"

"Sure, but if they were jealous—"

"No, Chris. They loved each other. I told you. The rules are different for us. Chad wanted to be with me. And with Josh. It would've been fine."

"Oh. Uh, nobody thought that was perverted?"

"Read about the Greeks and Romans. It's not perverted. It's classical. Do you think it's perverted?"

You shrug and hope you sound cooler than you feel. "Different strokes for different folks, right? But if someone thought it was perverted, would they kill—"

"We're nefs. No one else's rules matter."

"Not to you. But something mattered to someone, or Josh wouldn't be dead."

Thirteen

When you return to Rider House, for the first time in your life, you're grateful for homework. You don't want to think about missing girls or dead boys. You bury yourself in words and history and theory until ten thirty, when you climb into bed and fall asleep almost instantly.

Something wakes you. You look for the clock in the dark. You've barely slept for an hour. You think you should go back to sleep, but you listen.

Someone's in the hall. Probably on their way to the bathroom. You should sleep. But it doesn't sound like they go into the bathroom, because you don't hear water run through the pipes.

It doesn't concern you. Go back to sleep.

You hear another shuffling in the hall. How do you know what concerns you?

Levitz sleeps soundly. Envying him, you get out of bed. The hall light is on to make it easy for Fitzgerald to see boys sneaking in or out of their rooms. The floorboards are cold and the air is cool. You should've put on a robe and slippers.

No light shows under any door. You must be the only one who heard anything. If you heard anything.

There's a faint whispering upstairs and a taste of cigarettes on the air. At least two boys are awake, sneaking smokes. But you thought the sound came from this floor.

A slipper slaps softly on the landing. You're in the middle of the hall with no place to hide. You shouldn't care. If it's Fitzgerald, say you were on the way to the toilet. If it's a boy, he's more guilty than you. But you hate the idea of being caught.

It's Banner. O'Reilly follows him. They'll say something insulting. You wish they wouldn't notice you.

They look through you and keep coming down the stairs.

Is it a game? Did they agree to pretend not to see anyone they met?

You glance at yourself. You don't see anything different. The Invisible Man couldn't see himself, but can Invisible Kid or Invisible Girl? Or is the Amazing Elah Man's power like the Shadow's ability to cloud men's minds?

If you move, will they notice you? They certainly might hear you. You remain still until they go into Vaughn's room. O'Reilly closes the door quietly behind them.

You should go back to bed. There are no good reasons for O'Reilly and Banner to be out. There are plenty of reasons that have nothing to do with you. They wouldn't be happy to see you, no matter what they're doing.

But how many boys are in Vaughn's room? What are they doing? The tinge of cigarette is gone from the air. You don't hear any more strange sounds in Rider House.

You tap lightly on Vaughn's door, so lightly you'd have to be awake and listening to hear it. There's no answer. You try the handle. The door opens. No one is in the room.

Can nefs teleport? A Johnny Cash poster by Vaughn's window makes you remember the song, "Ring of Fire." Down into the burning ring of fire. That always seemed redundant, but the song is still cool.

Vaughn's window is slightly ajar.

You should go to bed. You cross to the window and look out. Shadows move under distant trees. They're not caused by wind.

You lift the window. Someone greased it; it lifts silently. You get onto the sill and leap. You think, Up, up, and away! You land hard on the grass.

You follow the shadows, walking on the balls of your feet, trying to feel what's underfoot before you put your weight down. If you can walk on water, you must be able to walk lightly.

The lawn feels like carpet. You could probably leap twenty or thirty feet easily. But bouncing across campus is not a subtle way to follow anyone, so you don't try that.

The shadows head into the woods. Will there be a midnight party with beer and dope and kids making out? If so, you can go back to your room, jealous and lonely and relieved. You don't want to find Josh's killer. You want to fail to find any hint that Josh was killed, because that is the closest you can come to proving he died by accident.

The shadows merge into the shadows of the woods. You'll lose them if you can't see them.

The woods grow brighter. Colors are muted, contrasts are greater, lines are crisper. Remember the effect for a painting someday.

The shadows are seven boys. Vaughn is their leader.

The trees rustle as you walk under them. The sky is cloudy. You think of campfire stories. The wendigo runs on treetops, something else you should try.

The boys come to a small rise in a field and cross over an abandoned stone fence. You come up slowly, not wanting to surprise them or be surprised. No one's there.

The trees are too far away for anyone to reach, except possibly Vaughn, if his nef powers are like yours. The grass is deep enough for boys to hide in. Did Vaughn realize you were following?

Something disturbs you, a faint vibration or a distant hum. Maybe it's pitched so high that humans can't hear it, but nefs can.

The stone wall is not a fence. A round building stood here, long ago. A tower?

You go to its center, following the strangeness. A big rock has been rolled aside. A stairway leads into the earth. The steps and walls are rough blocks, dark with dirt.

Staring down at the dark passage, you wish you hadn't found it. Maybe it's a trap. Maybe it's not meant to be a trap, but if they catch you, could you escape? Even if no one catches you, will you learn something you'll hate knowing? You want to come back in the morning with an army of Dumont's servants. And wait far away in the sunlight while they go down.

Whatever's disturbing you is there. You feel it like a cold draft.

You hear a murmur, a muted chanting. But that's a new sound, not the strangeness. Vaughn and his friends are down there with it.

If you trusted Mather, you would go tell him everything now. But you have to know what's happening before you can know who you trust.

You go down. The stones are firm beneath you. The air grows colder, damper. You smell decaying things, then a whiff of something burning. The strangeness is stronger with each step.

If someone comes up, you'll learn how fast an elah can run. But if someone comes down, you'll be trapped.

So go down fast, see what's here, and leave. You continue onward, thinking of traps a dark tunnel could hold: poison snakes, hidden pits, ceilings that collapse. You tell yourself the boys wouldn't come down here if it was dangerous.

But it might not be dangerous for them.

Something ahead is flickering.

How long can you stay unseen? You don't feel weaker. You need to know what's happening. Keep walking.

The seven boys are in a round, vaulted chamber. They're wearing sweat suits and running shoes. Light comes from candles in niches in the walls. Vaughn stands at the center by a high table made of rough stones, like the walls. It's the source of the strangeness.

You look closer. It's not a table. It's an altar. On it are a golden cup, a jeweled dagger, and a sheet of wine-red velvet draped over something like a pumpkin.

The boys are chanting. It must be Latin because it sounds a little like Spanish, but you don't recognize any of the words. No, you recognize *"deo."*

The chanting continues long enough for you to realize you can be the invisible prince of the world who might be killed if he's caught in a hidden chamber observing a mysterious ritual and still get bored. How do detectives endure stakeouts? Would it be foolish to go back to your room for an hour? Could you just ask Vaughn in the morning what was happening here?

The chanting stops. Vaughn raises the knife, cuts his wrist, and drips his blood into the cup. It would be anticlimactic if it didn't raise more questions: Who else knows about this? Did Mather hide this from you? Did Dumont? Is Vaughn breaking the rules of the nefilim by creating his own worshippers? Or do all nefs have worshippers? If so, why didn't Dumont tell you to start getting your own? Did he assume you would figure it out? Or did he think you weren't ready? Or did he start your group when his worshippers drank from you?

The cup goes from boy to boy. As each drinks, you feel a web of power grow with Vaughn at its center. Should you stop them? Could you? Even if your blood makes you the strongest nef after Dumont, you know so little. Karate taught you that skill means more than strength. What skill do you have? Vaughn was born to a family who knew what he was. The first steps he ever took may have been on water. Now his disciples magnify his power.

The cup returns to Vaughn. He sets it down, puts his hand on the cloth, says something in Latin, and lifts the cloth.

You gasp, then clamp your mouth shut. If you made a sound, it was covered. Several of the others gasp, too.

A bearded man's head is on the golden platter. Its hair and skin are almost translucent. You think you're looking at Josh Dumont, then remember: "scull" with a "c." They found him intact in the river.

The strangeness comes from it. Perhaps a nef 's power continues so long as flesh or bone survives. The force of the call says this nef was very strong. Was he an elah? How long has the head been here, calling for someone who could hear it?

Did Josh Dumont hear it? Is that why he was killed?

Its eyes snap open. You're too shocked to gasp. Several of the others aren't. A few boys stumble backward. You step sideways to keep from being bumped by Banner.

Vaughn calls, "It's cool! Our lord wakes!"

The eyes are so pale you can't see the pupils. Then you do see them, disks of ice floating in milk. It's watching you.

You wish it would look away. You can't see anything sane in its eyes.

Vaughn sets his hand on top of the head. He grits his teeth as if the touch hurts and pleases him greatly. Something flows from the mad head to him. He must have needed the ceremony with his worshippers to be able to tap it. He looks as mad as the head. If you screamed in his face, you doubt he would hear.

The head's eyes close. Vaughn jerks his hand away. His eyes roll back. He thrashes, then staggers. O'Reilly catches him. Banner grabs his hands as his body goes stiff, bending backward like a bow. Then he falls limp, gasps, and opens his eyes.

The others help him stand. He says, "Not yet. Not enough. But soon. We'll make a new way."

You press yourself against the cold wall as the boys file out. Vaughn drapes a cloth over the head, blows out the candles, and follows the others.

You study the chamber for clues to its history. You see nothing, so you start up the stairs.

The door stone rolls over the entrance. You dart ahead and touch it for no good reason: it's stone, and it's covering the entrance. You're sealed in a chamber in the earth with a living head.

The head's strangeness still calls to you. It has a quality now: despair. You shudder because you share it.

You do not want to go back down to the altar, but the head did not hurt Vaughn. It must be a perfectly harmless living head filled with elah energy.

You don't want to see it again. If it twitches, you know you'll jump, and you might squeal.

But it may have the answers you need.

You go back to the altar and touch the velvet cloth. Someone washed it recently. It smells of soap and sandalwood, or maybe the head does. Without light, the cloth seems black to you. You remember it in the candlelight. Bloodred.

You lift it. The pale head looks like someone made it from wax. The face isn't handsome or ugly. You would think it was just a man if you didn't feel its call. Is it right to say it's the call of the blood when the source looks bloodless and has no heart?

It opens its eyes. The blood is the life. It has life.

You say, "Uh, I'm Chris Nix. I'm the prince of the elohim. I don't have the slightest idea what I'm doing."

The face doesn't change. Someone said it takes more muscles to frown than to smile, but don't muscles get their instructions from the spine?

The eyes focus on you. You have to do something.

You put your hand over the head, say, "I hope you don't mind," and lower your hand. The hair looks wiry, but it's as soft as cotton. Who washes it? The hair could be hiding something disgusting, cockroaches or rats living inside the living head, but you can't let yourself think about that. You continue to lower your hand.

The skull is cool and hard and—

This is Sheol, where the dead go. Sometimes there's light, sometimes darkness. Sometimes you think you're being protected. Sometimes you think you're being used. Light brings different people. Some wear unbleached robes. Some wear armor under white cloth decorated with the red cross of the sun god. Some are boys. All of them dream of a time when peace will come. It's a good dream, but it's not enough to sustain you in Sheol.

Parsees say that when people die, Lord Wisdom judges their spirits. The bad go to torment. The good go to gardens. You wish you had died a good Parsee or a bad one. Even torment would be better than Sheol's emptiness. Surely someone will free you. Surely there's another mystery where you might go.

You loved the desert. You loved to wander through the land of locusts and honey. You bloomed there.

Your thoughts are hungry locusts swarming around a dry flower.

It's time to fly across the desert.

Gardens await you.

Fly—

You're a boy with his hand over a severed head. Its eyes stare at nothing.

You touch the lids. They're dry and delicate. You press lightly to close them. The skin is like dried moths. The head crumbles into powder. It smells like leather.

No, that smell is something else.

You circle the altar. You put your hands next to it as if feeling for heat. One stone is different. In candlelight, you might not notice it. In your shadowless vision, it seems to be outlined.

You touch it, then draw it out. It slides easily, revealing a small chamber that holds a shallow, wooden box.

You lift it out carefully. Whatever is in it makes no sound and doesn't shift. The cover has a gouge. No, an incised drawing. Of a knife.

You open the box. It holds sheets of paper with rough edges. The writing on them is in an alphabet that you've never seen.

But as you look, the words seem familiar.

You blink and look closer. It's like walking into the dark and wanting to see. Your eyes adjust. You can read.

You sit on the floor and begin.

BOOK THREE

The Gospel of the Knife

One

I, Eoda the Knife, write this. Of course you doubt me. Am I not twice dead, hanged by my own hand if you trust Matai, my guts burst open if you trust Luka? Read this as if I lie. Then ask who gains if I do.

In the days when Caesar's pawn, Herodes, ruled the land of Yahudea, the priest Zakaryah was chosen to serve in El's house. He entered the holiest place and saw El's agent by the incense altar.

Zakaryah was terrified, but the agent said, "Be at ease, Zakaryah. Your woman will have a boy. Call him Yohanan. He'll be a nazar who won't drink wine, but will be filled with El's breath. Many will submit to El because of him."

"How can that be? I'm old, and so is Elishaba."

"You question me? You won't speak until all I've said is true."

So Zakaryah became mute and Elishaba, pregnant. Because her man was old, she knew her neighbors would think she had not kept her wedding vow. In shame, she hid in her home, hoping the child in her would die.

Next El's agent went to Maryam, a young woman who lived in a camp of the Holy. He said, "Lucky girl! El will have you! Don't be afraid. They'll call your boy a sky child, a son of El."

She begged him, "Please. I haven't known a man."

The agent had no pity. "El will come. Your cousin is six months pregnant, though everyone thought she was too old. With El, nothing's impossible."

Knowing she had no choice, she said, "You see El's slave. I accept this." When he left, she prepared to flee, but darkness fell on her.

The next day, Maryam hurried to her cousin's home. Elishaba saw her and cried, "El's had you! The child in me jumped because it knows the one in you."

Maryam hid with her cousin for three months, but the seed in her did not die. After Elishaba's son was born, Maryam returned to the Holy Ones and begged Khalpai of David's line to take her. When Khalpai learned that she carried a child, he thought he'd been tricked into marrying a whore. He decided to send her away in the morning.

But that night, El's agent came and said, "Khalpai of David, keep Maryam. Her child is El's. Call him Imanuel so people will know El is with him, and fear and obey him."

Now, in the empire of Parthia, magi watched the sky for signs of what will come. They saw a fravashi, the star of a new soul being born. Its brightness said a saoshyant, a savior from their prophesies, had been born.

Two magi went west. At Hill Salem, they asked Herodes where the new prince lay. His surprise told them they'd been too trusting. They saw he wanted the child to kill or keep as a hostage. When the magi found Khalpai and Maryam, they told them to go south, where Rome and Parthia were weak and El had few worshippers.

In Egypt, Khalpai became Yosef and Imanuel became Esu, names as common as Maryam. For two years, they heard stories of how El punished Herodes. His loins bloated and filled with worms, his bowels burned when he shat, his body itched as if insects hatched in his skin, his lungs were like ovens.

When El let Herodes die, Rome divided Yahudea among

Herodes's heirs. Khalpai thought it would be safe to return if they found a quiet place in the north, in Galil, far from El's house in Hill Salem.

Esu grew up believing he was a common child. He never went farther from home than Sepforis. He only went there when the man he knew as Yosef needed help building a house or its furnishings. He worked when there was work. He watched over his brothers and sisters. He expected to become a builder. He was as content as any child can be.

Two

When Esu was twelve, Khalpai decided to take the family to Hill Salem for the flatbread feast. His hair was gray, and Maryam was stout; who would know them?

In the city, Khalpai told the family, "So much has been rebuilt it should be called Hill Herodes. See El's house there? Herodes doubled its size and expanded the fort at the corner. There in the high city is the old palace, and there, the new. That large pool was once two small ones. There's a theater and a stadium—"

Esu said in awe, "The whole city is El's home!"

Maryam said, "It's the home of the rich, not El."

Khalpai said, "When I show you Caesaria's harbor and theater, Hill Salem won't seem so grand. But there's nothing to rival El's house, not even in Rome. Herodes gave us that much."

"Gave himself," said Maryam.

Khalpai smiled. "But it's ours now."

In El's house, in the people's court, crowds buffeted the family. Bankers changed coins with images of people, beasts, or elahs for coins that had no images to anger El. Dealers sold cows, sheep, and birds to sacrifice. Under the porches, teachers from Yahudea's many sects taught anyone who would listen.

Khalpai bought incense and took the family into the sanctuary, past the wall with its signs warning foreigners in Greek and Latin:

NO STRANGER MAY PASS THESE WALLS. ALL WHO ARE CAUGHT BEAR THE BLAME FOR THEIR FOLLOWING DEATHS.

While Maryam kept the younger children in the women's court, Khalpai took Esu into the men's court. Esu stared in awe at marble walls and doors inlaid with gold and silver. He watched priests kill beasts and sprinkle the blood on the great altar, then give a share of each dead thing to El's fire, a share to themselves, and a share to the buyers for their feast. He saw the three golden wonders: the stand with seven lamps for the seven planets, the table with twelve bread loaves for the months, and the incense altar with its thirteen sweet spices.

Beyond El's bloody altar were the doors to the holiest place. Esu tried to peek in, but its curtain was closed. He studied the embroidery of sky blue, earth yellow, sea purple, and fire red, and all its mystical symbols, and he wondered if you covered a room, what were you worshipping, the room or the cover?

Khalpai gave their incense to a priest and took Esu out. In the women's court, Esu's brother Yakob begged to know what they'd seen. Khalpai said, "Needless death and wasted wealth." When Maryam looked at him, he said, "Let's make the most of this visit. I won't come here again."

Esu heard that and slipped away. In the shade of the porches, he saw people in the pale robes of the Holy. The youngest was a boy who looked like him.

Esu sat to listen, but the Holy Ones stared at him. The eldest asked the boy who looked like Esu, "Do you know him?"

"He's my brother."

A man laughed. "You have no brother."

"They look like brothers," said a woman.

"What's your name?" the eldest asked Esu.

"Esu of Yosef."

"The name means nothing," said the young man.

"He's the right age," said the woman.

"Teachers?" Esu asked. "The right age for what?"

The eldest said, "To be the lost Imanuel."

The boy nodded. "My mother and her cousin were visited by an agent of El who said they'd have sons, and I should be Yohanan, and he should be Imanuel. But Imanuel disappeared with Maryam and her man."

Esu said, "My mother is called Maryam."

The eldest asked, "What does Yosef do?"

"He builds. He's the best builder in Galil."

A woman said, "Khalpai built well."

Esu asked, "Why would Father change his name?"

The eldest said, "To keep you from your destiny."

Yohanan said, "He's not your father."

Esu said, "But if he's Khalpai—"

Yohanan smiled. "Our father is El."

Three

Esu spent the next days with the Holy in the people's court of El's house. The scrolls that had bored him were now a song to his glory. David had been a common boy, but El chose him to kill men, take women, and live in splendor. With Zadok helping him as priest, David had ruled Yahudea. Now Esu was chosen.

When the family left Hill Salem, Maryam and Khalpai thought Esu was in the caravan, but they'd only seen Yakob several times at a distance. When no one could find him, they sent the children on with neighbors and came back to Hill Salem.

They found Esu with the Holy Ones. Maryam called, "Son, why've you treated us so badly? We looked everywhere for you!" Then she covered her mouth in surprise as Esu turned to face her. With the sun in her eyes, she had spoken to Yohanan.

Esu said, "Didn't you think I'd be learning my father's business?"

The eldest of the Holy stepped forward. "It's good to see you well."

Khalpai and Maryam's despair pleased Esu. They had failed to keep his birthright from him. His hands would never be hard, dirty, and scarred like Khalpai's.

The eldest said, "You'll come back to us now."

Maryam said, "No."

The eldest said, “He’ll be lord of all Yahudea. What El wants, who can change?”

“No!” Maryam cried, so loudly that visitors across the court looked their way.

Khalpai stepped beside her. “I’ll go back. Whether you’re in the women’s camp or free won’t change my life as a monk. But I’ll be happier if you’re free.”

Maryam told Khalpai, “We should’ve died on our wedding night.”

“No!” said Khalpai. “You’ll stay free! Our children—”

The eldest said, “Let them decide at thirteen whether to join us.”

Khalpai said, “Who’ll support Maryam?”

“That’s her concern. You and Imanuel will come with us.”

Maryam cried, “No! Yosef, no!”

Khalpai said softly, “I treasure what we had. I always will.”

Maryam turned to Esu. “You were my greatest burden. Don’t make me sorry I bore you this far.”

Khalpai said, “Maryam.”

She whirled to face him. “Should I say I’m glad? I’m not! El’s won!” She looked at Esu, then ran from the court of the people.

Yohanan whispered, “Women are weak.”

Esu didn’t answer. His mother’s last look told him two things. If she’d had a sword and time, all the Holy would’ve fallen before her. But if she could only kill one, she would’ve chosen him.

Four

The Holy sent Esu to the camp called Damascus, like the city. He expected to be treated like a lord. Yohanan told him they were more than others, so they had to do more, not less. When they weren't studying, they worked the fields, trained with weapons for the war between the children of light and dark, and washed themselves for any foul thing done by intent or accident.

Yakob joined them a year later. He fit in so well that the Holy called him Yakob Zadok. But while Yohanan and Yakob Zadok won praise, Esu wrestled with the scrolls.

Why do the first words say elohim made the world and sky, not El alone? Who were the other elahs? Why was El often called Yahu? Who were the sons of elohim who took the daughters of men? What were the nefilim? Why do the sons of elohim disappear from the scrolls after Yahu flooded the world? Why did El say, *To Abraham, Izaak, and Yakob, I appeared as El of the Mountains, but I didn't make the name Yahu known to them*?

Why do the scrolls say elohim made plants, birds, and animals, then men and women at the same time as equals, but then say Yahu made a man, then plants, birds, and animals, and at last a woman to help the man? If the second story is true, why didn't Yahu know the man would need a helper and make the woman right away? Why did Yahu make a garden with a tree of life and a tree of wisdom, then drive out the people who chose wisdom? Why did he have to come down from the sky to learn what was happening in Sodom? Why did he stop Abraham from sacrificing a son, but didn't stop Jepthah from sacrificing a daughter? Why did he reward men like Abraham who lied, Yakob who cheated, Lot who took his own daughters, King Shaul who sent good men to die, King David who had a man killed so he could take the man's woman, and King Salemon who murdered his brother? Why did Yahu tell his people to kill their neighbors, rape their women, enslave their children, and take their goods and land? Why did Yeremiyah write, "How can you say we're wise because we have Yahu's rules, when the scholars' pens write lies?" What lies did scholars place in the scrolls?

Esu took his questions to the Holy. They said to trust them, for he was young and El hid meaning that only they could read. El's anointed prince did not have to understand. He only had to win the war between the children of light and dark. Then judging day would come, El's fallen warriors would be raised to glory, and their enemies would be tortured forever.

One day, following the way of the Holy, Esu took a waste shovel and walked three thousand steps outside Damascus to keep the camp pure. He dug a hole and, holding his robes around him to hide his nakedness, he squatted over it to shit. He knew the only ones who might see him were animals and El. He thought about the next day, resting day, when the Holy don't shit. For some, that meant a day of pain. For those who couldn't hold their shit all day, that meant many prayers and ritual washing to be clean again.

Esu saw the droppings of a wild dog nearby. Beyond them, a rock bore streaks from birds. He saw the grass and knew shit helps plants grow. As he covered his hole, he thought of the life ahead of him. If El made all things, did El make a person filthier than a bird?

Esu threw his shovel aside and walked away from Damascus. Let the Holy anoint a new prince. He would be a builder like the man who tried to save him from this life.

When he reached his home in Galil, Maryam looked on him with horror and fear. He begged her forgiveness. She fed him and told him how he was made by El and how magi called him a saoshyant. When she finished, she said, "Agents will look for you here. Find a land where El's names aren't known. Become something better than El wants you to be."

I was four then. My first memory of my brother is of a young man who ran crying into the night.

Five

Sometimes Esu lived as a builder, sometimes a farmer, sometimes a beggar. Wherever he wandered, his questions followed. His answers lay in the east, so he went there. He visited schools and temples and asked many Mazdans, "How may I learn your truths?"

Some ignored him. Some said their way wasn't for strangers. But in a market in Yazd, a scroll seller heard a magus reject him. When the magus left, the scroll seller said, "Study the Avesta."

Esu said, "I have no money."

The scroll seller laughed. "And I have no copies to sell. Find work with magi if you want to know the Avesta."

"How long would it take?"

"To read? A few weeks, maybe more. To know? A lifetime, maybe more." He saw Esu's face and smiled. "To know its heart? You know it already. Zarathushtra taught it long ago. Good thoughts, good words, good deeds. If you don't know that, the Avesta is worthless. If you truly know that, it's worthless, too."

"I wish to learn Mazda's way."

"Have you learned your own?"

"In the west, I studied many ways."

"Many ways lead to Mazda's gardens."

"And many lead to wastelands."

"Wastelands lie on many ways to gardens."

"But few travelers pass through them without guides."

"It is good to have guides," the scroll seller agreed. "And to be one. Sit, and ask."

Esu sat under the scroll seller's canopy. "Who is Zarathushtra?"

"A man who lived when people believed the world was ruled by many elahs. He said the only elah is Mazda, a name that means wisdom, and all others are false. He said wisdom made us free to choose between truth and lie. You feel those forces war in you whenever you choose between helping yourself or helping others."

Esu frowned. "I heard Mazdans worship many elahs. Mazda the Sky Father, his virgin mate, Anahita of the Waters, their child, Mithra the Sun, their chief agent, the Good Spirit, and many lesser agents."

The scroll seller nodded. "Zarathushtra's teaching left no room for magi who want wealth and praise. After he died, bad magi said Mazda is only the lord of lords. They brought back old elahs and made new ones. They said the temptation that leads us from truth, the Bad Spirit, is an elah, and the Bad Spirit's traits are agents who serve him along with all the old elahs of terror. In that way, bad magi made themselves necessary again."

"We have priests like that in our land."

"Zarathushtra said bad teachers warp the truth, mislead the people, and distract us from good thoughts and deeds."

"What's a saoshyant?"

"One who will come to finish Zarathushtra's work. Some say Zarathushtra will be born again."

"Do you think that?"

The scroll seller laughed. "They say the saoshyant will be born of a virgin and have power so great he'll give life to the dead."

"So it's only a story."

"A story is never only a story. Isn't helping the hopeless giving life to the dead? Isn't anyone who makes the world better a saoshyant?"

"The sects I know would rather help priests than the poor."

"That describes every sect. You're from Yahu's land? You also worshipped many elahs, as a city named for Salem of the Dusk should tell anyone."

"Our priests don't say that."

"I'm sure you heard one history from them. Would you like another?"

"Please."

"When Assyria conquered Hill Salem, they carried the rich Yahudeans to Babel, along with the golden bull statue of Yahu, the city's elah. Life changed little for the people left behind. They still farmed and paid taxes and praised your elohim, El and his mate Asherah, their son Yahu and daughter Anat, and the rest.

"But in Babel, the exiles learned Assyrian ways. They changed the shape of your alphabet. They taught their children old stories in new ways. They learned new holidays. When Persia conquered Assyria, King Cyrus was too clever to say that Mazda had beaten their elah, Marduk. He said Marduk was another of Mazda's names, and they had come, not to conquer, but to bring truth and justice.

"Cyrus sent governors, soldiers, priests, and the children of your exiles to Yahudea and played the same trick. The Persians said El and Yahu were more names of the one Elah, and 'Elohim' was only a title that showed Elah's greatness. They built a temple like those to Mazda, on a high place with a sacred flame, but they called it El's house. They didn't restore your gold bull statue because Mazdans don't worship images. A Persian named Ezra stood in El's house and read from scrolls that he said your people had forgotten. He has another name in your scrolls: Zerubabel, the seed of Babel. He planted Babel's seed in Yahu's land by teaching what magi believe, that Elah has many names and is served by many agents, that there's life after death, that the one Elah will judge everyone after the great war between light and dark. Thanks to him, your people call Cyrus an anointed, though he worshipped Mazda, not Yahu.

"In time, Persia fell to the accursed Alexander. He burned its capital and the world's greatest library, destroying the only complete copies of the Avesta. After Alexander's death, his heirs fell in turn. In Yahu's land, Zadokees took control of the temple from the Persianists, and the Holy Ones split from the Persianists, and each sect mixed old and new teachings to make their own. Now Parthia rules where Persia did, and Rome holds Yahudea, and every land is divided by sects who claim to teach the only true way."

The scroll seller sighed. "Perhaps a saoshyant will come. But even a saoshyant would look on the world's madness and despair."

Six

In Yazd, Esu found stories from many lands about elahs. They took women as they pleased. They favored virgins, widows, and women whose men were away. They showed no interest in their children. Their children grew up to kill monsters and become kings, or to kill kings and become monsters. If his mother's story was true, which sort was he?

One day, a woman stopped him on the street to show him a shawl. She whispered, "Your mother needs a son's help. Go home, live like any man, and no one will care about you. If you understand, pretend you don't want to buy this."

He had questions, but he gestured for her to go. For a day and a night, he thought about what she'd said. The next morning, thinking, Seek, and you'll find, he set out into the city.

When he saw the woman, she ran inside a house and barred the door. Thinking, Knock, and it'll open, he pounded until the door opened a crack.

The woman looked down the street, then said, "Come in," and barred the door behind him. "We'll have to give up this place, thanks to you."

"Who are you?"

"A friend of truth. There are those who'll help you."

"How'll I know them?"

"By their help."

"Do they have a word or a sign?"

"Agents of the Lie love words and signs. What comes will come without warning."

"Why tell me this?"

"Because you may be the saoshyant. Your deeds will tell us if we're right."

"And if I'm not?"

"There'll be others. Some stories promise three saoshyants, each a thousand years apart. Were you followed?"

"How would I know?"

She said again, "Were you followed?"

"No." He didn't know why he was sure, but he was.

"Good. Go."

"But I don't know what to do!"

"The answer isn't in Yazd."

"Is it in Yahudea?"

"It's in you."

"I don't feel it."

"You do. You don't trust it. Free what's in you, and free yourself. Keep what's in you, and kill yourself." She opened the door and pushed him out.

He asked, "What will the agents of the Lie do?"

"Nothing, so long as they don't know if you're Khalpai's son or Yahu's. Your mother has her story. Only you can prove it's true."

She slammed the door. He heard the bar drop and knew that no matter how long he knocked, the door wouldn't open again.

Seven

Esu went home and worked as a builder to feed our family. Mother found him a woman, Marta. He lived like any child of the people. In his thirtieth year, he heard that Marta's sister had left her man. They said she worked sometimes as a hairdresser and sometimes as a whore.

Marta told him, "She's not my sister now."

"Is that your decision to make?"

"She made it, not me."

"Why did she leave her man?"

"He's a bad man. But a good woman takes what El gives."

"No," Esu said, and he went to Hill Salem. He walked into Maryam Hairdresser's room and said, "I'm your sister's man."

She cringed before him. "Please. My shame is my punishment. Don't do more to me."

"I didn't come to judge you. I came to bring you home."

She stared in wonder. He said, "Your father asked me to eat with him. I'll come back for your answer."

Her father was a Persianist called Shimon Jarmaker who lived in the Place of Figs. While Esu ate, he saw the Jarmaker frown at the door. Maryam came in with an alabaster box. She knelt before Esu and began washing his feet. Her tears fell on his skin. She wiped his feet with her hair, and kissed them, and rubbed them with ointment from the box. To buy that box and ointment, she had spent all she owned.

The Jarmaker asked Esu, "Don't you know what kind of woman touches you?"

Esu looked at Maryam, who had nothing, and at the Jarmaker, who kept rich people's respect by throwing out his daughter. He told Maryam, "Let's go home."

They walked away from town. On the road, Maryam said, "You're a child of Elah."

He asked, "What's Elah?"

"The world. Its maker. Its conscience." She laughed. "Why ask me? Who made a woman a priest and forgot to tell her?" Then she saw his tears.

"People make priests," he said. "Elah makes sages, and you're one."

Near River Yordan, a crowd waited to be washed by one of the Holy's good teachers. Esu saw the nazar and knew him. Yohanan smiled back as if they'd been apart for fifteen days, not fifteen years. Yohanan asked, "Brother, have you made mistakes?"

Esu said, "Am I human?"

"If you are ready to be better than you were, mistakes may be washed away."

Esu stepped in the water. Yohanan spoke for all to hear, then pushed him under and drew him up. In that moment, Esu knew his mother spoke the truth.

Eight

That evening, Esu told the story of his life to Yohanan and Maryam Hairdresser. When he was done, Yohanan said, "Your mother took a hard way."

"What do you mean?"

"Her story is mad. Never expect truth from women or strangers. The Mazdans are right in one thing: The Lie is subtle."

"What did Elishaba tell you?"

"That El blessed her."

"Did she say she had a choice in the blessing?"

"El chose her because he knew she would accept."

"Because she wouldn't dare do otherwise."

"Because El knew she was good."

Maryam said, "A good elah gives children to women through the men they love."

Yohanan asked her, "Are you sorry that Esu and I live?"

"The child doesn't justify the mother's rape."

He sighed and turned to Esu. "You should have grown up in our camps and stayed far from women."

"Can you answer her?"

"What's to answer? El is good."

"The world is good. Is the world's elah good?"

"I had questions, too, when I was young. I asked El for clarity."

"In a dream?"

"In the country. I go out, and he finds me. You should go, too."

Esu laughed. "And be made mute, or a salt column, or worse?"

Yohanan said. "Are you afraid?"

"The scrolls tell us to fear El. What do I do?"

"Find a quiet place. Fast. Call for him. He'll come."

Nine

For forty days, Esu fasted with birds and beasts for company. Then a visitor came who walked like a youth but looked like a man of years. He said, "Are you a child of El?"

"Aren't we all?"

The visitor pointed at a rock. "Tell that to be bread."

Esu tossed his head back. "The scrolls say we don't live on bread, but on Yahu's words."

The visitor took Esu to El's house in Hill Salem, to the wall above Valley Kedron. "Jump. The scrolls say Yahu's agents watch over you. They'll carry you in their hands so you won't stub your foot on a stone."

"They also say, don't test Yahu."

The visitor took Esu to Mount Gad and said, "All lands are mine. They can be yours. All you must do is bow to show who you serve."

"Go away, tester. The scrolls say to serve Yahu only."

The visitor set his hand on Esu's shoulder. His face burned in the sunlight. "I am Yahu."

Esu stood before a fire that could consume him. He dropped to the ground, crying, "Lord, forgive me!"

"Rise." Yahu pointed to a rock. "Tell that to be bread."

Esu said, "Be bread," and the stone was a loaf so fresh he could smell it.

Yahu pointed at the rocks below. "Jump."

Esu jumped. Winds caught him like an open scroll and carried him back to the mountaintop.

Yahu said, "You and Yohanan will raise the people and drive out those who serve other elahs. Kill the men, take the women and children, and press on. Cross the seas and take far lands. With their gold and silver, build fleets and armies. Wherever you go, level strange temples, kill strange priests, destroy strange elahs. Ring the world in houses of my worship. Give the world my peace, and I'll be pleased with you, Imanuel, my son."

Ten

Esu returned and told this to Yohanan and Maryam Hairdresser. Yohanan said with satisfaction, "The end begins."

Esu said, "If we begin it. Yahu wants war."

"The war of light and dark. We saw it coming."

"Did you see which side you'd be on?"

"We're children of the light!"

"Who unleash war, death, famine, and plague?"

"Yes! The dark grows stronger every day!"

"Shouldn't we work to weaken it every day?"

"We do."

Esu laughed. "How? By hiding in camps like the Holy? We should go through towns and cities, teaching people to love and share."

Maryam smiled, but Yohanan frowned. "It's not what Yahu wants."

Maryam said, "Is war the only way to bring peace?"

Yohanan said, "Our enemies will attack if we don't."

"Maybe not," Esu said. "We have our power."

"Which threatens them."

"Then we should use it in ways that don't. Let the rich think we're sheep. Let's teach love and sharing. Let's build bands to spread our word. And when we're ready, we'll rise in such numbers that no one will dare oppose us."

"Is that what Yahu wants?"

"He said to raise the people and kill those who oppose us. If people join us, his agents will see us doing his wish."

"And if people don't answer your call for peace?"

"Then we'll give the call for war."

Eleven

At the Holy camp called Damascus, Maryam Hairdresser went with the women, and Esu went to the meeting house. When he said the war between the children of light and dark had begun, they cheered. When he said they would win with words, the cheers died.

The eldest said, "We've fought with words for years."

"You've waited for the world to destroy itself. That's a strategy for vultures, not eagles."

"The world would've destroyed us otherwise. Now you say it's time to win, but you'll avoid the fight?"

"If we call for fighters, Rome will come in strength. My power and Yohanan's are limited. Don't you think we would turn their swords into plows if we could? They're many, they're rich, and they know war."

Esu picked up a stone, turned it into bread, and took a bite. "But we can inspire people. We can feed them. We can gather so many to our side that the invaders will flee like a wolf chased by dogs."

"How long will your way take?"

"It comes when it comes."

"We've trained for war. We're ready now!"

"War can't tell good from bad or light from dark. That's why the Lie loves war."

"War will reveal the light!"

"Where's the light in death, maiming, torture, rape, robbery, and plague?"

"You say Yohanan agreed to this?"

"Yes."

"Then the good teacher is revealed as the bad teacher, and you are the man of the Lie."

"You won't help us?"

"If your way proves itself, we'll help. But we can't abandon our way. We're a refuge for good in this bad world. We have the scrolls. We can't throw that out for your whim."

"Am I your prince?"

The elder shrugged. "That's what we've wondered since we found you."

Twelve

Yohanan stayed by the river. Crowds came to hear him. Even Zadokees and Persianists came.

He taught, "Change yourself, because Elah's rule is coming. If you have two coats, give one to someone who has none. If you have food, share it with someone who's hungry." He told tax men to be honest. He told soldiers, "Don't hurt people, don't lie, and be content with your pay."

Herodes Antipas, Rome's tetrarch of Galil and Perea, saw the threat. Whose pay should his soldiers be content with? How can a ruler be served by soldiers who won't hurt people? What's left for the rich if everyone shares? What happens to Caesar's rule if Elah's rule comes? Antipas locked up Yohanan in Fort Black.

Then Antipas heard of a strange nazar called Esu of Father. He did not cut his hair or wear dyed clothes, but he kept company with women, tax men, and mistake-makers. Some called him a bandit, Rome's name for rebels. Some called him a rainmaker, the people's name for fakers. Some called him Yahudea's anointed prince.

He taught, "If you want to be perfect, sell all you have and give to the poor." But who will serve Caesar if hoarding wealth is wrong? He taught, "Give Elah what is Elah's, and give Caesar what is Caesar's." But if the world is Elah's, what's left for Caesar?

Antipas sent word to Pontius Pilatus in Yahudea, Herodes Filipos in the north, and Kaifa the high priest of El's house. All of Caesar's pawns knew to watch for the strange nazar and seize him if they could.

Thirteen

Esu learned from Yohanan's capture. He kept away from cities and wandered so no one knew where he might appear.

A band grew around him. Because they followed a nazar, they were called nazars. Because they lived simply and shared everything, they called themselves the Poor.

First Marta agreed to Esu's marriage with Maryam Hairdresser, and they were three. Then Andreas, who had followed the Washer, chose to follow Esu instead. Shushana, cast off by her family after she was raped, found a new family with them. Andreas's brother, a man so strong and simple that everyone called him Rock, quit the rebel Sons of Yonah to join the Poor. Yoana, wife of Antipas's steward, left her man for Esu's sake. Rock brought his wife, then convinced two of the rebel Sons of Thunder to become Poor. From the sea came the half-Greek, half-Yahudean Filipos. From the fields came Netanel, a worker who said it was easy to stop being poor in order to be Poor.

His family thought Esu was mad, but we soon saw his cunning. So Mother Maryam came with his sisters, Salema and Tabitha. Yosi came with his woman and children. Yakob Zadok came from the Holy.

Last to come were his rebel brothers. Shimon came from the

Zealots. And I, Eoda, sometimes called Twin because I look like Esu, came from the assassins called the Knives.

When we came, we knew only this: Esu was a child of the people, not a child of the rich. He had power from Elah because he taught we are all children of Elah. He said we would inherit the world. What did we care for the past? Let priests and scholars debate the nature of El, Yahu, and Elohim. We had Esu, Elah, and our mission to make a better world. We had more than we had known we could want.

As Esu wandered, he mastered his power. When the first blind man came to him, he spat on the man's eyes and touched him, but the man only saw people like walking trees. Esu had to touch his eyes twice to make him see clearly. Later, he used spit to heal a mute's tongue. But in time, Esu healed with only a touch, then with only a word, and then with only a wish.

Stories spread of his power. He told fishermen where to find a better catch. He made wine at his wedding to Maryam Hairdresser. He turned a few bits of bread into many. He calmed a storm. He walked on water. He raised the dead.

As the stories were told, his greatness grew. When people said he healed a madman, they said the madman was possessed by a demon named Legion who was cast into a herd of pigs and drowned. All who heard that knew what to think: Esu's magic could defeat a Roman legion. Who else should be anointed prince?

Fourteen

One day at Rock's house in Town Nahum, Esu said, "Let's scatter to spread the seed. Then we'll gather the crop."

Rock asked, "Who'll believe our words without seeing your power?"

Maryam Hairdresser said, "They don't need to see. They'll hear his truth."

Esu said, "You'll have both words and power." He took a knife, cut his arm, and held it over a cup half-filled with water. As the drops fell, he quoted the scrolls, "The soul of the flesh is in the blood. I've given it for you to make amends on the altar for your souls, because the blood atones for the soul."

He lifted the cup. "Drink and pass it on."

We were troubled, but we trusted him. I took the cup after Shushana and drank.

I was light bound in flesh, surrounded by uncountable lights, each caught in darkness. The brightest was Esu. My light was not as great as his or Maryam's or Yakob Zadok's. But I saw I was more than I'd known. In that, I was like every living thing, an eternal spark caught in something beautiful and delicate.

The light dimmed. I was only a man, sitting in a yard, lowering a cup from my lips. The yard pulsed with life. Nothing needed doing there. But beyond the walls were wrongs and illness and madness and death. We were warm in a room with family while friends were lost in a storm.

The rest of that day was the finest we had known. Water was made wine, and stones became bread, and we had songs and dancing. When night came, many pairs went walking with smiles that were wider when they returned to sleep in Rock's house.

Fifteen

Seventy went out in pairs to teach and heal. When the power of the blood faded, we returned to Galil and gathered by the lake. Our joy was great, until we saw Esu.

He placed a bundle before him. “This is the gift of the Herodians.” When he lifted the cloth, we saw the head of Yohanan Washer. Esu said, “Antipas has shown his masters that he can answer power with power.”

Andreas shouted, “They can't answer Elah's power!”

Rock shouted, “Call fire on Rome!”

Yakob of Thunder shouted, “Flood Caesar's cities!”

Yohanan of Thunder shouted, “Let the war of light and dark begin!”

But Esu said, “Can't they? The scrolls say the rich have always had their way. If Elah can do anything, why hasn't he changed that?”

“So we may be free to choose,” Maryam Hairdresser said. “If we are to learn, Elah cannot act.”

“Yet the scrolls say Yahu sent flood and fire.”

Rock said hesitantly, “Yahu stopped acting long ago.”

“Then where is the power of the sages from? Where is my power from?”

“From Elah!”

"Does Elah want an unjust world?"

Rock squinted at Esu and did not answer. Maryam shouted, "No!"

Esu looked at each of us, then said, "I must tell you things that are for your ears only." Then he told what he learned from his mother, the scroll seller, the Parthian woman, and Yahu. As he spoke, people gasped in pity or outrage. The only calm face was Yohanan Washer's.

When Esu finished, a man cried, "This is madness! El does not have human children! El is not like the gods of strangers!"

Yakob Zadok called, "Think! You know Esu's good!" But many of the seventy left then in shame and anger.

All who stayed were troubled. If Esu's story were true, how could we hope to win?

Rock stood. "Teacher! Do you know the one who appeared to you is Yahu?"

Esu looked at his hands, then at Rock. "He's like Yahu and El in the scrolls. He's more powerful than a storm. His power and knowledge have limits. His pride and rage don't."

Andreas asked, "Could he be the tester? Or a spirit? Or a magus?"

Esu said, "In the old stories, Yahu of the Mountain is the son of El, lord of all. The scrolls call Yahu a jealous elah. His jealousy may have driven him to steal El's name."

Filipos said cautiously, "In Greek stories, the sky father killed his own father to become lord of elahs."

Rock stared at him. "Yahu killed El?"

Filipos said, "Some who call themselves the Wise say Elah is the All-One, but a lesser elah rules the world and claims to be its lord. This lesser elah has many names. One is Yao."

Maryam said, "Like Yahu?"

Filipos shrugged. "It could be."

Esu said, "Even if Yahu killed his father, he could never kill Elah, the maker of all, who made men and women in the image of elohim." Esu looked around the circle. "Elah lives in you." He looked at the lake and the hills. "In everything. If Elah was dead, wouldn't the green die and the air rot?"

Rock said, "Is Yahu your father?"

"I felt that was true when he said it."

"Then Yahu can't be the Lie!" Rock cried. "Anointeds can't be sons of the dark!"

Esu said gently, "Anointeds need oil in their hair and people to rule. That's all the name means."

Rock's gaze never left him. "Please. Are you the Lie's son?"

Esu nodded.

Maryam called, "No! Mose said the child doesn't bear the parents' mistakes. What if Esu and Yohanan were fathered by Yahu? They're still Elah's children! Know them by their deeds, yes? You've seen their work!"

An older man stood and told Esu, "To rule the world, what bad lord wouldn't pretend to be good? You give us hard sayings. Who can hear them?" He turned to us. "If you follow him, you'll die, stoned as blasphemers or staked as traitors."

Maryam said, "The truth will live."

"What good's truth if those who know it are dead?" The man left with others, and our band was small again.

Sixteen

People said Esu was mad and only his maddest followers stayed with him. They said he claimed to be El's living son. Some said he claimed to be El.

Esu said, "Let's go where no one will find us," so we sailed to Dalmanutha. The next morning, people came asking for him. Shimon whispered, "It's good Esu's a healer. We would starve if he told fortunes."

We went into the house where Esu stayed. I told him, "You've been found already. More Persianists and Zadokees want to see your power."

"To see it fail. Send them away."

Rock said, "They'll think you're hiding."

"Even Persianists and Zadokees can be right."

Maryam laughed. "You're not hiding well."

"True," Esu agreed. He went out and told the crowd, "At dusk, you say we'll have good weather if the sky's red. At dawn, you say we'll have bad weather if it's overcast. You fakers can read the sky, but you can't read the signs of our time? Cruel and contrary people need magic shows. I won't give any more."

One of them shouted, "Because you can't!"

"If a fish swallowed me like Yonah and spat me out, what would it prove? That I'm good or wise? It would prove I'm poor food for fish."

We went north, following the Yordan out of Antipas's territory and into his brother Filipos's. We wondered where Esu would stop our flight, but we didn't ask. There was nothing for us in the old lands of Isroel and Yahudea.

We made camp near the Lone Mountain and the towns of Caesaria Filipi, where Canaanites had worshipped an elah of the storm. Later, Greeks came and said an elah's son was born in a cave at the foot of the mountain. They built a temple and called the place Panias in honor of him.

Esu said he would spend the night praying on the mountain. Many of us chose to do the same. I found a place not far from him.

While I was alone, I thought about the old elah of this mountain. Was he glad for Pan's company? Was he jealous of Pan's temple? Did Canaanites still worship him? Did he know Esu had come? Did he hope Esu would stay? Did people still sacrifice to him? Did he want the blood of animals or people? The scrolls say Yahu demanded Abraham's son, then spared the child as the knife began to fall. Was the story remembered because Yahu rarely spared children?

A sound made me fear for Esu's safety. I ran to see him facing a visitor. Esu's face was calm. The visitor wore a pale robe like Esu's. In the moonlight, it glistened whiter than snow, whiter than any bleached cloth. I wanted to flee, but I stayed. Call me brave, if you're kind, but I feared running would make them notice me.

Esu said, "I waited, Gavriel. You didn't come."

The visitor said, "What have you learned from Yohanan's fate?"

"The price of disobedience."

A second visitor stepped into the light. His robes glowed brighter than the others. So did his hair and beard. He looked like the Washer and Esu. I knew him before he spoke. Yeremiyah may be right that the scrolls include lies, but I will vouch for the terror in those who see Yahu.

Esu said, "Father. What should I do now?"

"What I've wanted."

"Is there another who can be priest?"

"Choose one, if it's useful."

"The scrolls say it's necessary."

"Scrolls say what we say they say. The Persian saoshyant and the Samarian tahev don't need companions. Why should an anointed?"

"Father, if you want war, I need the Holy and the Persianists. They expect two anointeds. Zekaria's scroll says two anointeds stand by the lord of the whole earth."

"Then choose someone you can remove when your sons are grown. Let Marta's start a new line of princes, and Maryam's, a new line of priests."

Seventeen

The next day, the band knew two men in white had met Esu on the mountain, and someone must serve as Esu's Zadok.

Yakob and Yohanan of Thunder came to Esu with their mother, Elishaba. Yakob said, "Let us sit by you. It doesn't matter who's on the right or the left. If one of us falls, the other can take his place."

Esu saw the band would be torn if this was not decided. He chose Rock to be his Zadok. Then he said we would begin Yahu's war by seizing El's house during the passover feast.

Maryam said, "You're willing to give Yahu praise and war?"

Esu said, "If we don't, he'll find someone worse to serve him. When the war's won, we'll convince Yahu to follow Elah's way. If not, we must kill him."

Rock said, "Can Yahu be killed?"

"Every land has stories of the death of elahs."

"What if Yahu is Elah?"

"If he knows everything and can do anything, he knows and wants us to do what we're doing."

Maryam said, "Must we fight his war?"

"The scrolls say Yahu doesn't turn from a goal or think past one. He burned babies and pregnant women in Sodom. He turned Lot's woman to salt for the crime of looking at her home. He flooded the world and only let a few worshippers escape. Now he wants the last war. We must survive to save as many as we can from his wrath."

Marta said, "Maybe Yahu said he wants war to test us, like telling Abraham to kill his son."

Esu said, "He tests for obedience. He loved Abraham because Abraham agreed to kill his son. He loved Yob because Yob praised him for every cruel thing that Yahu did."

Rock said, "He'll love you when you give him the last war."

"Only after he has it. Cain gave Yahu fruit instead of blood. Onan refused to rape his brother's woman. Yahu punished them both." Esu studied us. "If you want to go, go now. If you follow, be ready to lose your life. In this fight, I'll have no power to spare, not even to save one I love."

We all promised to stay.

Esu said, "When the war is over, the survivors will drink of health, life, and power. The war may be long. But some who stand here won't taste death until this people's child has come into his home, and the world is a garden again."

Eighteen

The next day, we went south to Samaria. At Shokar, the Samarians said Rome was too strong in Yahudea. They wanted the first blow to fall in their land. Esu said Yahu wanted the attack in Hill Salem. They said the city didn't matter because El's true home was their mountain. Esu said a victory in Hill Salem would bring the world to our side. They said a loss there would end all our hopes.

The Sons of Yonah and Thunder were loudest in their disgust. Yohanan said, "Rain fire on them, as Eliyah did!"

Yakob added, "When other towns hear, they'll obey you."

Esu said, "I serve Yahu, but I won't abandon Elah."

Andreas said, "Now you say we can serve two lords?"

Esu nodded. "Because we hate one and love the other."

The next day, as we were leaving Samaria, ten Samarian and Yahudean lepers stood far off, calling, "Of Father! Teacher! Pity us!"

Esu told them, "Go show yourselves to the priests."

As they went, their skin grew ruddy and smooth. One Samarian ran back and dropped on his face at Esu's feet, thanking him and El.

Andreas said, "I thought you weren't going to give more shows."

Esu said, "We might take Hill Salem without Samarians, but we'll never hold it without them. Those ten will tell everyone what happened here."

Nineteen

Yakob Zadok returned and told Esu, "Maryam says, 'One you love is sick.' It's Lazar. They want you to come."

But Esu said to wait. For two days, a band that could move in minutes waited for his word. Then he said at last, "Let's go to Yahudea. My friend sleeps. I must wake him."

Filipos said, "If he sleeps, he'll be fine."

Esu said, "He's dead."

Near Yeriho, a crowd waited. The failure of the seventy had not destroyed Esu's reputation. It gave new stories. What were the hard sayings that drove off his followers? Could a Galilean give endless life? Could the father of Of Father be El? Had someone come at last to drive Roman demons from Isroel's body?

A man climbed a sycamore to see us. Esu looked up and said, "Zakai, hurry down. We'll stay at your house today."

People murmured that the nazar was going to be the guest of a collaborator, a rich tax man. Zakai came down and told Esu, "Look, sir, I give half my goods to the poor. If I take anything by mistake, I pay back four times as much."

"Then you're forgiven. This people's child has come to find what was lost."

The crowd murmured louder. What we'd all lost was our freedom.

We left Yeriho the next morning. A blind man called Of Timai sat begging by the road. Hearing the crowd, he asked what was happening. When he heard Esu of Father was going by, he began to cry, "Of Father, David's son, pity me!" People told him to be quiet, but he cried louder, "David's son, pity me!"

Esu said, "What do you want?"

He answered simply, "Sir, I want to see."

Esu touched Of Timai's eyes. "Have your sight and go. Your faith has made you whole."

Of Timai looked around. "Thanks to Elah and David's son, I see!"

Of Timai followed us out of Yeriho, praising Esu and making the people cheer for David's son. They wouldn't go back until Esu said to look for him at El's house.

Esu sent most of the band to Efraim, where the rebels were strong. The rest of us went to Place of Figs, where Marta came out to meet us. She said, "Lazar's been in his grave for four days. You let him die."

"He'll rise again."

"Do you think I'm a Zadokee now? I know he'll rise on judging day. And I know you let him die now. You didn't come."

Maryam ran from the house. Shushana, Yoana, Salema, and some neighbors followed her.

Shushana told us, "She wanted to go to his grave to cry again."

Maryam fell down at Esu's feet, crying, "If you'd come, he wouldn't have died."

Esu's face was like a lake swept by a storm. "Where does he lie?"

"This way." Shushana led us out of town. We all followed. Esu walked alone and wept. A neighbor said, "See how he loved him!" But another asked, "Couldn't a man who opened the eyes of the blind have kept his friend from dying?"

Esu groaned when we came to a cave with a stone over the

entrance. Then he nodded, and his face grew calm. "Take away the stone."

Marta said, "By now, he stinks." She added more loudly for everyone to hear, "He's been dead four days. You brought the others back within a day of their death."

When we moved the stone, we found Marta was right. We covered our mouths and noses and hurried back.

Esu lifted up his eyes. "Maker. Thank you for hearing me." He cried out, "Lazar! Come out!"

We waited. Then a man wrapped in grave clothes walked into the light.

Esu said, "Help him." Only those who knew Esu heard the strain in his voice.

Esu saw me staring at him. I thought, You let a friend die and made his sisters mourn for days to give people a story. I said, "No one should envy you."

He nodded, turned, and started back. While the others helped Lazar, I followed Esu, close enough to catch him if he stumbled. He never did.

Twenty

The next day, we set off, rejoicing and praising Elah. Esu rode a donkey, and Rock rode its colt. People began joining us before we left Olive Hill. They cried "Bring peace from the skies!" and "Glory in the highest!" and "Bless the one who comes in the lord's name!" If Romans or Herodians asked, the lord was Elah. Yahudeans knew the lord was David, and Esu came in his name.

At Damascus Gate, Esu looked up at El's house and shouted, "Hill Salem, I bring you peace! You'll be the capital of the world."

In the city, we heard shouts of, "Who's this?" and answers of, "Esu of Father, nazar of Galil, son of David, son of Elah!" Some spread their clothes along the street. Others cut branches from trees and lay them before Esu and Rock. People shouted, "Save us! Bless Lord David's land! We need you now! Let the skies hear it!"

We rolled into El's house like a flood. The people's court was busy with worshippers, priests, bankers, sellers, and beasts for sacrifice. Blind and crippled people came to Esu. As he healed them, children shouted, "Save us, David's son, save us!"

A small man watched from the shade of a porch. When I worked in Hill Salem as my uncle's clerk, I served many Herodians. This one was called Shaul of Tarsus.

Twenty-One

The next morning, at El's house, Esu sat near the treasury chests. Near every gate were people from our band, the Holy camps, Galil, and Yeriho. Soldiers on Fort Antonia watched, smiling and calling to each other, as relaxed as armed men on watch can be. Esu told Rock, "We'll be anointed here, where all can see."

As he spoke, several Herodians cast shekels into the treasury. Then a poor woman threw in two lepta. Esu said, "She gave more. They gave from their wealth. She gave from her poverty." He looked at the bankers. "This is wrong."

Rock said, "It's El's house."

"It's not greed's house." Esu picked up pieces of cord and twined them together. "Tomorrow is Yahu's. Today is mine." He told the nearest banker, "Take this away! Our father's house isn't a market!"

The banker said, "I know you, Of Father. Don't worry. Your father gets his share. The priests collect it for him."

Esu slapped the cords on the table. "You made this a bandits' den!" He flipped the table, scattering boxes and coins, and shouted, "Clean our father's house!"

The people joined him. Tables and stools were turned. Sheep, oxen, and people were driven out. Priests, bankers, and Herodians fled. Within moments, we held El's house.

After Rock and Esu were anointed, Esu went on the wall. He

called, "The promises of the scrolls come true in me! I, Esu of Father, a nazar of Elah, am your prince! If you thirst, come drink. If you hunger, come eat. We'll open the storerooms and treasuries. There'll be enough for all!"

The crowd cried, "This is the anointed!" and "Esu of Father is Esu Anointed! Isroel has its anointed prince!"

Twenty-Two

Then soldiers came from Antonia's tower with shields and clubs. The people screamed. Esu told us to flee into the sanctuary.

We ran through the men's court and into the priests' court. The sacrificing had stopped. Beasts were still tied to the slaughter rings. Bodies lay on tables and hung on hooks. Bowls of blood waited to be splashed on the great altar.

Esu opened the curtain that hid the holiest place and led us in. The room was like an empty storeroom. Esu went to the wall near the incense altar. At his touch, stones slid back without a sound. They revealed a passage narrow enough to make a wide man turn sideways and low enough to make most men stoop.

As the women entered, I looked back into the holy court. Two Galileans were stealing the priests' golden tools. Soldiers ran in, and clubs began to fall. I started to look at the tunnel to see how many of us waited to go in. A club shattered a Galilean's head. His blood hit the great altar.

Esu gasped.

The clubs kept falling. A Galilean fell against the great altar, adding his blood to the gore on its side.

Esu gave another gasp. His eyes stared without seeing. I knew the gasp this time. It was pleasure.

He shook himself, and we ran into the tunnel. When he closed the way behind us, I asked, "What are you?"

"Your brother."

"Blood feeds you."

"Death feeds elahs. Worship, too. Temples and altars are granaries to us. Assyrians destroyed the first Yahu's house, and the sacrifice ended. Zerubabel wanted an incense altar, like in Persian temples, but the great altar was rebuilt. The slaughter resumed with animals instead of humans."

"Did you expect this?"

"No. I thought stories like the sacrifice of Jepthah's daughter were only about Yahu's cruelty."

"When two women claimed a baby, Salemon said to cut it in half. That satisfied one, so he knew the other was the mother. The story only makes sense if the first woman thought it better to sacrifice half a baby than none."

"Don't fear me, Eoda. I'm not my father. If I was, Romans would be fleeing, not us."

Twenty-Three

The tunnel ended in Valley Hinnom near the smoke and stench of the pits. I thought we would flee to the north. Instead, Esu took us up to the city. If anyone saw us, they thought we had used the latrines of the Holy. They passed through Holy Gate so often that many called it Shit Gate.

At the Holy house, the elder greeted Esu with, "Lord, welcome! Tomorrow, the war, and El will rule! Who can stop it now?"

"Who, truly?" Esu said. He looked at me.

In the evening, we met in the upper room. Esu said, "I'm glad we can have this meal together. We may not eat like this again. We face the great war, and war separates people."

Rock said, "Everyone's worried, but I'm not. I'll go where you go, to prison or death."

Esu looked at his hands, then at Rock. "Be careful. The tester wants you. When I sent you without money, sack, or shoes, did you lack anything?"

Yakob of Thunder said, "A sword."

Rock said, "Look! Here are two!" He showed us swords that the Holy kept hidden.

Yakob of Thunder said, "Can you make more from them, like with bread?"

When Esu didn't answer, Yohanan of Thunder said, "No need. I'll sell my cloak tomorrow and buy a sword."

"It's enough." Esu looked at us and said, "One of you must betray me. Today was the first day of Yahu's war. I wish it was the last. I see unending battle and unending blood. I don't have the power to stop it, only to fight it. But who does war feed?"

"The rich!" Rock cried.

"Caesar!" said Andreas.

"We'll bring Elah's peace!" Yakob of Thunder shouted, waving his knife.

Esu nodded wearily and looked at me. We had been eating like friends at a feast, dipping bread into bowls and offering bits to each other. He said, "One who dips his hand with me in the dish will betray me. Every people's child goes as it's written, but pity the one who betrays a people's child! He has more to bear than any other."

I asked with everyone else, "Is it I?"

"It's one I love." He dipped bread and offered it to me. "What must be done, do quickly."

So I ate the bread he gave me.

Esu said, "I have a new order. Love each other as I've loved you."

Andreas said, "You say this after telling us there's a traitor in the band?"

"Yes. Remember what I've said of love." Esu took a cup and filled it with wine and blood. "Take this, and share it." He gave it to me and held my eyes. Then he took bread and gave thanks, and broke the bread and gave pieces to us. "Eat, and remember me." He pointed to the cup. "This is the new pact in my blood. I shed it gladly to set things right."

I drank and felt the power of his blood burn into mine, and passed the cup on. We all glowed like one light in our love for all life. Then the cup returned to Esu.

He said, "You trust Elah, so trust me. If I fail, our maker will send more comforters, sages, saoshyants, tahevs, and anointeds. They'll always come with truth that the world denies, but you know."

I said, "Show yourself to the world! Tell the truth where all can see and hear."

He looked at his hands, then said, "This world's lord would burn it to hide the truth. But so the world may know its true maker, I'll do what I must." He smiled. "If my death comes, my life will still tell people about mistakes and goodness and justice. I have so much to say, but you can't bear it now. Listen to the spirit inside you. It'll guide you."

Rock said, "You can't fall. You're the anointed!"

"Ah, Rock. Elah loves you for your faith." Esu looked up. "Maker, the hour's here. Help us to help you. As you've given us power, let us show everyone the true elah. Fill us with the strength you had before the world was. Keep my brothers and sisters from mistakes and mistake-makers. Wash them with truth. And the power that you gave me, I've given them, so they may be one. Maker, the world hasn't known you, but I and my friends have. Let the love you've shown me be with them."

Then we sang a song that Esu loved and left the Holy house.

Twenty-Four

I found Shaul of Tarsus at Kaifa's house with my uncle Nikodimos, some men of the Sanhedrin, and some Zadokee guards. Kaifa asked them, "Why haven't you brought him?"

An officer said, "He disappeared in El's house."

"Because you let him slip away."

"He's no ordinary man."

Then I told them how to take him.

To know what happened to Esu while I did what he asked, I must sift through the stories that Constantine approved for use in his empire.

I can believe Esu told the band, "Sit here while I go and pray." Marta and Maryam would have let him go. They loved him. They wouldn't have let him go if they had known his plan. I loved what he wanted to be, and I could barely obey him.

Rock and the Sons of Thunder loved what they wanted him to be. They would have insisted on going with him. So I can believe he said something like, "My soul's very sad. Stay and watch with me." He might very well have fallen on his face and prayed loudly enough for them to hear, "Maker, all things are possible for you. Let this pass. Still, don't let it be as I want, but as you do."

I can believe he would have returned to find Rock and the others asleep. They would have wanted to rest for the next day's fight.

As for the agent who appears in some copies of Luka's story, an agent of Yahu may have come to warn Esu what would happen if he turned away from war. If so, in his agony, Esu would have prayed harder. His sweat might have fallen like beads of blood to the ground.

I wish I could think Elah sent an agent to say that all Esu believed about love and peace was true. But Esu would have been disappointed then. An elah who intervenes is not an elah who wants people to learn to be free.

I want to believe Esu told the sleeping band, "Sleep on and rest. The hour's come, and this people's child has been given into the hands of mistake-makers." But if he said that while they slept, who could have heard?

I can believe he said, "Get up. See, he's near." But the written words look like calm acceptance. If he spoke them, his voice must have mixed dread with his relief that I had obeyed.

Twenty-Five

I led Shaul, Kaifa's slaves, and soldiers from Antonia to the grove that Esu loved. We carried lanterns, torches, swords, and staffs. We were bright enough and loud enough to warn him, if he had wanted to wake the band and flee. But he waited for us.

Walking to him was easy. Talking was impossible. I stood still until he said, "Brother, do what you came to do."

I kissed him in greeting. "Teacher."

"Don't call me that."

"I couldn't do this for my brother. Only for my lord."

He smiled. "Ah, Eoda, are you betraying this people's child with a kiss?"

I couldn't answer. I couldn't finish his task. He had to go alone to the soldiers and ask, "Who're you hunting?"

The Roman said, "Esu Nazar."

"I'm he."

Two soldiers took Esu's arms. Around us, people were waking. Yohanan of Thunder raised his sword and called, "Sir, do we fight?"

The Roman said, "If you don't want to be taken, too, go now!"

Rock drew his sword. "I won't leave!" He swung at a slave named Maleh and cut off his ear.

Esu said, "Sheath that! I could have asked Elah for twelve legions of agents, if I wanted war!" Esu picked up Maleh's ear and healed it. While the soldiers watched in wonder, Rock sobbed and ran off.

Returning to Hill Salem, I wondered what happened to the elah Salem after Yahu came. Was he watching us now with joy because an upstart elah had failed? Or was he watching with sadness because Yahu would never be overthrown in turn?

Twenty-Six

One thought let me watch all that followed. Why had Esu shared his drink and power before he sent me to betray him? So that if he died on Caesar's stake, we could raise him.

They questioned and beat him through the night at Kaifa's house. In the morning, they took him to Pilatus, then to Antipas. The questions and beating continued. When his clothes were soaked with blood, the soldiers stripped him. Shaul gave me the bundle, saying, "We waste nothing."

I told myself Esu trusted me to do what was needed. I accepted the load.

The soldiers dressed him in a cheap red robe like a prince of fools and sent him back to Pilatus. As we followed, Shaul said, "Why did Pilatus send Esu to Antipas?"

I said, "I've drunk from Esu's cup. It's enough to let me know you and Pilatus have drunk from someone else's. Pilatus delayed to be sure Yahu wants Esu dead."

Shaul smiled. "Pilatus calls him Sky Father, but he stays the lord, however you name him."

At the judging hall, Pilatus talked with Kaifa's Herodians. In the yard, Yahudeans and Galileans were shouting, "Free Of Father! Free our prince!"

Pilatus turned to Esu. "Your people want you. Will you lead them to war?"

Esu looked away. Then Pilatus did as he done before. Soldiers dressed like Yahudeans mingled with the crowd. On their leader's signal, they attacked with clubs. Everyone fled. When only Herodians and soldiers remained, a new call began: "Kill Esu Nazar! Kill the false prince!"

Pilatus showed a bowl of water to us. Washing his hands, he said, "I'm innocent of this man's blood. You all see it."

What court would free a murderer who washed his hands? But in Pilatus's court, the murderer was the judge.

Then his soldiers tore the bloody robe from Esu, and Shaul gave it to me. They whipped Esu and put a crown of thorns on his head. They gave him a purple robe and said, "Hail, anointed prince of Yahudea!" They beat him and did all that's told in the four stories that the sun worshipper approved.

Then Pilatus wrote a sign in Greek, Latin, and Assyrian that read, THIS IS ESU NAZAR, LORD OF YAHUDEANS.

Kaifa frowned. "Don't write that. Write that he says he's lord of Yahudeans.' "

Pilatus shrugged. "I wrote what I wrote."

"Do you want to tell the world you knew who you killed?"

"Fools will think I'm mocking him. But those who matter will know what Pilatus has done. I hear the whispers. That I'm stupid. That I'm cruel. That I don't deserve a better post than this shit heap at the empire's ass. But who can claim a greater kill than mine? Put up the sign!"

As soldiers took it away, Shaul said, "Some may think it's a sign of repentance."

"Kill the son of an elah and apologize with a sign?" Pilatus laughed. "By Mithra's balls, let my next post be where people can think and wine is good!"

Twenty-Seven

Soldiers took Esu into the yard. Soldiers put a reed in his hand to go with the crown and bowed, saying, "Hail, anointed lord of Yahudea!" They spat on him and hit his bloody head with the reed. They beat him and abused him. Yet Constantine's church says Yahudeans are damned for what collaborators said, but Romans are forgiven for what soldiers did.

When the soldiers stripped Esu, I was given another blood-soaked bundle. They put unbleached robes on him to make him look like a nazar again.

In the street, Romans met us with eight prisoners, each dragging a stake half again as long as a man. Six of the prisoners had been with us in El's house. I never learned their names. The last were Timai Beggar and Zakai Taxman.

The rebels saw me and looked away. They thought they protected me from Pilatus by pretending not to know me. What could I do? I followed with Esu's bloody clothes and waited for the time to save him.

Outside Hill Salem, at the place called Skull, nine holes had been dug. The soldiers made the prisoners drop a stake into each and fill the holes. A small crowd grew. None of the men of the band dared to be there, but Mother came with Maryam, Marta, Salema, and Elishaba.

They begged the soldiers to let the men go. Esu called, "Don't cry for me! See how the rich treat a people's child!"

They stripped him. Four soldiers brought his bloody clothes to Shaul, so the pile in my arms grew.

When all the rebels were staked, the soldiers put Pilatus's sign above Esu's head and taunted him, saying, "If you're El's son, come down from the cross."

At mid-afternoon, he cried, "Elah! Elah! I thirst!"

A soldier filled a sponge with cheap wine, put it on a hyssop reed, and lifted it to Esu's mouth. But the centurion said, "Don't. Let's see if Eliyah saves him."

Sometime later, Esu cried, "Maker! Take my breath." His head fell on his chest.

Marcus and Luka say the world turned dark and the curtain of the holiest place tore from top to bottom. Matai adds that the earth heaved, rocks shattered, graves opened, and the dead walked into the city, where many people saw them. But Yohanan wrote nothing about unusual things happening when Esu collapsed. In this case, I can't say Yohanan was wrong.

The women beat their breasts and tore their clothes and wailed and finally left. They must have seen me standing near Shaul. That must have made them certain of my guilt. But what was death to us? Esu had given us the power of life. It was easy to make Shaul think I accepted Esu's death. The power burned in me to undo it.

After the crowd left, Shaul told the centurion, "Kaifa doesn't want bodies hanging overnight with the feast coming."

The centurion told his men, "Break the bandits' legs." With only their arms to support them, the rebels began choking to death.

When the soldiers came to Esu, Shaul waved them back. He took a silver cup from his purse, then drew his knife. Its blade was dark and shaped like a spear's head.

He gave it to a soldier who drove it into Esu's side. Esu jerked on the stake, bowing his body as he tried to escape the knife. He screamed and slumped again. Shaul stepped close to him with the cup to catch the blood and pale liquid pumped by Esu's dying heart. When the flow seized, all that happens to dead men happened to Esu.

I learned later that the blade came from a rock like Abraham's in El's house. At the time, I only knew what I saw. It killed the children of elahs. None of us would use Esu's power to spark the life in him. Nothing was left to spark. His body was meat. His spirit might return on judging day. It would not come back sooner.

Twenty-Eight

Shaul took Esu's clothes. He had me carry his body. If he thought that was a test, it was a poor one. The body isn't the spirit.

At Pilatus's house, I was given a room and a slave. I told the slave I wanted sleep, but I didn't. I thought about Esu giving us his cup. Had he planned to hang on the stake for days, showing that Rome couldn't kill him?

That night, Shaul told me to help Yosef of Ramah. I thought I should wonder about the name. Ramah is in the scrolls, but no one knows where it is. I did not wonder. I followed Shaul.

What waited was not a man. I saw its soul before its shell. The shell told me nothing. It was the likeness of a man. You would pass him on the street and forget him as you passed.

Mose wrote that elohim made men and women in their image. Had they made themselves in ours instead?

"Fetch the body," Yahu said. He trusted me. I had killed my brother for him. He should love me as much as he loved Abraham.

I obeyed. Nikodimos brought myrrh and aloes. We wrapped the body in clean linen, then took it to a garden where a new tomb had been cut from the rock. I understand then. Egyptians use myrrh and aloes to make their dead last for centuries.

We put the body in the tomb, rolled a stone to close it, and left.

I heard thunder, and Yahu was gone. Shaul said he would call when he needed me again.

I went to Shaul's room and took the knife that killed Esu. When I came back to the tomb, Rome's guards were there. The wild stories had begun. If Esu could raise the dead, couldn't he raise himself?

I stepped in front of the guards. My face was like Esu's. My clothes glowed like lightning. They fled. I took the body. A priest of the elahs of Egypt would have done my work more quickly, but not more thoroughly.

On the day after the passover, as the sun rose, I returned to the tomb. Maryam, crying, looked in and saw me. Mother and Salema followed her. I asked, "Why're you crying?"

She said, "They took away my man. I don't know where they put him."

"He's not here."

"If you carried him away, say where he is, and I'll take him."

I knew I could not tell her. I hid from their sight and left. I left Esu's grave clothes where they would be found, so Pilatus and Antipas would tremble when they heard.

Days later, when my madness was fading, I went in search of the band. I found them hiding. Rock said, "Esu?"

"Twin," Yakob Zadok said. "Eoda."

Andreas said, "You betrayed him."

Maryam said, "What happened?"

I showed the knife I had taken. All of them stepped back. The blood we had tasted told what blood it had drunk.

I said, "Do you have food?"

Marta said, "We can't feed him!"

Maryam said, "I can." She brought fish weed and a honeycomb, and she stood by me while I ate to clean the taste from my soul.

When I finished, she asked, "What happened?"

I met her eyes. "I drank the blood. I ate the flesh."

Her horror began as a question she couldn't ask and I couldn't answer. When she turned away, Yakob Zadok said, "Go, Eoda. In Esu's name, leave us in peace!"

So I went.

Esu had looked for peace in the wild. I sought it there, too. Animals would come and linger, trying to learn what I was. People would flee. I saw spirits and elahs, but if they were real, I can't say. Far from the places of people, beings of power are as real as sand or water. Some fled when they saw me. Some watched from far away and left. Some whispered promises and told me to join them. I ignored them all. I only had to wave the knife, and even the boldest would go.

I thought my peace lay in the knife. I tried to take its peace for myself. I could put the blade against my skin. Then my hands would weaken and the knife would fall. I could bury the hilt in the ground and fall forward onto the knife. Then I would float a finger's width above its point.

One morning on the shore of Lake Galil, Rock, Netanel, the Sons of Thunder, Marta, and Maryam talked about what to do. I didn't look like Esu then. I looked like a madman who lived in the wild. I went to them and asked, "Do you have any food?"

Rock glanced at me. "No."

I said, "Go out and throw a net on the right side of your boat. You won't be able to pull it out because you'll have so many fish."

Netanel said, "We're nazars. We don't eat Elah's creatures."

"That's so," I said. "I forgot."

Maryam squinted at me. Then her eyes widened. "It's Eoda."

Rock gasped, ran into the lake and began swimming. I knew I should be amused or sad. I only envied him. He could feel terror. He could feel cold. He could know that he might drown, and if he did, his death would come from his choice.

The others ran to the boat and set out. Only Maryam stayed. She said, "They can't forgive you. They can't understand. I understand, but I can't forgive, either."

"Esu took the narrow gate."

"You took a narrower one."

"He didn't force me to it."

"He wouldn't. It might've been kinder if he had."

"Then I would've hanged myself. Then I would've hated myself so much, my guts would've burst open."

She nodded. "Sit." She gave me bread and fish weed, then sat across from me. When I'd eaten, I said, "Where's Shushana?"

"Gone."

"With the women of the Holy?"

"She wouldn't want me to say. The band is pulling apart. Yakob Zadok wants to follow the Holy. Andreas and Rock prefer the Persianists. They've met one named Paulus who wants to help us."

"And Marta?"

"Gone, too. She wouldn't say where. She fears for her child. And herself. And everyone she loves. If Esu can be killed, who's safe?"

I drew the knife and put the hilt in her hand. "This kills nefilim. It may kill elohim."

She stared at the knife, then at me.

I reached for her hand. "I'm done." I drew her hand toward me. "Please." I pulled the tip of the knife close to my heart. "For the one we love. I've tried. I can't—"

She threw the knife into the lake.

I lifted my hand. The knife rose from the water and came to me.

Her eyes flicked wide. Her hand covered her belly.

I said, "I should've gone to Shaul. He would do it." I stuck the knife in the sand between us.

"Why didn't you?"

"Because you would be sorry."

Maryam looked out at the water. The boat was turning back. "Did you kill Yahu? Are his agents dead?"

"No."

"Then you're not done."

I drew the knife from the sand. It burned so hot that Maryam shielded her eyes. I said, "For each one that falls, there'll be another who'll draw power—" I stared at her.

Maryam nodded. "What are they, without their power?"

"What am I?"

"The answer's in you. Will you free it?"

I stood. How long would it take to find every source of their power and destroy it?

I let the knife cool. "Yes," I told Maryam and the still, small voice within me.

Twenty-Nine

I have written many words about one year. Now I must write a few about many.

In the first days, we shared all things equally. We used his flesh and blood to heal as we had when the seventy went out. The nazars grew in Yahu's land. We thought Esu's way would survive his death. We did not know there would be a traitor among us.

The newcomers included a man and woman, Ananias and Safira. They said they sold their land and gave the money to Rock. He said they kept some money for themselves. He used Esu's power to kill them.

If Ananias and Safira did as Rock said, Esu would have pitied them, not killed them. The murders woke the band's old division, the Sons of Thunder and Yonah against Esu's family.

I could not imagine why Rock chose to kill. Some whispered he kept the money and killed the couple to shift the blame. Then I met his new friend, Paulus. Paulus was Shaul's attempt to have an honorable name.

I told the band that Paulus was our enemy. Paulus said that was true until he had a vision of Esu. He, who had never known Esu in life, claimed to know him better now than we. The Sons of Thunder and Yonah supported him.

Paulus saw he could not win in Hill Salem, where people knew Esu's teaching and knew a nazar like Yakob Zadok should lead the

Poor. He took his work to other towns. To weaken Yakob Zadok, he said men should have short hair like Romans, not long hair as Mose wrote. To weaken Maryam, he said women should not teach. To weaken me, he said I had betrayed Esu, as if Elah and Esu were so frail that I could make them fail. To weaken the Poor, he said Elah gave us masters, so slaves should obey. To weaken Esu's teaching, he said beliefs mattered, not actions.

The rich of Rome and Yahudea liked Paulus's way. Maybe they simply liked that it weakened Esu's. They helped Paulus.

While Yakob Zadok stayed in Hill Salem to guide our people there, the rest of us set out to share truth with all who seek it. In Egypt, they called us Knowers, because we knew wisdom waits to be wakened in everyone. Some called us magi because we were like Mazdans, the wise ones.

Shimon took Esu's words to Rome, where Paulus and Rock had gone to be rewarded. Emperor Claudius wanted to hear Shimon Magus, brother of the elah called Christus. Paulus said Shimon's teachings were false because his power was weak, as if truth and force are one. Shimon used the blood to fly before Claudius. Paulus and Rock used their power to throw Shimon to his death.

When we heard this, we thought Paulus and Rock won because they outnumbered Shimon. Then we heard more stories. Though Esu had said to call no man father, Rock became a Pater of the Mithrans. In the service of Sol Invictus, he and Paulus drank an elah's blood. That living blood was stronger than Esu's dried flesh.

Yakob Zadok chose to stay in Hill Salem and teach, so Herodians killed him. The nazars continued to grow, so Rome destroyed Salem's city and did not let any Yahudeans return.

We continued to wander. To the world, we were no one. But we told our stories of Esu, and the Paulians told theirs.

A hundred years after Esu's death, Tertulian began teaching that Elah was three, Father, Son, and Holy Spirit, just as bad magi taught that Ahura Mazda is Mazda, Mithra, and Spenta Mainyu.

Three hundred years after Esu's death, Emperor Constantine said Mithra and Esu are the same and should be worshipped together. The cross of the Invincible Sun became the Roman stake of Esu's death. The Fathers of the Invincible Sun became the Fathers of the Anointed Esu. Elah's worship was moved from the sabbath to Mithra's day. Four contradictory stories about Esu's life were declared to be the only true story about him. Writings that disagreed with the Paulians were burned. So were people.

A thousand years after Esu's death, the Father of the Paulians said Esu's priests could not marry. Yet they said their church was built on Rock, a married man.

They slaughtered tens of thousands of peaceful Cathars to prevent the coming of a second saoshyant.

Their love of death continues. They war on those who worship many elahs, and those who worship only one, and those who worship their threefold elah in ways that do not make them richer. They make war because they love profit and Yahu loves war. In the scrolls, slaughter is a sweet savor to him.

Now is a good time to die. My old friends are dead. I wish I had not eaten when Esu's flesh was so potent. I wish I had not lived to see the things done by the heirs of Paulus and Constantine in Esu's name.

What comes next, I do not know. I would like to face the loving Elah of Esu's teaching. But I will be content if the Zadokees were right, and there is nothing after death. As Esu said, Elah's gardens are in us.

But if I face the judge of the Paulians, let him sentence me to torment. Better to be forever in torment with Esu than in gardens with Yahu's cruel servants.

Wherever I am, I will treasure truth's voice.

Reader, may you do the same.

BOOK FOUR

El Elyon

One

You put the pages back into their box, slip the box back into its place in the altar, and go up the stairs. When you reach the stone covering the way, you think, Nothing is locked to me.

The rock rolls aside. The sky is still dark. Dawn is hours away. You feel life all around you, plants, animals, insects. You cannot imagine a better world. But you could wish for better caretakers.

Walking back, you think Josh Dumont must have walked here. Did he visit that chamber? Was his death plotted there? Was he killed there, then thrown into the river?

Elverado must have walked here, too. His death may have been more than the removal of a nuisance. It may have been the most recent of many sweet savors unto the Lord.

Judas said the nazarenes and magi who helped Jesus are dead. Do they have heirs? Did Josh Dumont die because someone wanted to avenge Jesus's death? It is usually easier to kill a prince than a king.

You should be terrified. But you think you know how Jesus felt in Gethsemane. You see the course before you. Follow it.

At the Academy's campus, your sadness deepens. What kind of school would Jesus make? One that taught students to share, to serve, to call no one master.

At Rider House, you look at Vaughn's dark window. You don't need to return that way. Nothing is locked to you.

You go in through the front door. When you enter your room, Levitz says, "Nix?"

The clock says you were out for two hours. When did Levitz notice? Does it matter? "Yeah?"

"Where were you?"

You want to laugh. How do you answer? You were in the woods. You were in the truth. You say, "Walking."

"You risked getting expelled to go walking?"

"It's nice out."

"Yeah, right. Good night, Nix."

"Good night, Levitz."

You lie in your bed thinking about gods. What makes Yahu more powerful than the nefilim? You think you'll be awake for the rest of the night. But what good would that do?

That may be your last thought before you sleep.

Two

You hear a voice. You're in darkness.

You're the world's prince. You can see in darkness.

You're in your room in Rider House. Levitz stands by your bed. He's in his pajamas. He's whispering, "Chris. Hey, Chris. Wake up. Something cool's about to happen."

"What?"

"You got to see. Come on!"

The clock says you slept for twenty minutes. You want to tell Levitz to forget it. You don't care if girls have snuck over or if he has cigarettes or weed. Nothing will seem as cool to you as to him. You start to tell him so.

But he's your roommate. He's sharing something with you, or he wants your help. And maybe it is something cool. You would love a distraction from the Academy and the elohim and love and death and being you.

You stand. When your feet touch the cold floor, you're completely awake. You wish you were still asleep, but you're awake.

Levitz peeks out the door, then waves like he's seen too many army movies. You follow him. If Fitzgerald catches you, he'll punish you the same as Levitz, so you better not get caught. You realize you're grinning. It's good to be an ordinary boy breaking stupid rules. Stupid rules exist for the joy of breaking them. You wish you could tell Elverado that.

You lose your grin. Running into Vaughn or one of his disciples would end your joy. But there's no light under his door or anyone else's. The house is quiet.

Levitz heads upstairs, looks around the landing, and waves for you. You hesitate. How many of the boys up there are with Vaughn? Not all. And if this is a chance to learn more about his group, you should take it. You go up.

Levitz tiptoes to a door, opens it silently, and slips in, leaving it ajar for you. You step in after him.

And you sense a nef as someone grabs your shoulder.

You're shoved into the middle of the room. It's a double, tidy, bland, decorated with football posters, and not what you're noticing.

Vaughn is leaning against one desk. All his disciples are here. In pajamas, slippers, and robes, they look like a parody of a *Playboy* party. But if this is a joke, they're playing it straight. Their faces are grim. They're spread out around the room, ready to grab you no matter which way you might run.

Banner closes the door. O'Reilly leans against it. Vaughn says, "Welcome, Nix."

You look at Levitz. "Et tu, Brutus?"

He says, "I thought you'd call me Judas."

You say, "I'm not that vain."

Vaughn smiles.

O'Reilly says, "Don't get all pissy, Nix."

Vaughn tells him, "You, neither, O'Reilly." He looks back at you. "I said I wanted you to join us. That's why we're here. To prove our good intentions."

"You could've sent flowers."

"We're a club. You're invited. This is how it's always been. A verbal invitation in the middle of the night."

"And if I refuse?"

Vaughn shrugs. "You mention this to anyone, we don't know what you're talking about."

O'Reilly says, "You don't want to refuse. But if you do, you really don't want to talk about this."

Vaughn looks at him again. "Christ, O'Reilly, can you say anything that doesn't sound like a threat?"

O'Reilly says, "What's the point of a mysterious club if you can't sound mysterious?"

You smile, though you don't relax. "Does the club have a name?"

Vaughn nods. "You don't learn anything more unless you agree to join."

"But I don't know what I'd be joining."

"Sure you do." Vaughn gestures at the others. "Us."

Levitz says, "It's cool, Chris. I wasn't lying."

"What if I don't think it's so cool after I join?"

O'Reilly says, "We kill you." When Vaughn frowns, O'Reilly tells him, "Man, come on, it's a fucking secret society!"

Vaughn says, "Yes, it's a secret society. That's why we'll keep it secret." He glances back at you. "I can tell you this much. No one has ever chosen to leave us after joining."

O'Reilly says, "Or dared," then grins at Vaughn.

Banner adds, "Beaucoup useful connections, man. If I told you some of the people who've been in the club, you'd shit yourself."

You say, "I can walk away now if I want?"

Vaughn nods.

You turn and walk out. You go downstairs quickly. You put your hand on your door handle and think the surest way to learn what's going on is to go through with this. You walk back up to the jocks' room and open the door.

No one has moved from their places. You say, "Is there a secret knock?"

Vaughn smiles. "Join us and see."

"Okay. I'm in."

Vaughn laughs, walks over, and claps your shoulder. Everyone's grinning. This would feel great if you weren't sure there's an initiation.

Vaughn says, "Let's drink to that!"

One of the jocks goes to the wardrobe, then returns with a bottle of Boone's Farm Strawberry Hill and the goblet from the room in the woods.

Vaughn sees you staring at it. He says, "Pretty cool, huh? The club's had that forever."

O'Reilly adds, "If you go looking for it tomorrow, it won't be there." He glances at Vaughn. "That's true."

Vaughn nods. "That is true. Sorry about the Boone's Farm. We gave twenty bucks to a college kid and said if he got us something good, he could keep the change. He got that and kept the change."

You don't want to ask what's wrong with Boone's Farm. Or say that your concern is not with the quality of the wine.

Vaughn unscrews the Boone's Farm and pours it into the goblet. The first sound might be liquid striking liquid. He sets the bottle down, raises the goblet high, and says, "To the lord of the world!"

Everyone repeats it in a loud whisper. They look at you. You say, "To the lord of the world."

Vaughn hands the goblet to Levitz. "Why don't you take a taste to show it's all right?"

Levitz's eyes open wider as he smiles. "Thanks!" His Adam's apple bobs as he swallows. He stands still, gazing at something infinitely far away. Then he shudders, looks at you, and comes to offer the goblet in both hands. "Here, Nix."

Knowing all eyes are on you, you put out your hand. You feel the blood in the cup before the cup touches you. You drop your hand and shake your head.

"What?" O'Reilly says. "You want the rest of us to taste it first?"

Vaughn says, "That wouldn't change things."

Banner says, "So drink."

"Chris," Levitz says, "it's fine. Drink!"

"He won't," says Vaughn.

You nod and ask him, "What do we do now?"

"Who do you serve?"

"I'm working on that."

One of the jocks says, "What's going on?"

"He's a nef," Vaughn says. "From a strange line. El sent him. I want to know why."

You say, "Can I take the option where I go away and don't tell anyone?"

Vaughn shakes his head.

O'Reilly says, "Chad? We can't force him—"

Vaughn says, "If we have to."

You look around. Nine boys. Except for Levitz, they must all have been disciples for years.

Vaughn says, "Drink."

You reach for the goblet in Levitz's hands, realize what you're doing, and jerk your hand back.

"Drink," Vaughn repeats.

"Drink," the others whisper.

Your fingers touch the goblet. You don't feel it. You feel the blood.

"No," you say. But the goblet is in your hands and rising toward your mouth.

"Drink," Vaughn says. "Join us."

The goblet is before your mouth. The smell of strawberry wine is in your nose. So is the smell of iron. So is the smell of power.

"Join us," the disciples whisper. "Join us now."

Sweetness and bitterness are in your mouth. If you swallow, they'll fill you.

And what will happen to CC? What will happen to your family? Vaughn has people who believe in him, but you have people who believe in you.

You spit the drink out and throw the cup to the floor.

A hint of surprise crosses Vaughn's eyes. If he gestures to the others or says something, you can't tell. But you know they're throwing themselves at you because they're limbs of his body.

So you slip away. They lunge where you are not. One disciple flails and manages to catch your elbow.

Nothing can hold you. You ease from the boy's grip like an eel.

Only Vaughn's eyes follow you clearly as you walk to him. You see fear, smell fear, bathe in fear. You are who you are. All should fall before you and tremble.

You lift a letter opener from the desk. Vaughn's fear grows. If you plunge it into his heart, all he has will be yours. Why shouldn't you? Didn't he kill Josh Dumont? Wouldn't he kill you? Dumont's people could cover up his death. You deserve a sacrifice. What sacrifice would be more pleasing than the death of one of the nefilim?

You're the elohim's prince. You're the top of the food chain, king of the hill, lord of all you survey, the big kahuna, the big boss man, he who must be obeyed, master of all and servant of none. You're the anointed. You're the man. You're the god. Vaughn's power should be yours.

You slash the letter opener across your hand and thrust it against his face. He thrashes, trying to twist free. You tighten your hand on his jaw, pressing your palm against his lips, and say, "Drink."

"Please—"

"Drink!"

He gasps and swallows. You feel it, not on your palm, but in your blood. His flesh is your flesh. His disciples are extensions of your will. He has other worshippers in the world. They are yours and part of you. You don't know who or where they are. You know what matters. If you call, they will come. If you call strongly, they'll let nothing slow them but death. Kill Vaughn and keep them.

No. There are things you must know. You say, "Who am I?"

Vaughn says, "The consort."

"When did you know?"

"Now."

"When did you suspect?"

"Now."

"Why did you pull that shit with the sit-ups?"

"Dumont sent you. I thought you might be one of his agents. I thought if you got mad, you'd reveal yourself."

"Did I?"

"Not until dinner."

"When you tried to make me trust you."

"Yes."

"Could you lie to me now?"

He smiles. "Yes. But why should I?"

"To keep me from telling Dumont who killed Josh."

Vaughn stares, then laughs.

"What's the joke?"

"Why would I want to stop you from telling him something he knows?"

"He knows you killed Josh?"

"Me?" Vaughn rolls his eyes. "I killed Josh?" You can't tell if he's laughing or crying. You don't think Vaughn can, either. He rubs his eyes, shakes his head, and says, "I would've died for Josh."

You study him. He said he can lie. That's the only thing you know you can trust. Would Dumont hide the killer's identity from you? If he had a reason. But what reason could he have? Is Vaughn only trying to make you doubt Dumont more than you already do?

"Who did?"

He shakes his head.

"Tell me."

"If El didn't, I won't."

"He wants me to find out."

"Does he?"

You frown. Why would Dumont say Josh was murdered and make you hide your identity from other nefs? So you would hide your identity from other nefs. What does that gain him?

Trust nobody. Nobody can help you.

Vaughn says, "Just forget it, Nix. Everyone will be happier."

You look at the others. "Do any of you know who killed Josh?"

Some shrug. Some shake their heads. You say, "Go back—" You catch yourself. "When I tell you to go, all of you except Vaughn will go to your beds and sleep. When you wake, you'll forget anything happened here after curfew, and that anyone planned for anything to happen here, and that there was any reason why anything might happen here." You look at Vaughn. "Will that cover things?"

He smiles. "Good enough. You don't have to get it perfect. They'll rationalize the little things."

"Thanks." You look at the others. "Go."

They move like soldiers sleepwalking. Banner and O'Reilly get into their beds and fall asleep as the rest file into the hall.

You tell Vaughn, "I can make you talk."

"Sure. But no way I'm going against El. So I'll keep from giving a name as long as I can, and then I'll give you names like crazy."

"Like?"

"Like anyone except the person who did it."

"Man, I wish you hadn't said you can lie."

He laughs. "I nearly said I couldn't. But I want you to trust me."

"Why?"

"You're the anointed. If I'd known, I never would've tried to claim you."

"Do you mind, uh, what I did?"

"Yes and no."

"Can I undo it?"

He blinks, studies you, and finally says, "I suppose."

"No one's done it?"

"Not that I've heard. It would just weaken you."

"Seriously weaken me?"

"I doubt it. You'd just give up what you won when I drank. I guess."

"How would I do it?"

He frowns. "You're serious?"

You nod.

"Huh. I suppose it'd be like putting power in something. Only the place you'd put it is where it came from."

"Okay, I'm guessing that makes sense to you."

He gives you a glance again, then smiles, but it's friendly. "Sorry. I keep assuming the consort—" He hesitates.

You offer, "Would know how to do shit?"

"Yeah. Where did El find you?"

"Florida. Putting power in a thing would be like making a magic thing? Like the knife that killed Jesus?"

Vaughn hesitates at that, then nods.

You think about power swirling around you and within you. It's a cloud of purple smoke. Let it slow and settle. It's purple sand. See the grains. Some are blue. Some are red. Each is unique.

The blue ones are the worshippers from Dumont's dinner. Keep them.

The nearest red one has many many paler red grains clustered around it. That's Vaughn with his disciples. Snip the strands.

Vaughn's eyes flick wide. He says, "I didn't think you would. I—" He adds with a hint of annoyance, "You freed my people, too."

"Seemed fair."

"I gave them a free choice. I'm not like some nefs."

"Can they know what they give up?"

He squints at you. "You serve El, you've got your own worshippers, and you're asking that?"

"I don't serve anyone."

He laughs. "Tell that to El."

Retorts are tough when the other person's right. You say, "What's the secret room in the woods?"

Vaughn's face grows blank.

You say, "What's with the head? He was El's enemy. Does El know about him?"

Vaughn holds your gaze, then says, "I shouldn't say anything more you don't know. That'd be presumptuous. What you learn should come from El."

You smile. "That's good."

He nods. "I'm a faithful subject of the elohim."

"I can make you drink again."

"Sure. Just say so. Now that I know who you are, I'd be glad to drink."

"Because you're a faithful, et cetera."

He nods.

"Then stay in your room until morning to prove it."

He bows. "Yes, my lord."

You walk downstairs together. At his door, he says, "Nix?"

"Yeah?"

"Josh took me to that room."

"How'd he find it?"

Vaughn shrugs.

You say, "You didn't ask him?"

"Sure. He said nobody showed it to him. He must've felt it out there."

"Who knows about it?"

"So far as I know, just us."

"Which you would say if someone else did know about it."

He smiles and nods.

You say, "Fair enough. I read *The Gospel of the Knife.*"

His eyes widen. "Did you tell El?"

"Not yet."

"Will you?"

You shrug.

Vaughn says, "It's nothing to concern him. It's probably a forgery. I hear there are enough pieces of the True Cross to build Noah's ark."

"So I shouldn't tell El?"

"I didn't say that. But does he really want to be bothered with trivia?"

"Did Josh read it?"

Vaughn looks away, then nods. "Sure. It was a goof."

"And the head was a goof?"

"The head is power. Nefs collect power, however we can."

"It's gone now."

"Oh. I thought I felt something. Didn't you want it?" He looks at you a little longer. "No. You wouldn't have freed me, then."

You shrug.

He says, "El killed Josh."

You keep your face still.

He asks, "What'll you do?"

You shake your head.

He says, "Nix? I would serve you."

You nod.

He repeats, "So, what'll you do?"

"I'm working on it. Why did El kill him?"

He shrugs. "Nobody can tell you."

You nod and walk away.

Three

The eastern sky is lighter, but the night is still cool. The wind smells of rain. You should be wearing more than pajamas. You should be wearing shoes. But you're not planning to be seen, and it's good to feel the world.

Seek, and you shall find. You walk through the town thinking, Trust nobody. Nobody can help. Nobody cares.

The moon is dim through the clouds. Trees sway. You could walk like this forever.

You come to a neighborhood that reminds you of home. The trees don't have Spanish moss, and the houses are two and three stories tall, but most cars are old and few lawns are tidy and what doesn't show signs of repair shows need of repair.

You walk up to a house that might be a little better kept than its neighbors. You climb its steps and press its doorbell and wait.

When the porch light comes on and the door opens, you say, "I'm sorry to disturb you so late, or so early, or now, but I think I finally figured it out."

Mrs. Medeiros, in a thick red robe and pink pajamas, squints at you. "Who're you serving?"

You say, "Nobody."

She smiles. "Then what are you doing out in your pj's, boy? Come in out of the cold!"

The light goes off and the door opens wider and she's guiding you into a hall with faded floral wallpaper and a flight of cherry-wood stairs.

Someone is on the landing. She's beautiful in a long green T-shirt and a white terry-cloth robe. You say, "It wasn't on purpose. I mean, I wanted you, but I never wanted to force you. I just missed you. Like, really missed you. I didn't know what I was doing. I'm sorry."

You watch her, and think you may paint this someday, the light from the hall falling on mystery and beauty. Then you turn for the door.

CC says quietly, "Where're you going?"

"Away."

"I figured that."

"Away from Dumont."

"Can you?"

"I'll find out."

As you start to go out, CC says, "Can you do it alone?"

You shrug. "I got to."

"No. You don't."

You look back. She smiles, and there's no mystery, just beauty.

Mrs. M heads into the house, saying, "I'll put tea on. You got a minute. I don't think you can get into much trouble in a minute. Well, I know you can get into a lot of trouble in a minute, but you best not."

"Yes'm," CC says. As soon as Mrs. M is gone, CC's coming down, and you're afraid she'll fall, and you're going up, and you stop just short of each other. She nods and steps into your arms. You kiss, a very light kiss that says you're sorry for everything you misunderstood, and you look into each other's eyes, and you kiss again. You taste salt and smell soap, and it's the best taste and smell that has ever been.

When you separate, you say, "What line are you?" She frowns, so you add, "Martha's or Mary's? Or did the Baptist marry? Or—"

She laughs. "What, you think Israel's the only place that has gods?"

"You're a god?"

She looks down, then looks up at you. She's darker than Nefertiti and much cuter. She looks like a queen. What was the name of the Egyptian cat god? Bast. When CC glances at you from the corners of her eyes, she could be Bast or her daughter.

She says, "I never got to tell you why I'm CC. When I was little, so little I don't remember this, we stayed at Granny Carter's farm. I got off on my own, and they couldn't find me till they came to the pen of a mean old boar. I was sleeping curled up beside him. Auntie said I had Satan's mark. Granny laughed and said every three or four generations, there's a Carter with a gift. Said I was a regular Circe."

Mrs. M calls from the kitchen, "You stop what you're doing and come have some tea now!"

You say, "Mrs. Medeiros knows about you?"

"She knew before I did." CC takes your hand and leads you through a living room filled with painted porcelain figures of appallingly cute children in costumes from around the world. The kitchen's style is older than the front of the house: black and white linoleum squares cover the floor, the walls are white with red trim, a clock above the stove looks like Felix the Cat.

CC tells Mrs. M, "Tell him how you found me."

Mrs. M sets out cream and sugar and fills your cups with tea. "Wasn't me, exactly. We knew Mather was sending Mr. Fitzgee down to Florida. Someone came up from Miami to tail him. Kept watch on the Nix place. Saw you run off and started circling the area. Saw a hippie van pick you up and tailed you to the Carter house."

You say, "I'm surprised we didn't spot him in the black neighborhood."

Mrs. M smiles. "Did I say this was a white man? They went to the Carters' after the police took you home. Told them some of what was going on. CC wanted to stay for your sake, but her aunt wanted to get far from there."

You say, "A guy at the airport had a note saying nobody could help."

Mrs. M nods. "One of us."

You say, "Who's that, exactly?"

She sips her tea, sets it aside, goes to the counter, and pulls out a drawer near the floor. As she rattles through the contents, you can see in: spatulas and spoons and knives, all stained with age, some with chipped handles or broken edges. She pushes aside a cleaver and takes out a knife.

Its handle has been wrapped in black plastic tape. Its shape is odd. The hilt is a long cylinder that ends bluntly, as if it snapped or someone cut it. The blade is a long leaf, sharp on both sides. Kitchen knives usually have one edge.

Mrs. M says, "You know your Bible? John 19:34?"

You shake your head. So does Mrs. M. "All that tuition, and they can't even teach you the Bible?"

CC says, "One of the soldiers with a spear pierced his side." When you glance at her, she says, "Quoting the Bible was the best way to reason with Auntie. Didn't always work. She'd say the devil can cite scripture. I told her that was Shakespeare, but she said that proved her point."

Mrs. M sets the knife on the table before you. You think, That killed Christ. When you think that, you can feel it, not like something alive, not like a living nef or the head of the Baptist, but like their opposite. Does it eat life or give death?

You touch the hilt.

You're Esu bar Abba. You hang on the invaders' stake with a blade in your side. You wanted people to care for each other. This is your father's answer.

You're Caesar's soldier. You would rather serve in the Ten Cities where they speak a sensible language and worship sensible gods. The only thing you share with these people is your hatred of your master. Pilatus has a talent for making people hate him, which makes them hate Caesar, which makes them hate you. He gives insane orders, like the one you're carrying out. The rebel is on the stake. He'll die in a few days. That's why rebels are put on stakes. Why should this one be stabbed? Are they afraid he'll escape? And why should he be stabbed with a particular blade?

You are who you are. You're making a tool for sacrifices. Sacrifices please you. A slave brought you grain, but you didn't praise him. Another brought creatures that bled and died. You rewarded him. Your favorite slave offered his eldest son. You promised to make his numbers grow. You will stand by your pact. You want a world of slaves like him. You tell slaves to serve their lords and honor their fathers. Your son says to call no one father and no one lord. When the world was young, you showed your power by killing those who displeased you. Now you hide your power and send others to kill for you. The world grows more complicated, but you stay its master.

You're Mark Christopher Nix. There's a knife in your hand. You want to show its maker how well it works.

Someone's squeezing your other hand. It's CC. You say, "He killed Josh, too."

Mrs. M says, "Not with that."

CC says, "Who?"

You say, "Jay Dumont. Yahu of the Mountain. He killed his son. Two sons."

Mrs. M says, "More than that."

"Am I next?"

"Depends. Is he done with you?"

"He says he wants an heir."

"He wants someone in that seat. He's not planning to turn over his job to anyone."

You look at the knife. "Where does your group fit in?"

"What do you know?"

"I read *The Gospel of the Knife.*"

"Then you saw the Baptist."

You glance at CC. She says, "Mrs. M told me about him."

You tell them both, "He's gone now. He was trapped, so I let him go."

Mrs. M smiles. "Good. We never could."

"We?" you say. "Vaughn is part of your group?"

"If there's a group. It's more like he's not part of them."

"Them?"

"The elohim."

"So how does it work?"

Mrs. M stands. "More tea? Maybe some scones?"

CC says, "Mrs. M!"

She shrugs, sits, sips her tea, sighs, and says, "People know people who help if they can. Mostly, we get inside their organizations and try to make things better. You know about Ezra in Jerusalem?"

"The guy who wrote the Bible?"

Mrs. M smiles. "One of the guys who wrote one of the versions of the Bible. He served Yahu, but he served us, too. Like Isaiah, Jeremiah, and Micah. They preached about a god of love and justice, so the nefilim had to behave better. They turned a few like Elijah, John, and Jesus to our side." She sighs deeply. "But Yahu keeps winning. Until now."

"What do you mean?"

She looks at the knife. "You can end it."

"That can kill Yahu?"

"It's one of the ways he got rid of competition."

You put your hand above the blade. There are more deaths there than you felt before. They're tangled together, and their thoughts are strange. F. Scott would say the gods are different than you and me. Ernest would probably drink more.

CC says, "You can't do it."

You hate the idea, but you also hate the idea she thinks you can't. You pick up the knife. The voices in it are quiet, now that you know them. The power burns. It's like getting into a hot springs that's so hot it hurts, at first. The longer you hold the knife, the more you like holding it. You thrust it once in the air. "It'd be easy."

"It'd be murder."

"Who's murdered more than he has? How many will he kill? Even his worshippers admit he destroyed the world once. You want to let him do it again?"

"But killing is his way."

"You got a better one?"

CC looks down and shakes her head.

You picture the knife sliding into Jay Dumont. No, not Jay Dumont. A thing that feeds on the world's suffering. But what you see is a man with an unhappy wife and a daughter who wants him to love her.

You squeeze CC's hand. "I hate it, too."

Mrs. M says, "You can get closer to him than anyone."

You say, "Did Josh try?"

Mrs. M nods. "Poor boy thought he was the third saoshyant. Thought there was some kind of guarantee, like the third time's the charm. My guess is he tried to talk to that devil. And his own father killed him."

"What about Vaughn?"

"He's too weak. And he can't get close enough. I think he'll try, because he's like that. But he'll fail."

You remember Dumont showing his glory to you. You couldn't even stand up before him.

You set the knife on the table and shake your head. "I can't do it."

CC squeezes your hand. "Maybe there's another way."

Behind you, Dumont says, "No. There's no way at all."

CC looks back in surprise. Mrs. M looks back in fear. Dreading what you'll see, you turn.

Jay Dumont stands near you in a gray cardigan, blue polo shirt, and tan trousers. Mather is behind him in blue pajamas, black slippers, and a blue robe. He looks around as if he's studying a dream.

Mrs. M lunges for the knife. Before her hand touches it, she gasps and falls onto the table. Her eyes are open and dull.

You reach for her without thinking. Dumont says, "Don't touch her. She died over breakfast. Cholesterol and cigarettes are a bad combination."

You say, "I can bring her back."

He nods. "And I can send her away again. It'd be cruel, but if you hate her, we could do that." His attention is on CC, who watches him warily. He says, "Interesting. The little gods stay far from my path. I haven't seen one of their get in ages." He glances at you. "Well done, my boy! We'll present you as Solomon and Sheba!"

CC snatches the knife from the table. "Don't plan a big wedding." She holds it toward Dumont, ready to thrust or parry. In her anger, she's fearless. Your terror is great enough for both of you.

Dumont opens his arms, inviting an attack. "Why not? You'll be one of his mates or mine."

You say softly, "CC—"

She looks at you, nods, and lets the point drop.

Dumont says, “Good. I thought you would—”

She turns, thrusting the knife at his unprotected stomach. His eyes widen. You know you see surprise. You might see fear.

An inch from his belly, the blade glows, too brightly to look at. CC screams and releases it. The tape around the hilt burns. The knife hangs in the air, vibrating like a hummingbird.

You call, “CC!” and pull her into your arms. Her hand has been seared, but you think it should be made right. You feel her power merge with yours to heal her skin.

Dumont plucks the knife out of the air. It melts into his palm like water into dry earth. He glances at Mather. “Keep her at your place until we return.”

You say, “No.”

Dumont says, “She won’t be hurt if she’s not foolish. We’ll wake her power properly. Why shouldn’t you have two daughters of gods for yourself?”

CC stares at Mrs. M’s body. She says, “Save her. Save her, and I’ll go with him.”

Dumont says, “You’ll go, and I won’t save her. Would she save me? She thinks chaos is freedom. She doesn’t see the price that rulers pay. She’s mad in a way that no god can cure. Let her stay where nothing troubles her, and she troubles no one.”

You say, “CC—”

And all is darkness and silence.

Four

Everyone and everything has gone.

No, you've gone.

And not alone.

"This may be my favorite place," Dumont says.

You're under the stars. You hear the wind. The ground is rocky and dotted with grass. The trees are small, tough scrubs. You smell pine sap mixed with the scent of the earth. You see lights low in the distance, towns or cities. You're on a mountain.

"I may have been born here," says Dumont. "I don't remember. I read once that to remember a thing, you must keep remembering it. Then the act of remembering changes the memory. We constantly revise our past. If the past concerned me, I would worry about that."

"Where are we?"

"Here. Call it what you want. It's had many names. I never gave it one." He's quiet for a moment. "No. I called it home."

"How did you find me?"

"Fitzgerald saw you weren't in your bed. I called Heller. She said you'd talked, but you still wouldn't have her. So I followed your blood. I thank you for dealing with the Baptist. The cult that served that head has been a nuisance for two thousand years."

"Do you kill all your sons?"

"I kill none of them. You killed John. Pilate killed Jesus."

"And Josh?"

"Mather."

"Because you wanted it."

He smiles sadly in the starlight. "I'm God. God kills. I'm the king. Kings kill usurpers."

"I don't want your place."

He makes a small sound like a laugh.

You say, "I never asked for this. I don't want to be the world-prince. I just want to draw comic books."

Dumont nods. "And I just want to live forever. But time is the last assassin. They told you I killed my competition. That's true of some. Others died thanks to wars or accidents or age. Some were no threat to me, so I let them wander."

You wonder if that means he couldn't find them all. You decide to keep quiet.

"I love my daughter. If I were younger, I would make her my mate. That's another thing gods and kings do. But I like leaving her free. She'll think better of me, if I do."

"She doesn't think she's free."

"Not now. She compares herself to me, not to those who have less than she does. Someday she'll know how free she was, and how much a prisoner I've been."

"You're a prisoner?"

He laughs. "Compared to those who have less, no. I'm a prisoner of my passion. I act when I wish. Sometimes I regret that."

"Do you, uh, want to kill me?"

"Killing you wouldn't win much, but your death would feed me. On the other hand, I want Heller to have a son who's strong in the blood. As the mother of the next El, she would be secure among the nefilim then."

"If she had a son, would you let me go?"

"I could say yes. Would you believe me?"

"I'd try really hard to."

He nods. "You see how it is."

"I don't! You could do so much good, but you hoard all you can and you let bad things happen—"

"We're just like humans, Christopher. They wouldn't worship us otherwise. They don't want us to be better than they are. If they wanted a world of love, they would've followed Buddha or Jesus or any of a million fools. They want the world they have."

"Because you encourage it."

"It's easy enough to do. They love privilege and power and feasting on creatures slain for them. As I said, we're just like them."

"Can't you be better?"

"Of course. You see what we take, but you miss what we give. They lived under the sky eating grubs and plants. In six thousand years of war, their life spans have tripled. They live in comfort. Shouldn't they be grateful? Don't we deserve the fruit of our harvest?"

"War is the only way to get progress?"

"Of the kind that feeds us, yes. When I was young, killing a hundred people could take all day. Now they can sacrifice millions in an instant. Destroying the world in fire will be far easier than flooding it. Sometimes I see no reason to let it continue after me."

"Heller would die."

He nods. "That troubles me. Do I kill her, too? Or do I give her the world when I go?" He laughs. "If I worshipped myself, I could kill her and think I was giving her heaven. Or if I thought life didn't matter, I could kill her and think I wasn't stealing anything at all."

"Life matters."

"Yes. I wouldn't cling to it otherwise."

"People will keep worshipping you."

"That's so."

"It's a good time to go. With Heller's place secure."

"It is." He glances at you. "But I am who I am."

His face becomes a blaze. The light searing your eyes doesn't brighten the darkness on the mountain. It burns for you. There's only the light that is Yahu, and a voice that says, "You'll be my good and loyal servant. You'll take my daughter. What I decide, you'll do. I am who I am."

In the beginning is the word. Words make worlds. You say, "No. You're not."

You feel his surprise like being soaked with slush. You add, "You say you are who you say you are."

You reach for the strength of the people who were there when you were anointed. The people who worship one god under many names. The people who drank your blood. The people who funnel the world's worship to him. The people who are tied to you, the heir.

You feel the strength of the web of the world.

The ones who live in palaces and claim to be poor.

The ones who say being children of prophets makes them princes.

The ones who claim to have truth to sell.

The ones who feed Yahu with praise.

The ones who say he and his heir are one.

The ones who say he and his spirit are one.

The ones who say all his names are one.

You tap that strength because it's yours. You tell Yahu, "You're a word. Your name is your power. But you anointed me. You gave me your name. I am the word now. Mine is the praise. Mine is the power. Mine is the glory."

And you take all that's yours.

And you feel Yahu dying.

Tears are on your face. The light before you is dim. No, it's raining, and a cloud has crossed the moon. No, both are true.

There's laughter. It's not yours.

He says, "You are who you are."

And you know he's pleased.

And you're alone on the mountain.

The world lies before you. People die with your names on their last breaths. They die in beds and cars and wars. They feed you power. They feed you life. You are who you are.

You remember the Academy.

And you're there.

You walk into Mather's house. The furniture could have come from the mansion of a sixteenth-century New England governor. You could know its past, if you cared about the past.

The kitchen is modern. All the appliances are avocado green. Mather, dressed for school, sits at the table, eating a breakfast of eggs, sausage, and toast. CC has the same meal before her, but she has not touched it.

She sees you. Her eyes flick wide. That's enough to make Mather look up.

He says, "Chris?"

You say, "I am who I am."

The fear grows in him. You pity him. You say gently, "You've had a long life," and you release him from the web of your worship.

CC stares at the dust that was a man.

You say, "It was like with the Baptist. I let him go."

She nods, but she doesn't smile. She says, "What do I call you?"

What are you now? World King? Elohim Lord? El Elyon? "Whatever you want."

"What about Mrs. M?"

"She's gone."

"But you can bring her back—"

"Then I couldn't stop with her, could I?"

"It wasn't her time."

"It happened. Either it was her time, or no one has a time."

You see her grow sadder, and then suddenly hopeful. "Can you bring everyone back?"

You think of Mrs. M and Elverado and Josh Dumont and Grandpa Abner and John F. Kennedy and Marilyn Monroe and Vietnam and Hiroshima and the fields where people are buried and the fires that consumed them and the places where fish or birds or insects ate the bodies of those who fell or were left behind. You say, "That's the end. When everyone has learned—"

"What?"

You shrug. "The lesson of life."

"And death?"

"That's just part of life." Then you tell her what you must do.

She says, "You don't know it'll work."

"I don't know it won't."

"War's a habit now. This might not change that."

"But if I don't try, I'll be—" You shake your head.

She says, "You're not someone who doesn't try."

You say, "I love you."

She kisses you gently. You hold her until you realize that if you don't act now, you'll never act.

So you and she walk hand-in-hand across the Academy. Students and masters would stare at a pale boy in his pajamas and a dark girl in her robe, so neither of you lets anyone else see you. You only want to see each other.

On the boys' campus, you go into Chad's room. You tell him to forget you were the world's prince or one of the nefilim.

On the girls' campus, you tell Heller the same.

You walk into the woods. There may be better places for this. There are worse ones, too.

You reach the field with the broken stone wall. Young people come here to make love and get high. Old people come here to be grateful for life. The best people come here to be here.

You sit with CC as the dawn comes.

You set your hands on the grass. You press your fingers into the earth. Your power drains into it. All of the power that comes to El Elyon. All of your power as one of the nefilim. All of the power born of praise and death.

Until the only power left is the power to call it back.

CC says, “Maybe you shouldn’t give it up.”

You say, “I’d rather be wrong about giving it up than wrong about keeping it.”

She smiles, though she’s begun to cry. She says, “I love you.”

You hug her. After a moment, you manage to say, “I won’t forget what’s important.”

She kisses you. “I know.” When she leaves, she runs. You think she’s as fast and as beautiful as a gazelle. You hate that you can’t tell her that. You want to shout it after her. But if you do, she might come back. You couldn’t bear to watch her go a second time. You can’t bear it now.

But you watch her go.

Like a gazelle.

When she’s gone, you go back to the Academy.

And in every free moment, you write this. When you finish, you’ll hide it with *The Gospel of the Knife.* You’ll leave that hiding place and forget all you know about elohim and nefilim. You’ll forget there’s a secret room with an altar that holds these pages. You’ll forget that you chose to forget anything.

But you’ll remember this: You loved a girl called CC. She loved you. Life separated you, but that’s not losing. That’s learning.